All Of My Days

By

Elizabeth Castle

Copyright © 2019 by Elizabeth Castle

All rights reserved. No part of this publication may be reproduced, distributed, or transmitted in any form or by any means, including photocopying, recording, or other electronic or mechanical methods, without the prior written permission of the publisher, except as permitted by U.S. copyright law. For permission requests, contact Elizabeth Castle @ elizabethcastle22@gmail.com.

Name: Castle, Elizabeth, author

Title: All Of My Days, 2021

Description: Series: All Of Me

Publishing History: China Blue, 2019

Publisher: In The Air Publishing

Identifiers: ISBN 9781967731084 (ebook) | ISBN 9781967731091 (paperback) | ISBN 9798304881838 (amazon hardcover)

Cover Designer: betibup33

The story, all names, characters, and incidents portrayed in this production are fictitious. No identification with actual persons (living or deceased), places, buildings, and products is intended or should be inferred.

No generative artificial intelligence (AI) was used in the writing of this work. The author expressly prohibits any entity from using this publication for purposes of training AI technologies to generate text, including without limitation technologies that are capable of generating works in the same style or genre as this publication. The author reserves all rights and license uses of this work for generative AI training and development of machine learning language models.

Chapter One

Lian Albright used her bright red mitten to wipe the frost that was forming on the inside of the window of her small coupe before burrowing deeper into her black wool coat. "So what do you think?"

"I think he's hot." Mindy yawned but kept her eyes on the man down the road heading into his apartment building.

Lian couldn't help but smile at her counterpart's comment. They'd been watching Jonas Cole for the past week. Most of Mindy's comments were about Jonas's appearance, rather than why they were following him. Lian had to admit he was indeed hot, though she would use the adjectives rugged and handsome to describe him. And sexy. Very sexy. She had his profile and several surveillance photos. He was six feet even. His hair was so dark it looked black. That feature, she knew, he got from his mother. The height would be his father. He was an interesting mix of his parents. He had chiseled cheekbones and a square jaw, though under his five o'clock shadow it was hard to see it in the fading daylight. That was his father. His nose and mouth were also from his father. But his eyes, with just their hint of an almond shape, and the deep, deep brown color, were from his mother.

Lian just hoped that when he was finally confronted, he would have the temperament of his mother.

Mindy made a note on her tablet. "I have to say, for a guy who looks like that, it's really sad that his social life is as pathetic as yours is. It's just not natural."

"For him or me?" Lian took a snap with her surveillance camera. Mindy had it right. So far, he had done nothing more exciting than go to work and make a stop at the grocery store. They hadn't seen him with anyone that raised red flags. He commuted alone, he ate lunch alone, on the rare occasions he left his office during the day, and he went home alone.

"Him. I've given up hope for you." Mindy tugged her bright blue coat tighter around her neck. Her bright blonde curls framed her pixie-like face.

Lian had heard this lecture before, so she didn't ask again. Mindy was only twenty-six, but she'd done some hard living in those years. Last year, Mindy had decided she needed to get married and start a family, so she was constantly on the lookout for a suitable candidate. It seemed Mindy had her eye on the man they were watching, which, as far as Lian was concerned, was a bad idea. As for Lian, dating was low on her priority list.

Lian zoomed in with the camera she held and took another photo. She certainly wouldn't mind breaking her pattern if the man looked like Jonas. She supposed that made her a bit shallow, but she had found herself immediately attracted to his image the first time she'd pulled up a picture of him on the internet. In person, he was even better looking. She had casually walked past him on the sidewalk the day before while he was heading towards his office building, trying to get a better look at him. On the off chance he remembered her passing him, she had a valid excuse for being near the building.

Startled out of her reverie, Lian set her camera aside. For a moment she thought Jonas's eyes had met hers across the distance from where she was parked down the road from his apartment building. But he went inside without a backward glance. Lian let out the breath she held. Tailing an FBI agent could be dangerous work. She didn't want to imagine his reaction if he caught them.

Lian pulled the red cap that matched her mittens further down on her head. It was freezing, and the car was only a few degrees warmer than the air outside. Her nose was probably pink, and her face was going numb. She imagined her cheeks and lips were also the same bright pink shade as her nose. Shivering, she flicked her long French braid behind her back and settled back against the seat. It was easier to keep her waist-length platinum-blonde hair, several shades lighter than Mindy's, in a braid when she worked.

Mindy's quivering voice reflected how cold she was in the quiet of the car. "I think we can call it a night. If he sticks to his pattern, he's going to stay inside until he leaves for work tomorrow. I say we head back to the hotel. I need a hot bath to soak the chill from my bones."

Lian started the car, hoping the heat would kick in quickly. They had been sitting outside his apartment for the last two hours. The pair had been tailing him for the past week, but earlier today she had managed to lose him. He'd taken his car to lunch, but at some point, she had lost him in the busy afternoon traffic, and he had not returned to work. Lian wished she knew where he'd gone. Had he met with someone? Was he involved with his brother, Bo? Was his brother in the U.S.? She found herself desperately hoping the answer to her questions was no.

When they arrived back at their hotel, Mindy went straight to her room. By the time Lian had gone across the street to grab dinner and got back to her room, she had no doubt Mindy was already in the tub and had been for the past twenty minutes. Shrugging off her coat, Lian sat on the edge of the bed, pulling her laptop from where she had stashed it in the dresser drawer. She pulled up the file she was keeping on Jonas Cole.

He was forty-one, nine years older than she was. He was the adopted son of Abby and Henry Cole. His birth certificate said he had been born in Chicago, though Lian knew that wasn't the case. And he had not been born Jonas Cole. He had been born Jiao Lee in a private hospital in Hong Kong. He had been given a different name by the state of Illinois when he'd gone into foster care when no documentation on who he was could be found, or how he'd come to the U.S. The young boy could tell the caseworker his first name, but not his last, nor where he'd come from. But the boy spoke English and didn't look Chinese, so the caseworker decided that Jiao became Jonas and gave him a proper American surname to make it all legal. When he had been adopted, he had legally changed his name to Cole instead of the impersonal name chosen by the overworked caseworker.

Her file on him also told her that he had grown up in a government-run home, one for children who had been deemed unadoptable. He had run away from that home at age ten. He had been missing for the next four years, deemed just another statistic. But he had eventually resurfaced at fourteen and had been adopted two years later. It had taken the Cole family that long to get the state's permission to adopt him. It had not been an easy task, given young Jonas's social services record had recorded several illegal activities he had been involved in as a child as young as six, hence the reason he hadn't been adopted. Prospective families hadn't wanted to adopt the home's troublemaker. The older kids had used him to steal, lie, and do whatever else they could think of. Lian wished she could say otherwise, but it was not outside her knowledge that children of any age could be used and manipulated, especially when they were desperately seeking acceptance and someone to care for and about them.

Lian kicked off her shoes and climbed under the covers. She pulled her laptop closer. It was time to get closer to him. Time to see if she could uncover his secrets. Everyone had them, some innocent and some sinister. Everything in her screamed that he was innocent. But she'd been wrong before. And just because he was a lead FBI agent with the counterintelligence division didn't mean he hadn't turned against his country, or that his job there wasn't an elaborate ruse to get him access to some of the government's most powerful secrets.

It had only taken a small favor to get her assigned to his team. She was being hired on as a contract linguist. She would be on the FBI payroll, but not a member of the FBI. She'd done similar assignments over the years for the FBI, and one memorable assignment with the CIA. Mostly she worked for American businesses that had relations with businesses in China. Before that, she'd been an interpreter for hospitals in her youth.

A few years back, she had tried to get a more permanent position with the FBI. Americans who could fluently speak Mandarin and who knew the culture and local dialects were not easy to find, though competition for actual language analyst positions was tough in the FBI, where jobs were not easy to secure. She'd applied but had not been offered the job. Contractor positions were more easily obtained, as this one had been. Getting on Jonas Cole's team had been a bit trickier.

Her phone beeped, and she grabbed it off the nightstand. Her phone was as secure as it could be, but she still felt uncomfortable. She responded to the cryptic message with one of her own. She was operating without government sanction, and she felt like she was doing a trapeze act without a net. But she had made a promise, and she intended to keep it.

* * *

Jonas Cole watched impatiently as the recruits settled in. Though he had mostly settled into his new job as a supervisory special agent of a counterintelligence unit, he still got itchy feet when he had to deal with newbies. On top of that, he was used to seeing a bit more action. Counterintelligence was mostly done with computers these days. He had some skill in that area, but he was by no means a hacker. The twenty-two-year-old kid sitting at the station across from him, with pimples still decorating his skin, likely had more skills than he did.

His superiors wanted him in this role because of the many years he spent in the field and the instincts he'd honed over the years. Whether listening to a conversation through an amplifier across the street from his quarry or listening to him from thousands of miles away, the results were the same. His former boss called him a human lie detector. And with the injury he'd sustained two years ago, his superiors had pulled him out of the field and promoted him. Not that Jonas could blame them. But at only thirty-nine, Jonas had not been ready for a desk job. But at forty-one, that was where he now found himself, and he still hadn't completely adjusted.

The people assigned to his new project were an interesting lot. His superiors hadn't deemed his current quarry as significantly dangerous or important enough to get a full team working on the case. Jonas had a feeling about their quarry, so his boss had allowed him to gather a small but inexperienced team. His superiors had learned to trust his instincts, but budgets were tight and resources were hard to get.

The kid was a student; one was a lower-level agent hoping to get promoted and gain experience in counterintelligence, and one was simply a contractor on a short-term assignment. He potentially had a Chinese arms dealer supplying weapons to gangs and other assorted riffraff. The man had started with supplying gangs but was now upping the ante. Jonas was worried he was supplying munitions to potential terrorists, but he didn't have much proof; the man was not yet a great interest to the FBI, so he hadn't gotten seasoned agents assigned to the case. He also had hours of audio that needed to be interpreted, and miles of financial documents in Chinese to run through the computer system to decode if Jonas was to find out where he was operating.

He pulled the files of the team members up on his tablet as they patiently waited for him to get started.

He pulled up the kid first. He was twenty-two, maybe a hundred thirty pounds, six foot two, and so skinny he looked like a good breeze would blow him over. His sandy blond hair was ruthlessly combed back, probably in an attempt to tame the curls that were popping up all over his head. He wore a tan blazer, a white button-up shirt, and navy slacks. Jonas thought of it as the uniform of students. He'd seen a few of them in his day.

Jonas took a step in front of the kid. "Donaldson, Andrew. Says here you're an accounting and finance student. Just one month shy of graduating with your master's. Passed all of the tests with high scores. Very impressive for a man your age."

"Thank you, sir. I was honored to have been chosen for the Honors Internship Program. I'm looking forward to helping in any way I can."

Jonas nodded and went to the next. He didn't know the agent personally, but the man had come recommended. He wore the uniform of an FBI agent. The black slacks, black jacket, and plain blue shirt wouldn't stand out in a crowd. His dark brown hair was cut short. He was just shy of six feet, probably a hundred seventy pounds, fit and muscular.

Jonas took a step so he stood directly before the man. "Special Agent Rhodes, Matthew. Says you came from our Forensic Accounting division. Why counterintelligence?"

Agent Rhodes got to his feet. "I passed all the necessary exams and want to move into counterintelligence. I think my skills can be applied to this job, sir."

Jonas nodded at the vague answer. The man was sweating bullets and looked so nervous Jonas didn't have the heart to press him. He then took a step over to look at the striking blonde watching him with a smile on her face. Her bright blue eyes held his.

This one wasn't so easy to assess. She wore a wool skirt that skimmed her knees, black tights in deference to the cold outside, knee-high brown leather boots, and a sweater that accentuated her small waist and high breasts. She had her almost waist-length hair pulled back in an elaborate braid. She wore minimal makeup but knew how to enhance her natural beauty. Her file said she was five foot six, but the boots would add some height, as he was sure was her intention. She weighed around one-twenty and appeared to be fit.

Eyes on hers, he spoke. "Albright, Lian. Contract linguist. And what brings you to this assignment?"

"I speak fluent Mandarin and Cantonese, and I need money." Lian kept her tone bored, as she wanted to project the guise of just another linguist looking for work.

What she didn't want was for him to get too curious about her and start digging into her past. Her file with the FBI was slim. She had the necessary requirements to work as a contractor, and as far as the FBI was concerned, that's all there was to her. The time she spent with the CIA was classified and not mentioned in her FBI file. And the time she'd spent in China this past year was also classified. Her counterfeit records showed her working at a university in Maryland during that time, but for a man in counterintelligence, it wouldn't be hard to rip that cover story to shreds.

Jonas studied her face. Her accent, which spoke of her years spent in China, was incongruent in the face of a woman of obvious European descent. The face itself was not stunning. Her mouth was a little too big, as were her eyes. But the sparkle in her eyes and her low, sexy voice were enough to get his attention. Her almost white hair was braided down her back in an intricate weave. Her features were distinctive, as was that hair. Something about her was nagging at him. He thought he had seen her somewhere before, but her file said she was new to the Virginia area, and he didn't recognize her name.

"That's honest enough. All three of you have been assigned to help track down a man simply known as Kang. He's anywhere between thirty and forty years old. He used to operate out of Hong Kong but has made his way to the U.S. His last known address was a mansion in Beverly Hills. He likes to make money, and he likes to spend it. We're hoping to track him through his finances. Ms. Albright, you're assigned to sift through the statements and use the system to translate the most important ones first. Your next task will be to listen to some recordings and interpret those."

"What about us, sir?" Agent Rhodes interrupted.

Jonas gritted his teeth. "We have some of his records from American and Swiss bank accounts, along with some of his Chinese account records translated for you to start with. You'll get the rest after Ms. Albright processes them."

"Yes, sir." Rhodes fell silent once again.

Lian watched as the other two team members turned in their chairs and got to work on the files in front of them. The assignment was easy enough, for which she was grateful. It would be hard to deliver good work on a difficult assignment while keeping her eyes and ears on Jonas.

"Is there a problem, Ms. Albright?" Jonas took a seat at the station next to her.

"No. I like to get a feel first. Would you mind answering some questions?" Lian gave Jonas her most professional smile.

"Depends. You have clearance, but some things are beyond your clearance level." Jonas scooted closer in his chair and tapped a few keys to bring up her screens.

"Just tell me no if I get past my level. What is your interest in this guy? I would think running guns to gangs would be more at the local level in Los Angeles."

"It might if he weren't smuggling those weapons in from Hong Kong. And if he weren't selling those guns all over the country. I have reason to suspect that he has ties to some notorious triads."

Lian nodded. "Organized?"

"Highly."

Lian nodded again. There were generally two types of triads. Some were loosely organized, mostly operating as small groups but without much power. The other type was highly organized. They controlled most of the crime in local markets and often had police protection, though not legally.

"Our guy Kang likes to think of himself as part of a secret society, like in the early days of the Chinese triads in the eighteenth century. Rumors are that he spent a fortune when he arrived in the U.S. decorating his home with ancient Chinese art and antiquities. I have a feeling he ticked off the wrong people and fled Hong Kong, leaving his possessions behind. He's found himself quite a lucrative business here in the West." Jonas tapped a few keys and pulled up some files.

Lian grabbed the mouse and enlarged some of the files. "So you have a low-level ex-triad member living the American dream."

"That about sums it up. Local authorities haven't been able to pin anything on him. There were also a couple of homicides I'm sure he had a hand in. I'm hoping some of the recordings might reveal either his involvement or those who were. The homicides crossed state lines, but I haven't played the federal jurisdiction card yet. The two local police captains have been keeping me apprised of their progress."

"Which I'm guessing isn't much." Lian pulled up

the file with a picture of Kang. It was grainy, and unfortunately, it wasn't good enough for accurate identification. All it gave was an impression of hair color, which was dark brown given his Chinese heritage, and an idea of how tall. She took a closer look and saw a ring on the man's hand. The close-up of the ring was fuzzy but identifiable.

"I haven't had a chance yet to identify the symbol on his ring. That's another thing I need you for." Jonas saw where her attention had drifted.

"It implies he is an enforcer for the triad he is a part of. Puts him one step above your general triad members, but not so far up he's in line to be the next dragon head."

"Dragon head?" Jonas looked closer at the ring.

"Leader. I take it you don't speak or read Chinese."

"No. The cases I worked on in the major crime unit were domestic. The work I've done so far in counterintelligence has also been domestic. Kang's name kept popping up on a case I was working on."

Lian opened a browser and did a rudimentary search. "This is the symbol on his ring. It's simply Chinese for 'red pole' or, in English, enforcer. Our guy is very literal and probably likes people to know he is not to be reckoned with. He would have been one of many, but he was probably the most ambitious of the group."

Jonas was impressed. "Is this your first assignment with the FBI?"

Figuring the truth was her best bet, since she was sure he'd read and memorized her file, she shook her head. "No. I've worked a few cases with the FBI over the years. It pays well, and I get to do my duty as an American."

"But you weren't born here." Jonas had read the files on all three. Lian had been born in China. Beijing to be specific.

"You read my file, so you know I was born in Beijing. My parents were missionaries. It was only sheer luck that had my parents in Beijing when I was born. They were on the verge of being deported and were working on renewing their paperwork to stay in China. They were also meeting with friends. I came early, or I would have been born in the village where I spent most of my childhood."

Jonas scooted back to his desk. He had an unprecedented urge to touch. Normally when he worked, he was all business. Something about Ms. Lian Albright had his fingers itching. He got back to business. "Any more questions?"

"No. Knowing his level in the triad might help. He's most likely working with someone his level back in Hong Kong, or with someone higher up trying to get even higher. I think you'll learn a lot once Andrew and Agent Rhodes start tracing his money."

"Focus on that then. And when you get cross-eyed running the software program to translate them, the recordings are already in a file on your desktop." Jonas rose and walked to the center of the room.

The trio turned and looked at him. Donaldson looked excited. Agent Rhodes was poorly concealing his. And Lian Albright looked at him with big blue eyes that held secrets.

Chapter Two

"Well, well. If it isn't the chink wannabe." Agent Trevor White entered the gym where Lian was finishing up her run on the treadmill. Figured she'd run into him. It had probably been too much to hope she wouldn't. She'd heard he had been let go from his last assignment and was back in Virginia. She had hoped the FBI leaders would realize the guy was a useless slug and fire him, but no such luck.

Agent White was under six feet, had brown hair, and a nondescript face. Nothing about him stood out. She hadn't seen him since she had worked with him almost two years ago, and he now sported a bit of weight around his midsection, probably from spending time at a desk.

"Agent White. Glad to see you survived your last assignment." Lian gritted her teeth and didn't react to his incredibly ignorant, racist comment. She wasn't sure if Agent White was a racist or just a jerk. Probably both. Lian kept her pace, barely breathing hard.

Agent White scowled at her. She had witnessed his screw-up and had reported it to his superiors. He had been reassigned after serving a one month suspension. And because of her, he had not gotten the promotion he'd been hoping for. "Heard you got another contractor gig. Just can't cut it as a real FBI agent."

Lian increased her pace. She knew he would stand there and goad her all day if she let him get to her. He had a couple of his buddies behind him. White always liked to put on a show.

Agent White took a step towards her. "Hear you've been working at a college. Quite the comedown."

Lian stopped the treadmill and stepped off. She took a step to go around him. She took a step back when he crowded her. She subtly shifted her weight to her back leg. "Back off."

"Or what? You got me suspended with your little stunt. It's payback time."

Jonas, who had been watching the byplay from the doorway, yanked Agent White by his t-shirt and threw him to the mat. "Take one more step towards her and you'll be eating your teeth."

Lian came and stood next to Jonas, the fire in her eyes directed at the agent who was scowling at her.

"Do you want to press charges?" Jonas handed Lian a nearby towel.

"He didn't touch me. Just being his usual self. A class A jerk." Lian wrapped the towel around her neck, blotting the sweat that had formed on her chest.

Jonas directed his comment to Agent White. "Get out. And I had better not see you near Ms. Albright again. I've about had it with you and your attitude."

Agent White picked himself up from the mat,

muttered some expletives under his breath, waved to his cronies, and left.

"Thanks. Agent White and I go way back. I worked with him on my first assignment with the FBI. I also worked with him on my last."

"You testified in a hearing against him."

"Guess that was in my file, too." Lian walked to the nearby fridge and pulled out a bottle of water. She tossed one to Jonas, who caught it one-handed.

"Agent White requested a transfer to counterintelligence last year. I vetoed it. I'm not exactly high on his list, either. But I outrank him, so there's little he can do about it."

"Probably comes in handy. He hates your guts but keeps his mouth shut. Wouldn't mind having that power myself." Lian took a large swallow.

"He could be brought up for improper conduct, especially given what he called you." Jonas dropped onto a nearby weight bench.

Lian scowled at the doorway Agent White had exited. "He's a real peach, but it's his word against mine. His buddies will swear he never said a word to me."

Jonas spun the water bottle in his hands. "I heard him."

Lian shrugged. "I've been called worse, and in more than one language. He's not worth the time or effort."

"If he bothers you again, I expect you to tell me." Jonas rose to look down at her.

"The intimidation routine might work better if you weren't wearing gym shorts." Lian gave him a small smile.

Jonas looked down and gave her a light laugh. "You may be right. Are you done working out?"

"No. I just finished my warmup run. One of the best things about a job here is that I get to use the facilities." Lian set the towel down and took the weight bench next to Jonas. She selected some light weights.

Jonas watched Lian as she did some arm curls. She wore a t-shirt instead of the more revealing outfits several of the other female agents in the room wore. She was also wearing a baggy pair of sweatpants. He knew he shouldn't, but he thought she looked adorable with her hair back in a twist, sweat glistening on her brow and upper lip, and the baggy outfit covering up her curves. And though he couldn't see her curves, he knew they were there.

"How about you? You don't look like you've worked up a sweat yet." Lian couldn't help but notice the thick, ropy muscles on his legs and arms, nor could she miss how broad his chest looked in the tight-fitting white t-shirt.

"Waiting for a friend. We spar on Tuesdays. Speaking of which." Jonas turned to see his friend.

"You're going to want to watch your back, boss. White is out there running off at the mouth for all he's worth. Seems you made his blacklist."

Jonas looked at the doorway. "He's going to be a

problem."

"Don't take it personally. He's a problem for everyone."

Jonas looked at the younger man. "Agent Bartlett, I'd like you to meet Lian Albright. She's been temporarily assigned to my team."

"Lian?" The agent looked over at the woman on the bench next to Jonas. "Well, I'll be. How are you?"

Lian was lifted into a huge bear hug by the large dark-haired man who stood beside Jonas. "I'm good, Dex. Been a while."

Agent Dex Bartlett set her down, his dark brown eyes looking her over. "It's been at least a year, if not longer. How is your friend?"

Lian patted his cheek. "Here."

"Here? Why is Mindy here?"

"She decided she needed a break. She's on vacation, and since I was coming to Virginia, she decided to tag along. I didn't know you were reassigned."

"Yeah. I got a transfer to Jonas's team. When I heard there was an opening, I jumped on board."

Jonas watched the pair. "I take it you two know each other."

Lian glanced over at Jonas. His tone was strange. "I helped find a missing Chinese boy, one of several that disappeared in the Chicago area. FBI coordinated with the local branch of missing and exploited children. My friend Mindy called me in to help. Dex here headed up the team and brought me on officially."

"Yeah, along with White. Now I know what got him in a twist. He and Lian went a few rounds. Did he threaten you?" Dex automatically made a fist.

Lian put her hand over his fingers. "No. He didn't get that far. Plus, he's not an idiot. He wouldn't threaten me in front of so many witnesses. He was just a jerk."

"And he won't be again, or he'll be out." Jonas was one of many superiors who were working on getting Agent White tossed out of the FBI. He had a bad attitude; he didn't work well with the public, and he spent a lot of time causing trouble, both on and off the job.

"If you wouldn't mind giving Mindy my number, I'd love to see her while she's here."

Lian took pity on him. "Stop by later today and I'll give you her cell number. I'm sure she'd like to see you."

"Thanks." Dex's eyes lit with anticipation. Then his eyes lit with a different type of anticipation. "Ready to go, boss?"

"Yeah. And get the number after work hours. Your love life can wait until after work."

Dex winked at Lian. "No worries. If I know you, Lian will still be here when I clock off. You're a slave driver."

Lian tried to concentrate on her workout, but there was no chance of that. Jonas and Dex had taken to the sparring mat. Several different people stopped to watch. The two men were well matched. Dex was a few years younger and a bit faster, but Jonas wasn't exactly slow on his feet, and he had more power in his attacks. Both men pulled their punches, but they fought hard. Both men were drenched in sweat by the time the match ended. It was hard to tell which one had won.

"Want to go a round?" Dex dropped onto the bench next to Lian.

"I think I'll pass today. I'd hate to take you on when you're all worn out. Wouldn't be a fair fight." Lian bumped her shoulder against Dex.

Dex bumped her back. "Wouldn't mind seeing you take on Jonas. Bet you'd get a few good licks in."

She didn't say anything. She couldn't beat Dex in a fair fight, so she had no illusions when it came to Jonas. Dex fought her at her level when they sparred in the past, but he was just too big and too muscular for her to take down easily. "I think I like my head where it's at."

"He's good. Almost as good as I am." Dex gave her a wink and stood. "I'm going to hit the showers. I'll be by later for that number."

Lian gave him a small salute and turned her eyes back to Jonas, who was showing a younger man a few of the moves he had used on Dex. Though tempted to spend the rest of the morning watching Jonas, she had a job to do. He would probably be here at least another half hour. Then he'd hit the showers. Lian grabbed her stuff and headed for the showers herself.

She kept her eyes on Jonas as she crossed the room, even when he caught her staring. She didn't take her gaze off him until she hit the doors.

Realizing she had probably lost her mind, staring at him the way she had, she quickly headed for the showers. Now was not the time for her latent hormones to kick into gear. He might be the sexiest man she'd seen in a long time, but she had a job to do. And that job might find her turning in evidence against the man.

Lian showered and changed back into her street clothes in record time. She passed several people she knew, but simply nodded at them. First stop was Jonas's office. As a supervisory agent, he had his own space. He would probably head straight to where Andrew and Rhodes were working. They were due in the office within the next half hour. Lian hoped to beat Jonas back to the room where they were working. She didn't need to stay in his office long. She just needed to put a small tracker on his keyboard. She knew his office would be swept for bugs, but according to her sources, the sweeps were done off-hours. She couldn't know how often his office would be swept, but she planned to get it back before she left today. She needed his laptop code. Once she had that, she would find a convenient time to mirror his computer drive and take it back with her.

As she neared his office, she hugged a nearby wall, pulling a dark coat over her clothes and pulling a hat over her hair. She easily slipped into his office, doing her best to avoid the hall cameras as she went. There were not many people here at this time of the day. She had noticed that there was little activity early in the morning. She quickly planted the device. She also took the opportunity to do a quick check. His file cabinets were locked, as was his desk. He was not the careless type. There were awards on his walls, as well as pictures of him with other agents. Looking closely, she saw a picture of him with an ex-president and first lady. Impressed, she stepped back and slipped from his office. She smiled when no one was around.

She ditched the coat and hat and slipped behind her desk five minutes before anyone else arrived.

"You're making us look bad." Andrew dropped into his seat and booted up his computer.

"If you're interested in getting a recommendation, you just need to get here before the boss." Lian gave him a friendly smile. He was earnest and truly interested in learning whatever he could. He didn't understand Mandarin, but he had picked up a few keywords and was helping to sort a pile of paper records.

"Then we're good." Andrew quickly turned and got to work.

"Morning." Agent Rhodes came in.

Lian and Andrew said good morning back but didn't linger in conversation. Rhodes was a bit of a snob. He felt he was smarter than the two of them because he was an agent, and they weren't. He acted like he'd been insulted by being assigned to such a small project, but only when Jonas wasn't in the room. Once Jonas arrived, Rhodes would put on his game face. It annoyed Lian, but she let it go. She didn't have the energy to care. Andrew was so excited to be here; she didn't know if he even realized that Rhodes was being insulting.

"I have the pile you gave me yesterday. Should I keep with it?" Andrew pulled the stack from the locked desk.

"That would be great. I finished scanning and translating what you gave me yesterday, so I can give that to Rhodes. Right, Rhodes?" Lian timed her comment as Jonas walked into the room.

"Certainly. If you two have a few pages for me, I can look them over." Rhodes took the stack. "Good morning, Agent Cole."

"Morning. I see we've made some progress." Jonas walked past Rhodes's desk, checking his desk as he went. The agent had gotten started on the bank files, but there didn't seem to be anything worth noting on them yet.

Andrew turned eager eyes at Jonas. "Morning, Agent Cole. I was helping Lian. We just have a couple of piles to finish sorting."

Jonas raised his eyebrow at Andrew. "Learning Chinese?"

"Yeah. Lian's a great teacher. We were chatting yesterday. It's hard to imagine having to learn how to read and write Mandarin. She made me a cheat sheet in Pinyin and English so I could help identify which documents to start with first."

Lian saw the question in Jonas's eyes. "Pinyin is Chinese letters in the English alphabet. The cheat sheet will help him recognize both."

Jonas nodded in approval. "Good. There's probably a lot of duplicates in those piles and documents that won't be much help. We've not had much luck with the American and Swiss accounts."

"We'll get Andrew reading and writing Mandarin in no time." She squeezed Andrew's shoulder and went back to her desk.

Jonas saw the admiration in Andrew's eyes as he shyly looked at her under his lashes. The poor kid had a crush. And the kid had good taste. "So what are we looking for?"

"I'll print you a sheet." Lian pulled up the document she made for Andrew and printed a copy. "The ones in bold are the ones I think have the most promise. There are several mentions of a global trade company out of Hong Kong, but the phone number has a U.S. country code. Rudimentary search didn't pull much up on it. I'm hoping you or Agent Rhodes can dig further into it. Not sure it's legit."

"I'll see what I can dig up. I might send this to one of our other agents." Jonas looked and noticed a Chinese letter overlay on Lian's keyboard.

She glanced up at him. "Habit. It's easier to translate this way. I sometimes confuse my English letters."

Jonas took the empty seat at the desk nearby. "Your file said you were fifteen when you came to live in the U.S. The file didn't say why."

"My parents were killed in a boating accident on a remote river. My parents made my uncle, my dad's brother, my guardian. He wasn't about to live in China, so I was sent to live with him when they were killed."

"I'm sorry to hear that. You said they were missionaries?" Jonas listened as he looked over her cheat sheet.

"Yes. They were traveling and a monsoon hit late in the season. They were delivering medical supplies to a small village in desperate need. They were killed along with a dozen others." Lian dropped her hands in her lap.

He heard Lian mutter something, but he was sure it wasn't in English. Sorry he had pushed her; he changed the topic. "Let me see what I can dig up. Turn the files over to Rhodes as you finish them."

Lian watched Jonas for a moment, then got back to work. She pulled on the headset provided for listening to the recordings. She had been listening to them on and off when her eyes couldn't focus on the papers before her. She quickly typed out what she was translating, another reason she was good at her job. She could type almost as quickly as they spoke. She paused the recording now and again to clean up the copy and moved on.

Two hours later, she set the headset aside. She saw Jonas watching her. She stretched and spoke. "Anything on your end?"

Jonas looked back at his screen as he spoke. "Nothing concrete. But you're right. Something is fishy about the Hong Kong trading company. I'm turning it over. You?"

"Just boring stuff. Many of these calls are Kang calling his girlfriends. Let's just say he has a lot of them, and the things he told them would make a whore blush. There were a few routine business calls. I translated those, too, but nothing stood out. But you may get lucky, and an analyst might find something. Right now I don't have anything to compare the transcripts to."

"That would be where I come in. I've been watching him for the past year. Unfortunately, it took that long to get enough evidence to get even this small team investigating him. I know names and the businesses he deals with. With your transcripts, I can start piecing it together."

That answered that question for her. She would have to be careful. She had heard a few things on the calls that had made her question what Kang was up to. Jonas said guns. But she wondered if there was more to it. Or maybe she was just seeing patterns where there were none. She had already sent an encrypted file to her personal email. She had installed a program that would wipe out the trail, but she knew it wasn't foolproof. If the FBI caught her transferring files, she'd have a lot of explaining to do, and the FBI had much more sophisticated tools than she had.

It was almost seven when Jonas finally called it a day. "Everyone go home and get some rest."

Lian, as well as the other two, was more than ready. She bid everyone good night. She made a stop at Dex's desk since he was still working and gave him Mindy's number. She used the time she spent chatting with Dex to keep an eye on Jonas's office. She left Dex around eight, and Jonas and Dex left around nine and were the last to leave. She gave it another half hour before she quickly snuck into his office. The password tracker gave her what she was looking for. She accessed his computer with no issue. Smiling to herself, she plugged in the drive and installed the program to mirror his drive. She was only interested in his personal files. With her clearance, she already had access to the rest of the database he accessed. It took longer than she expected, but eventually, the mirror was complete. She slid the drive into a hidden pocket of her jacket and slipped out of his office.

She carefully made her way through the quiet hallways. Just as she had earlier, she made her way down the hall, careful to avoid the security cameras. She had once again tucked her hair out of sight. Other than her height and weight, she could be any female agent in the building. Her badge would log her leaving late, though, and that worried her a bit, but only if Jonas realized someone had messed with his computer. She had already worked late several nights the two weeks she'd been here, so her leaving late tonight wouldn't be out of the ordinary. She had plenty of work completed to show should she be questioned about the late nights. Nothing in them would slow down Jonas's investigation, so she wasn't worried about holding onto them a little longer.

Exhausted, she climbed into her car. Mindy had left her a message on her other phone. She picked up Jonas's trail when he left at nine. He had gone home. Mindy made another comment about his "pathetic" social life and thanked her for giving her number to Dex. They were having lunch. Going on a real date with Dex would be difficult with Mindy trailing Jonas at night, while Lian trailed him during the day. Lian would have to cover for her. Dex and Mindy had gone out a few times while Dex had been in Chicago working the kidnapping case, but they both had agreed a long-distance relationship wouldn't work. Neither had been willing to change jobs.

She deleted the message and headed back to the hotel. She was too tired to worry about Mindy's and Dex's love life. She needed sleep.

Chapter Three

"You need a break. You've been muttering to yourself in Mandarin for the past four hours." Jonas hit the power button on Lian's monitor.

"Shén?" Lian rubbed her brow and looked up at Jonas with a frown on her face.

"See what I mean. You need a break. Everyone else left two hours ago."

Lian looked around. "I see you didn't."

"Boss should be the last to go. Come on, I know a place where we can get dinner."

"Dinner?" Lian furrowed her brows. "Are you asking me out?"

"If I am, would you say yes?" Jonas collected her bag for her.

Lian figured she had two options. She could say no and go get the sleep she desperately needed, or she could go with Jonas and see if she could learn anything about him. Telling herself the only reason she was going with him was duty, and not because she liked the way he looked in his suit, she nodded. "I suppose since it's just dinner."

"Just dinner. This time." Jonas helped her with her coat.

Not sure if that was a warning or a promise, Lian buttoned her coat, keeping her eyes down. "I'm not going to touch that one."

Jonas led her out of the building and to his car. "I'll bring you back for your car after dinner."

Lian slid into the passenger seat of the nondescript sedan when Jonas held the door for her. She kept her eyes on him as he rounded the car.

"Like seafood?" Jonas locked his weapon and badge in the glove compartment and started the car.

"Love it. I've not had a chance to explore much."

Jonas glanced at her. Her face was half hidden behind the hood of her black wool coat. He brushed the fabric back with his free hand so he could see her eyes. "I haven't been out in quite a while, myself."

"I'm sure it's not for lack of a date." Lian tried to keep her eyes off his after her first glance. They were intense as they focused on her. It had been a long time since she'd been the object of such obvious male desire, at least from a man whom she wanted to return it.

Lian couldn't resist turning her gaze his way. "Aren't there rules about fraternization?"

Jonas touched a finger to Lian's lips. He'd been aching to touch her in some way since the moment they met. Her lips parted slightly. "If you were an FBI agent, it would be. I'd be your superior. But you're not FBI, and so long as relationships are kept discreet, no one cares."

Lian shivered from that slight touch. "Jonas, I'm not looking for anything but dinner."

Jonas dropped his hand and put it back on the

steering wheel. "And that's all I have on the agenda tonight."

Lian was impressed when they entered the restaurant. This was a cloth napkin kind of place, and she bet the wine selection was impressive. She thanked the hostess for seating them, and a waiter immediately appeared.

Lian ordered a glass of white wine and looked questioningly at Jonas when he ordered sparkling water with lime.

"I don't drink in the middle of a case."

"I probably shouldn't. I feel like I could lie down and go to sleep right here."

Jonas waited until the waiter left before responding. "Cases like these never have enough resources. My superiors won't give me a bigger team until I find some concrete evidence that the FBI should spend time tracking him, but I need a bigger team to find the evidence quickly enough to move on any leads."

"You seem pretty sure he's dirty. If you do prove your theory, will you get more men?" Lian looked over the menu; everything on it looked delicious.

"We'll see. It depends on what else might take priority. What made you come back to the FBI? Why not stay in academia?"

Lian caught herself before she answered. She had to remember that, according to her cover, she had spent the past year behind a desk at a university, not in China working undercover off the books for the

CIA.

"I've done a lot of things over the years. There's never a shortage of work for a professional interpreter. I've worked in hospitals, universities, assorted businesses, and embassies in both the U.S. and China, and the FBI. The universities are nice, but the projects are usually short-lived. My last assignment was research, and I have to say it got a bit boring sometimes. One thing I can say about the FBI is that the jobs aren't boring."

"You don't do it for the money." Jonas kept his eyes on hers.

"No?"

"No. If you were in it for the money, we wouldn't be here together. You do it for much more complex reasons. I'd guess the very reasons most people join law enforcement." Jonas couldn't keep his eyes off hers.

Lian gave up the pretense. "All right, no, I don't do it for the money. When I work for businesses, the players are working various angles, trying to get the best deal, to one-up the other players. It gets old fast, but it pays well. Universities are okay because the people I choose to work with care about history and people. But when you interpret for an embassy or the FBI, what you do matters. People's well-being, and sometimes their lives, rely on your skills."

"You ever work with the Chinese government?" Jonas still couldn't seem to get a handle on her. Sometimes she watched him with suspicion in her eyes. Sometimes she watched him with banked desire. And other times, like now, he couldn't tell what was behind those bright blue eyes.

"Yes." It was all she said.

Jonas broke off when the waiter appeared. He gave his order for the grilled salmon and a steamed vegetable side. Lian gave her order of shrimp in a wine sauce tossed over pasta.

"I take it you don't want to talk about your time working for the Chinese government?" Jonas leaned back in his seat and waited for her answer.

"No, I don't. What I did was classified. And it was years ago."

That got Jonas's attention. What he had read hadn't hinted at any classified assignments. "I find it interesting that the FBI will allow you to work for them if you have close ties to the Chinese government."

"Quite the opposite. Many would hire me because I did. I'm open about the time I spent working for them, and there are people in the FBI who know exactly what I did for the Chinese government. There is no conflict of interest in what I did for them and what I do for the American government. But if it worries you, I've been thoroughly vetted. And the U.S. government was aware of what I was working on." Lian flicked her braid behind her back and dropped quiet. She had to be very careful with Jonas.

The last thing Jonas wanted was for her to clam up. "Just curious. Lian is an interesting name."

Lian gave him a slight nod in thanks for dropping it. "My parents loved China. Had they not died, I might never have come to the U.S. My parents named me Lian, which means the graceful willow. They wanted me to fit in."

"But they taught you English."

"English is what they spoke at home. But I went to school with the rest of the Chinese children. I learned to read and write both. Believe me, it wasn't easy. The village we lived in didn't teach English, so when I finished regular school, I had English lessons at home. My mom taught the children of the village to read and speak English, too. Though they loved China, they still loved their own country."

Lian took another sip of her wine. "My turn. What about your parents?"

Jonas grinned. "My parents are great. They've been nagging me to come visit. I promised them that for my next birthday I'd take time off. My sister is pregnant with her first child, and my brother has two kids. I missed Christmas, so they want to have a reunion when I can get free for more than a couple of days."

Lian had read the file. His parents had two natural children. Jonas was their only adopted son. She wanted to get as much information from him as she could so as not to slip later. "Are you the oldest?"

"No. I'm in the middle. My brother is older, but only by a year. My sister is the youngest by seven years."

"Do you have pictures?" Lian finished her glass of wine.

"I do." Jonas made no move to show her.

Lian realized that an FBI agent wouldn't have pictures of his family on him. "Sorry, I wasn't thinking."

"Maybe if you make it to my apartment, I'll show you."

Lian ignored that. "I watched you spar with Dex. You've studied some martial arts."

"My dad signed me up for lessons when I was fourteen. I was a handful, and he thought it would teach me discipline."

Lian gave him a light laugh. "I can see that. The FBI would have ironed out any other rough edges."

"That they do. My parents were horrified and very proud when I joined the FBI. My brother is a cop." Jonas fisted his hands at his side to prevent himself from touching the loose strands of hair against her cheeks.

"Is your dad a cop?"

"No. He's an electrician. My sister is a pediatrician. My mom is a homemaker. Any other questions?"

She had dozens but couldn't ask him the questions she really wanted to know the answers to. She couldn't trust him. She had yet to find any evidence that pointed to his innocence. Of course, it was easier to prove guilt than innocence. But her experience had been that no evidence just meant the person had done a good job hiding it.

"I think that covers your family. Where did you go to college?"

"Nearby at West Virginia University. Figured I'd come to the source."

The waiter interrupted, bringing their meal. Lian thanked him. Without hesitation, she dug in. "This is amazing. I can see why you like this place."

"Like I said, it's been a while. But this is my favorite place."

Lian took another bite. "My favorite place is a Chinese restaurant in Chicago. It's not as fancy as this place, but the food is amazing. I used to eat there when I was feeling homesick. It was also my first paying job."

"You worked in a Chinese restaurant?" Jonas slipped a piece of his fish onto Lian's plate that she had been eyeing.

She smiled and took a bite. "The best Chinese restaurant in America. My uncle and I weren't getting along, and I needed to get out. I found myself in Chinatown one day. I had a little cash, and the sign said authentic, so I popped in. When I walked in, the owner was having a hard time communicating with an extremely belligerent man at the counter. Turned out he was a vendor. I translated for them. Quan, the owner, offered me a job, and I took it. I worked there until I left for university. I still visit anytime I'm in the city."

"I delivered pizza for cash." He finished off his fish

and vegetables. Lian looked like she was still savoring her meal.

"Something in common, then."

Jonas leaned back in his seat and watched Lian finish her meal. "That and seafood."

Lian gave him a small smile. "That's probably more in common than I have with most people here in America."

Jonas took Lian's hand from across the table. "Will you go back to China, then?"

"Ever been at a crossroads, unsure of where to go?"

Jonas thought about the day he met his future adoptive parents. "Yes."

"I left China when my parents died because I had no choice. I went back to China the moment I turned eighteen, trying to recapture what I'd lost. It didn't work. I found myself back in the United States at twenty-five, with a fresh master's degree in my pocket. At twenty-nine, I found myself back in China. A year later, I was back in America. Now at thirty-two, I'm working on a case for the FBI that involves a Chinese criminal. I've also been offered a full-time position at an import business in China."

Jonas dropped her hand. "I imagine the job at the import business pays better."

"That it does. But working for the FBI might get a criminal off the streets and save lives. But my job here is short-term. The other is not." Lian pushed her plate back, no longer able to continue eating.

"And the university? Would they take you back?"

Jonas found himself extremely interested in her answer. Something about this woman drew him in a way unlike any other woman had in a long time.

Lian tipped her head, her eyes narrowing as she watched him. "They might. But again, any job there would probably be short-lived. Then again, like I said, I'm not interested in the games men play in the business world."

"But you'll play the games the government plays?" Jonas found himself very interested in her answer.

"I don't play the games governments play. I just help create the game pieces. Men like you take those pieces and play."

Jonas signaled the waiter, his eyes not leaving Lian's. "That's an interesting way to think of it. And you might be right."

Lian watched as Jonas paid the bill. When he held his hand out to hers, she took it. She let him lead her back to his car. She slipped into the passenger seat, feeling mellow and content after the delicious meal and a couple of glasses of wine.

Lian relaxed as they chatted lightly on the drive back to her car.

Jonas pulled up beside her car. "Are you okay to drive back to your hotel?"

Lian nodded. "I'm fine. Just tired."

Jonas went around and opened the car door for her. "You know you don't have to come in so early."

Lian took the hand he offered and let him help her out of the car. She pulled the strap of her purse over her shoulder. "I just might sleep in a bit tomorrow."

Jonas closed the car door, but caged Lian's body between his and the vehicle. She didn't pull away or appear alarmed. She simply watched him with eyes that held secrets.

"There's something about you I can't quite put my finger on." Jonas stroked her cheek with his index finger.

"There's nothing special there." Lian shivered a bit at his touch.

"I'm not buying that. I don't know what it is, but it's there." Jonas leaned closer, bringing his mouth to hers.

Lian felt her eyes close as he came closer. She knew it was madness to let him this close to her, to let him kiss her, but she had no resistance in her. The touch of his lips on hers was soft at first, then became more ardent when she didn't pull back.

Jonas lifted his head for a moment, then dipped back for another taste. This time he pulled her body against his. He couldn't feel much of her through the layers of his and her coat, but he felt an impression of curves. Instead of pulling away, she wrapped her arms around his neck, bringing herself onto her toes for better access.

Jonas could feel Lian's hands trembling around his neck when he finally broke off the kiss. The sound of his breathing was harsh in the quiet of the night. "I'll see you tomorrow."

It took a moment to get her bearings, but she

realized she was once again leaning against Jonas's car. She was a bit unsteady in her heeled boots but made her way around him and to the driver's side door of her rental car without stumbling. "Good night, Jonas."

"Good night, Lian."

Jonas followed, closed her car door, and waited until she had left the parking lot before he got back in his own. It was late, but he wasn't tired. Instead of heading home, he headed to a friend's apartment.

* * *

"That was quite a show last night." Mindy yawned as she relaxed on her bed.

Lian felt heat rise to her cheeks. She sat with her laptop at a small desk in Mindy's room. She hadn't gotten much sleep after her dinner with Jonas, so she had gone to visit Mindy before heading to work. "You didn't need to tail him. You knew I was with him."

"Had you gone home with him, instead of back to your own lonely bed, I might not have. But I know you, and it was inevitable that I'd have to follow him home. Except he didn't go home, not right away."

Lian straightened and turned in her seat. "Where did he go?"

Mindy handed Lian a slip of paper with an address on it. "I don't know what apartment he went to, but that is the address. Maybe something in his files will tell you."

Lian shook her head. "So far, there is nothing on his computer that is out of the ordinary. There is the normal correspondence a man in his position would have. There are the types of files you'd expect from a man like him, too."

Mindy yawned and let out a puff of air. "As normal as they can be for an FBI agent, I suppose. Nothing sticks out at all?"

"No." Lian pushed her loose hair back from her face. She hadn't braided it since her shower.

"Maybe there isn't anything to find. We have no proof he's involved with Bo. We have no proof that he even knows he has a brother at all." Mindy yawned again, her eyes starting to drift closed.

"Maybe. But he was the only lead I had. So if he doesn't know where Bo is, then I need to rethink my plan." Lian entered the address into her file and shredded the paper.

"Maybe he can help us. Or maybe Dex."

Lian rubbed the ache in her brow. "If you tell Dex, then I can guarantee he'll tell Jonas. Those two are close. And if Dex tells him, and we're wrong about Jonas's innocence, we'll put Dex in danger."

"How long do you think it will take to finish going through his files?"

Lian inhaled deeply and exhaled slowly, trying to relax her tight muscles. "A couple more days. And let me find out who he might have gone to see at this address. Maybe it will be a clue."

"Or maybe he just wanted to get laid, and since you didn't oblige, he went somewhere else."

Lian blushed again but didn't rise to the bait. But she supposed Mindy had a point. Jonas had felt pretty virile pressed up against her, even through the layers of their clothing. "Just get some rest. You're having lunch with Dex. You don't want to look haggard. Just keep what we're really doing here to yourself."

"Have it your way. I still think they can help." Mindy snuggled deeper into the bed.

"Or maybe they'll go to their superiors, and I'll be arrested for the theft of an FBI agent's classified files."

"We don't have to tell them that part. You get to work before Jonas gets suspicious." Mindy drifted off.

Lian made a few more notes on her laptop and saved the file. She looked over at Mindy, who was now snoring softly. She was grateful for Mindy's help. When she had come back to the U.S., she had known she could count on the woman's help. Though Mindy knew Lian was looking for Bo, she didn't know all the reasons why. And though she had told Mindy that Jonas was Bo's brother, she hadn't elaborated on how she had come to know this. Mindy had accepted Lian's secrets and agreed to help. Lian only hoped she wasn't putting her best friend in danger. And perhaps Jonas as well.

Chapter Four

Lian arrived at the FBI offices around nine. After leaving Mindy, she had stopped for some coffee before heading over. When she arrived, there was extra security at the door, and there was extra security outside the office she and the rest of Jonas's team occupied. The agent at the door double-checked her badge before he let her in.

"What's up with the goon at the door?" Lian set her coffee down and stripped off her wool coat. Her stomach was in knots. She had a feeling she knew exactly why.

Agent Rhodes just grunted and kept at whatever it was he was working on.

Andrew didn't wheel over in his chair as was his custom, but he did turn to glance at her before turning back to his computer. "Rumors are there was a security breach. Not a lot of details floating around, but rumors are that it was Agent Cole's files. I was frisked when I came in this morning, and the agent outside the door is listening in on us."

Lian turned to her computer and kept her guilty face away from Andrew. "Do they think we have something to do with it?"

"Nah, just extra precautions, I imagine. But it could be because of what we're working on. If this guy Kang is as dangerous as Agent Cole thinks, it's possible he hacked the FBI computers."

Lian booted up the computer and pulled up the files she'd been working on. It was in her best interest to just keep working. "We haven't found anything concrete on Kang yet, but that doesn't mean we're not close. Men like him have lots of resources and lots of spies."

"That they do, Ms. Albright." Jonas came into the room, his eyes on the trio.

"Agent Cole. Is it true?" Andrew turned earnest eyes to Jonas.

"Yes. It looks like my files were hacked. So far, the data that was taken seems to be isolated to my files, but we have our cyber division combing through the system looking for any other files that may have been taken. And finding out how he got to them in the first place."

Andrew looked away from the anger on Jonas's face. "So what do we do?"

"You keep doing what we're paying you to do. Keep trying to find any shred of evidence that Kang is a criminal."

Lian turned enough so she could see Jonas's face. His jaw was clenched, and his fingers were crushing the file he was holding. She wished she could go to him, but not only would that be inappropriate at the office, but she had a feeling he wouldn't welcome her attention.

"So what do we have?" Jonas tossed the file onto the empty desk beside Lian.

Lian glanced his way, then back at the screen.

"Nothing concrete, but on Tuesday, June 15th, last year, Kang made his first mention of a man named Ping Biao. That name appears repeatedly from June through last December. I did a quick scan of the audio files. There are fourteen calls in total."

Jonas booted up the extra computer. He entered his credentials and pulled a search on Biao. "Well, well. You might have found a thread."

Lian leaned in closer to Jonas, to not be overheard. "Are you sure it's guns that Kang is running?"

Jonas nodded, keeping his eyes on the screen. "Fairly certain. In one of my earlier investigations, I found a list of serial numbers in a computer file that one of the local police precincts confiscated at a crime scene. There were crates of weapons on the premises."

Lian knew she should drop the subject until she had more evidence, but she couldn't help pushing. "Did the serial numbers match the guns found?"

"No. But that just means that the guns on the document they found had already been sold. What the police found was a new shipment."

"But they didn't find a file of serial numbers for those guns?"

Jonas faced Lian. "What are you getting at?"

Lian sat back in her seat. "Nothing. I just can't help but wonder if there is more involved."

Jonas shrugged and went back to his search on Biao. "There's always something else with men like Kang. They'll do almost anything to make a buck. I would bet there are drugs involved, or illegal gambling, or something along those lines. A man like Kang would have his hands in several dealings. But the serial numbers and the guns found were the first major clues that something was going on with Kang, and that his power in the western states was growing."

Lian went back to her screens. "I'll finish translating these calls first and see if anything else stands out."

"What about the bank files?" Jonas said while he focused on his search.

"The ones Andrew and I deemed most likely to be useful are translated and with Rhodes."

"Good. I need the three of you focused on this. I have to take a break from this and focus on the breach."

"Any clue as to who?" Lian casually asked the question, but her heart was pounding.

"Depends on what the cyber division finds. I can only hope it has ties to Kang, but the reality is that it could be anyone. And we can't be certain that my files were the only target, though it seems likely. The team should have something in the next few hours."

Lian dropped silent and put the headphones on to stop the conversation. Periodically she'd glance over at Jonas, who was completely focused. A couple of hours later, he instructed the team to continue working and to email him if anything of interest needed his attention.

Lian watched Jonas as he left. He briefly turned to her, and for a brief moment, she could see in his eyes that he was remembering the kiss they'd shared. Then he left the room without another backward glance.

"He's pretty ticked." Andrew spoke in the quiet of the room.

Rhodes grunted from his desk. "That's a mild word for it. When he finds out who did it, he'll have their head on a platter."

"Can't say that I blame him. Do you really think it was Kang?" Andrew spun to look at Agent Rhodes.

"He's a likely suspect, but as Agent Cole said, it could be anyone. Cole has quite the reputation in the bureau. Top brass has been grooming him for a while to take over a leadership role. His heading the counterintelligence unit is the first step to the top."

Lian considered that. And if that were true, she could see why. She'd only had those files three days before their theft was noticed. She was now on borrowed time, and she had very little to show for her efforts. So far, everything in the files didn't point to any wrongdoing on Jonas's part. And everyone here seemed to respect and admire him. And Mindy hadn't found anything suspicious while she followed him in the evenings. Lian told Mindy not to bother tailing him anymore. Other than his trip to that apartment building last night, there was nothing else to show for Mindy's efforts. It was looking like her only lead to Bo was a dead end.

Tonight she would track who lived in the apartment building Jonas had visited last night just as a final precaution. And it would only take another day or so after that to go through the rest of his files. Once she had done that, she could put Jonas in the clear.

Lian put the headset back on. Even if she cleared Jonas, she couldn't walk out on this assignment. Jonas's gut was right. This Kang fellow was indeed dangerous and becoming more and more so as the days passed. As she listened to the recordings, Biao's name popped up again. If she wasn't wrong, Biao was Kang's Hong Kong contact.

Jonas didn't come back the rest of the evening, and she left around eight. Security searched her and checked her phone before she walked out. She got in her car and pulled out of the lot. As soon as she hit the hotel parking lot, she pulled out her other phone she had stashed in her car.

She sent a quick text. "Need anything you have on a Ping Biao. Hong Kong. Related to J case, not B."

A minute later, the response came. "Twenty."

Lian tucked the phone in her pocket and headed to Mindy's room. She knocked, but when a minute passed and no one answered, she knocked again. Worried, Lian pulled out Mindy's spare key. They had swapped room keys in case of an emergency.

Lian had taken only two steps into the room when she realized Mindy was not alone. There was no mistaking the sounds the couple was making.

Embarrassed, Lian backed out of the room, quickly shutting the door behind her. Cheeks still flushed, she opened her own door.

Lian tossed her purse on her bed and set her second cell phone next to her computer. She had just kicked off her shoes when her personal cell rang. She recognized the number calling her, though it wasn't programmed into her phone.

Heart pounding, she answered. "Hello."

"Hope I didn't catch you at a bad time." Jonas's voice came clear over the line.

Lian smiled and dropped onto the bed. "No. I left the office a little while ago. I just got back to the hotel about ten minutes ago."

"I'm sorry I didn't get a chance to talk to you today. It was a crazy day."

Lian heard the weary tone come through. "You have a lot on your plate. I'm sorry to hear about what happened. It must be very worrisome."

"You don't know the half of it. Our cyber unit concluded that someone copied the files from my laptop. The question now is how in the world they managed to not only get in and out of the FBI offices unseen, but also how they knew my password?"

"I imagine it won't take your team long to find out." Lian closed her eyes as she said it, knowing he would surely hate her if he knew it was her. And she doubted he'd believe her reasons were honorable.

"It won't. But that's not what I wanted to talk to you about. I enjoyed dinner last night. I was hoping we could do it again."

Lian squeezed the bridge of her nose between two fingers. "I enjoyed dinner as well. But I won't be staying past this assignment, and it might sound like a cliché, but I'm just not the type of girl who hops into bed with a man, knowing full well it won't last."

Jonas was quiet for a moment. "No, I don't suppose you are. How about dinner Friday night after work? Just dinner."

"I don't know if that's a good idea, Jonas."

"Going to make me beg?" Jonas kept his tone light, but there was a serious edge to it.

"No, I'm not going to make you beg. But I'm serious, Jonas."

"I know a great Chinese restaurant. I can't guarantee it will be as great as the one you worked at, but I can guarantee you'll enjoy the meal."

Lian gave in. "I certainly can't turn down an offer like that."

"Good. That was my hope. I may not see you in the office tomorrow, but I'll come to get you on Friday around six."

"Six. Good night, Jonas."

"Good night, Lian."

Lian heard him hang up, and she set the phone down. Oh, she knew she was playing with fire. But there was something about him that drew her in and made her throw caution to the winds. She just hoped she didn't regret it.

Lian slipped from the bed and had a shower. She

then headed for her laptop. She booted up a hidden program and typed the address Mindy had given her into the search. There were over a hundred apartments in that building. It would take time to pull up all the names on the leases. She set the program to pull the information and opened up another window. As soon as she took the case for the FBI, she had her contact at the CIA pull a file on Kang. They weren't terribly interested in his activities, either in Hong Kong or in California. But from the email her friend had just sent her, it looked like they did have an interest in a man named Ping Biao.

The file said he was a well-known triad member, having been caught with guns and drugs over the years, but no charges had stuck. The man had a lot of power behind him, but it was only speculation as to who that power was. It was probable that whoever Kang used to work for, Biao was still a member. Or she supposed it was just as probable that both men had gone rogue and were operating solo. If so, that was a dangerous game to play, and both men would know that.

The file had a photo of Biao, but she didn't recognize him. She saved the file, attached it to a new email, and sent it off. She knew it was a long shot, but there was one person who, if she recognized the man, could tell her if he was involved with Bo. Lian knew she was probably grasping at straws, but it was worth a shot. She had run the name Kang through the woman, but his name hadn't rung any bells. But names were easy to change, faces a little harder, though not impossible.

An hour later, her query stopped. She took the list of names from the lease agreements and fed them back into a second database. While that ran, she went back to Jonas's files. Two hours later, her eyes crossing, she closed them. There was still nothing out of the ordinary in them.

Eyes gritty and tired, Lian took a look at the query. There were several women who lived in the building, many within the age range of someone Jonas might date. There were a few people with some minor criminal charges in their backgrounds, but mostly minor drug possession charges and domestic assault and battery. Very typical for an apartment complex of that size.

She then saw a name she recognized. Laughing lightly at herself and laughing in relief, she highlighted Dex's name in the file and put it in an email to Mindy to send out in the morning. She didn't want to risk sending it now and having it fall into Dex's hands. Besides, his hands were currently occupied, and she hated to disturb them.

* * *

Across town, Jonas sat in bed with his laptop. It irked him that he was sitting up late on a Wednesday night looking up any information he could find on the woman he currently wanted. It had been too long since a woman had caused him to lose sleep. And this woman wasn't even trying. She was even trying to discourage him, not that he planned to let her do that. Lian intrigued him, and for him, that was more attractive than anything else about her.

Her résumé and background check and the FBI files confirmed everything she had told him about herself. Her parents were missionaries, very devoted ones if the files were to be believed. There were images of old newspaper clippings of her parents in a few publications that highlighted what the couple had done for the people of China. They had lived in some of the most remote parts of the country. They had had only one child, and there had been a few pictures of her from her youth. There had even been an obituary honoring the couple, saying how they would be missed, as well as the young daughter they had left behind who was going to go live with an uncle in the U.S.

There was a picture of Lian when she graduated with a Master of Arts in Language at a renowned university in China. There were documents tracking her comings and goings from one country to the other. There were employment records, tax forms, and copies of articles she had written for university newsletters and alumni publications.

But a year ago was when the documents got a little vague. There was no record of her returning to the U.S. last year, only a record of her going to China two years before. There was also no concrete documentation that she worked for a university in Maryland. There were no publications, no mention of her assistance in any research in those publications, nor any records at all, other than pay stubs, to show she actually worked there. He couldn't find her faculty ID, her résumé, or an application to apply for the position.

Closing the lid and setting it to the side, he leaned back against the pillows. Perhaps he was getting jaded. His ex-fiancée had accused him of that. Said he couldn't trust anyone, that he was always looking out for the people around him to betray him. Of course, she had eventually betrayed him, finding comfort in the arms of a man she said had real passion in him, one who could trust her without proof of innocence and didn't always have one foot out the door.

The only part he had taken issue with was the one foot out the door. He had been committed to her, though he supposed in hindsight he could see how she might have thought otherwise. He had been gone a lot, and the work he did was dangerous. He couldn't sugarcoat the work he did, and he didn't elaborate on his day when he did come home. She told him she had come to hate his job, said she hated that she was always worried that he might not come home. The night she told him about her affair and that she was leaving him was the day he had gotten the promotion to lead the counterintelligence unit. It had meant less danger, steadier work hours, and less worry for her.

Once she had confessed the affair, he hadn't told her about the promotion. He had watched numbly while she packed a few things and left, leaving her marquise diamond engagement ring on their dresser. She had taken advantage of his work hours to finish emptying out the apartment later that week.

So here he was, spying on Lian. His gut said she wasn't dangerous, but his mind told him she was hiding something. The thought that she might not be what she seemed had driven him to pull up her full FBI file, the one that she probably knew they had on her but didn't know what was in it. He closed his eyes in disgust and slid down to lie flat. He really was an untrusting bastard. He just couldn't seem to help himself. And now he couldn't help but wonder what Lian had been doing for the past two years. Had she really been working in Maryland after a year-long stint with the U.S. Embassy in China? Or had she been doing something else?

Chapter Five

"So now what?" Mindy lay on Lian's bed, her eyes closed.

Lian sat at the desk, wearily rubbing her brow. Her head ached from being up all night finishing going through Jonas's files. She should have gotten some rest, but she couldn't spend another night wondering if she would find evidence against Jonas. "You already stopped following him, so there's no risk of him catching you. And we know he was visiting Dex, not a contact or a woman. His files show nothing out of the ordinary. I guess we go back to the drawing board."

"What if the FBI figures out it was you who hacked his files?"

That was still a risk, but she had been as careful as possible. Nothing tied her to the theft. The drive she used to download the files was destroyed. The password tracker had also been destroyed and was not traceable to her. She hadn't hacked the FBI using her own laptop, so she was clear there. Unless someone confiscated her laptop and found the copied files, there was no way to tie her to the theft. She knew parts of her would be on the security footage, but again there were way too many women in the building to narrow it down to her, assuming they could even determine it was a woman on the camera. Her hair was hidden, her clothes were masculine, and she was average height in her heels.

"If for some reason they do figure it out, I'll be immediately placing phone calls to my contacts at the CIA." Lian shut the file down and locked the laptop in the desk.

"Do you think Jonas would help us if you told him what is going on? I know Dex would." Mindy sat up on the bed, facing Lian.

"If you tell Dex or Jonas that I hacked the FBI, they are obligated to arrest me. And if they figure I'm a terrorist, I won't get that phone call criminals are entitled to or see the daylight again. You know nothing; you saw nothing. You thought you were just coming with a friend to enjoy an overdue vacation."

"Yeah, yeah. I'm just an innocent bystander. But I really think if you explain why you did it, they can help."

Lian shook her head. "Swear to me you won't say anything. Any hint of it from you to anyone, and you'll be arrested with me."

"It's just not fair to you. You're just trying to help."

Lian felt compelled to tell her again the facts of life. "You don't know who I'm working for. You can't know if they are innocent or criminals."

"I don't believe for a second that you would work for a criminal."

Lian laughed, but it was a harsh sound. "Depends on whose definition of criminal you use."

Mindy rose and placed a hand on Lian's shoulder. "You scare me when you say things like that."

"Good. That's my intent. The good guys are not always good, and the bad guys are not always bad."

A knock at her door had Mindy jumping.

Lian stood and took a look through the peephole. "It's lover boy."

Mindy turned bright red. "I guess I should tell you he spent the night with me."

Lian waved a hand at that. "You're a grown woman. You can do what you please. I'm happy for you, for what it's worth."

Lian opened the door. "Come on in, Dex."

Dex nodded at Lian, but his gaze was on Mindy. "I didn't want to just take off without saying goodbye."

Lian grabbed her wallet. She gave a quick warning look at Mindy before she spoke behind Dex, who was between her and Mindy. "I think I'll go get some coffee."

She closed the door behind the pair. She went down and downed a cup, then fixed another. She was sitting at a table by a window when she saw Dex come in.

"Mind if I join you?"

"Sure. Coffee isn't great, but it's drinkable." Lian waited while Dex fixed a cup.

Dex took a sip, made a face, then took another. "I've had worse."

"Like I said, it's drinkable. What's on your mind, Dex?" He looked like a man with a question.

"I'm not sure. But you look like crap. Have you slept at all?"

Sometimes Lian hated cops. "I'm fine. I wasn't feeling well last night, and no, I didn't sleep much."

"Is it the case? Jonas can get pretty focused when he's working. He forgets the rest of us are human." Dex was skeptical but kept it to himself.

"No, it's not the case. I must have caught a bug."

"Some bug. You've had it a couple of weeks if that's the case." Dex finished his coffee.

"I'll be fine. I think we've found a lead for Jonas to follow. Once the job is finished, I'll sleep for a week."

Dex changed the subject. "Jonas asked a few questions about you."

"Such as?" Lian couldn't help the jump in her pulse.

"Personal ones. The kind a man asks when he's interested in a woman."

Lian leaned back and smiled. "He asked if we were involved?"

"That was one of his questions. I told him no, that I was interested in Mindy."

"I'd say you're more than interested since you spent the night in her bed."

Dex shrugged. "It just sort of happened. We hadn't gotten that far when we were together in Chicago. We both knew a real relationship was impossible."

"But now that's changed? You told me you asked to be assigned to Jonas's team. I can't see you giving that up and moving to Chicago."

"No. But Mindy isn't as opposed to moving in with me as she used to be."

That was news to Lian, though she wasn't completely surprised. Mindy had been in need of a break when she'd agreed to help her and follow her to Virginia. Social work burned out many a person. "I wish you both luck. She was looking forward to coming with me, just to get away from the daily grind."

"So what about you and Jonas? Mindy said you two had dinner."

Lian raised a brow but figured it couldn't hurt. "He took me out for seafood. We're going out for Chinese on Friday."

"Is it serious?" Dex crushed his coffee cup and tossed it in a nearby trash can.

"No. I'm not staying."

"But you could. Mindy would like to have someone nearby whom she knows, besides me."

"You're assuming Mindy will stay."

"We discussed it already. She can move out of the hotel and in with me. See how it goes while she's here, and then she can decide if she wants to stay or not."

Having Mindy move in with Dex could present a problem, so long as Mindy was involved in the investigation. Then Lian realized it was the perfect excuse to get Mindy out of it. Lian knew she could very well end up in prison for what she did, and she had been doing everything in her power to keep Mindy's name out of it. All she had to do was destroy the phone she had given Mindy, and no trail between the two could be found.

Dex was quiet for a moment. "Are you going to tell me what's really going on? Mindy seemed cautious about talking about you and why you're here. She isn't as good at keeping secrets as you are."

Lian finished her coffee and rose. "Need a ride to work?"

Dex rose as well. "No. My car is in the parking lot. You can trust me, Lian."

Lian nodded. "I know that."

"Good. And for goodness' sake, get some rest tonight. Enjoy dinner tomorrow."

Lian watched Dex leave. She made sure he was out of the building before she headed back upstairs. She knocked on Mindy's door.

"What's up? I thought you would have left."

"Give me your phone." Lian closed the door behind her.

"Sure. Why?" Mindy handed the phone to Lian.

Lian pried the phone open and pulled out the memory chip. She tucked it into her purse, then the phone. "I hope you know what you're doing with Dex."

Mindy opened her mouth, but it took a moment for the words to come out. "He told you I was going to move in with him."

"He also asked me what was going on. He said you

don't hide things well. This phone and this chip are the only things tying you to me should I get caught. You're out."

"Really, Lian. You're overreacting."

"No, I'm not. You don't know what I've seen, or what I've done. And it's staying that way. You got me the information I needed. Now we go back to just being friends. Got it?"

Mindy sighed and dropped onto the nearby bed. "I guess I'm not as slick as I thought. I guess I should know better than to try to lie to an FBI agent."

"More like you shouldn't try to lie to the man you're sleeping with."

"What about you and Jonas?"

"We're not sleeping together. And he isn't the first FBI agent I've lied to, though I can hope he's the last."

"Come on, Lian. You really like him. I can tell when you talk about him."

Lian tugged her purse higher on her shoulder. "And because I do, it's best if I keep him out of this."

"It's a harsh way to live, Lian."

Lian shrugged. "It's a harsh world."

Lian heard her phone beep in her pocket. She pulled it out and read the reply to the email she'd sent out last night. It looked like her long shot had paid off.

* * *

Lian arrived at the office an hour later. Andrew

and Rhodes simply said hello and continued their work. Lian was still reeling from the email she'd received. Her contact recognized Biao and had simply said he was dangerous and to stay away.

Lian turned on the computer and pulled on the headset, but she wasn't focused on her work. She couldn't help but wonder what the chances were that she'd get assigned to an FBI investigation that led back to a man involved in her investigation of Bo. Her contact didn't say that Bo knew Biao, but Lian would bet money that they were at least acquainted, if not more fully involved. Her contact wouldn't have recognized Biao otherwise. And if Biao was involved with Bo, then it was possible Kang was involved somehow with Bo, too.

Her simple FBI assignment had just gotten a lot more complicated. It was possible Jonas would pull her from the case once she finished translating the paper documents and audio files. Lian needed to stay on this case, but she could do that remotely through her CIA contact. Perhaps it was possible to lead Jonas in the right direction without giving herself away. Lian knew she'd eventually have to come clean, but she planned to be out of the country and far away from Jonas when she did.

Lian was practically falling asleep at her desk by the time the end of the workday came. She finished the translations on all conversations with Biao and turned them over to Jonas. She hadn't seen him all day, just as he had said. She stood still while being searched on her way out and numbly made her way to her vehicle. She smiled when she saw Jonas sitting on the hood of her car.

"Good evening, Lian."

"Wǎnshàng hǎo, Jonas. I didn't expect to see you here."

Jonas stood while Lian unlocked the car door. He opened the door but blocked Lian from climbing inside. "I wanted to see you. The call last night wasn't enough."

"Jonas, I already told you I don't want to get involved."

Jonas tugged off his gloves and cupped Lian's face. "I think it's too late for that."

Lian stood stock still when Jonas kissed her. She tried to resist the kiss, but her resistance faded quickly as he coaxed her to participate. Lian found her gloved fingers clutching Jonas's shoulders.

Jonas heard a few snickers as people passed by, but he didn't care. He knew it was unprofessional to kiss Lian in the parking lot at work. But it was either out here or in the building where the likelihood of someone seeing them increased. And if he had gotten her alone in a secluded space, like his office, he wouldn't have kept his hands to himself.

The kiss grew heated and Lian found herself pulling her body as close to his as their bulky coats would allow. She wanted to throw caution to the wind and take him back to her hotel room. Of course, she then ran the risk of his snooping and finding the files she had on him and the files she had copied from him. The thought had her common sense breaking through.

Jonas let Lian break off the kiss. "Like I said, we've already gone too far."

Lian took a step back. "Maybe. But I don't have to let it go any further."

"What are you afraid of?" Jonas tugged his gloves back on but kept his eyes on Lian.

"I'm not afraid. I'm just not willing to start something we can't finish."

"I'm not buying that either." Jonas took a step so Lian could climb into the car but held the door so she couldn't close it on him.

"So what then? Are you going to follow me back to China? Are we going to fall in love, get married, and have babies? Come on, Jonas." Lian pulled on the door handle, but he wasn't letting her go just yet.

"Are you always an all-or-nothing type of woman?" Jonas leaned over so he could see her face in the faint light of the car's dashboard.

"Yes. Maybe once upon a time, I might not have been. But like you, I've seen too much, know too much about how the world works. I'm not willing to risk having my heart broken by a man who isn't what I need."

Jonas thought about her life as the daughter of missionaries. He supposed she probably had seen more of the world than most people did. And having lost her parents at such a young age would have cemented her views of the world. "All right. I'll back off unless you give me the go ahead. I'm still picking you up at six tomorrow."

Lian found she could smile at that. "Of course you are. Good night, Jonas."

Jonas closed her car door and watched her drive off. He went back inside to finish up his work. The cyber team had footage from the cameras of someone entering and leaving his office twice in one day while he was not in it. They surmised that someone had put a tracker on his computer and then returned later to copy his files. The footage didn't show a face or any distinguishable features. The camera did catch a glimpse of the thief's neck, so they knew he was Caucasian and of average height, but that was all they could tell. There were dozens of people who worked at the FBI that fit the criteria.

Everyone in the building had been subjected to a background check and a thorough investigation. But people changed; things changed. Jonas was having further investigations run on everyone who had been there less than six months, at least to start. And he was having Agent Rhodes, Andrew, and Lian investigated first, since they were currently the closest ones working with him and focused on the investigation into Kang. He also tossed Agent White on the list. Anyone with the kind of grudge that man held could lead them to do things they might not have done otherwise.

Once any other information that might have been

missed before was compiled, a surveillance team would follow their activities outside the office. Jonas figured that by Sunday morning, if any one of them was guilty, he would know.

Jonas was just about to leave when his phone beeped. He had a new email, but the sender was unknown.

"Hey, Dex." Jonas poked his head out of his office.

"Yeah?" Dex rose.

"I just got an email from an unknown source. Can you check it out?"

Dex nodded and went to Jonas's office. He pulled up the email on Jonas's desktop.

Jonas watched as Dex ran some checks. Dex wasn't on the cyber team, but not for lack of skills. Dex was a valuable asset to his team. He was extremely proficient with computers and had proven he had a knack for counterintelligence.

"Unknown address. Unknown name. Nothing I can trace to a sender. There's a document attached, but there isn't anything else attached to it or any trackers on it. You can open it."

Jonas took the seat as Dex vacated it. The email said from a friend. He opened the file. Several parts of the document were blacked out, but the name Ping Biao was at the top of the file.

Dex swore. "That's a CIA file."

"Yes, it is." Jonas continued reading the file. "Did you contact them?"

"No. I took the name and ran it through our

database. The guy is bad news, but we don't have much on him. But if he's involved with Kang, then we've got the proof you need to get more agents on the case. But this looks like the CIA has been following him for a while, and it has nothing to do with our case."

Jonas and Dex read over the files. Biao had been involved in everything from drugs to weapons to antiquities to human trafficking. The CIA had been watching him in hopes of finding out more about his boss, a man named Alexander Howard. Howard was an American living in Hong Kong. Supposedly he was a respected businessman, but the CIA believed otherwise. It looked like their case went cold a year ago when Howard was murdered. The Hong Kong police had no leads, and Biao had gone off-grid. The CIA was now watching Howard's son, a man named Bo Lee. Very little was known about the man, other than there seemed to be no ties between Bo and the triads, at least as far as the Hong Kong police were concerned.

Jonas copied the file to his drive. The second half of the file stated that Biao had finally resurfaced and had recently popped up in Hong Kong. The man was making deals left and right, and the CIA believed he had a contact here in the U.S., somewhere in Los Angeles. There was speculation as to who his American contact might be, and Kang's name was one of many other names on the list. It wasn't proof that Kang was involved with overseas arms dealing, but it was enough to take to his superiors along with the recordings Lian had translated, with Biao's name popping up in conversation. But what Jonas really wanted to know was who sent him the file. Jonas didn't have any contacts at the CIA, but it was a good bet his boss did.

"Let's see what else my team can dig up on Biao. Lian found other audio that mentions him. We should analyze it first, then take the next steps."

Dex nodded. "Got it."

"Do you think you can trace who sent this?" Jonas closed his laptop and locked it in the desk.

"Not likely. But if we find the person who sent it, we can match their computer to yours."

Jonas walked Dex back out to the bullpen. "I want to finish gathering any other evidence we can before I turn this over. And I want to know who hacked my files."

Dex nodded. "The cyber team is working on that, and I'll have surveillance in place on Saturday night. It's totally going to ruin my social life for the next few days."

"Still seeing Mindy?" Jonas waited while Dex gathered his coat.

"She's moving in with me." Dex gave Jonas a grin.

"That was fast." Jonas shook his head. Dex had a way with the ladies.

"She's living in a hotel and wasting money when she could move in with me. Maybe you should try that on Lian." Dex held the door open, and the two men headed to the parking lot.

Jonas pulled out his keys and unlocked his car. "Lian is proving a challenge. I don't think she'll fall for it."

"You never did go for easy. Good luck tomorrow."

Jonas looked over at Dex. "How do you know I have a date with Lian tomorrow?"

"She told me." Dex relented when he got a good glimpse of the scowl on Jonas's face. "I met her for coffee after I said goodbye to Mindy. They have rooms next door to each other."

Jonas waved at Dex, then drove off. When he arrived at his apartment, he was tempted to call Lian but headed for the shower instead. He would see her soon enough.

Chapter Six

"This is delicious." Lian took another bite of the massive meal in front of her. Jonas had ordered a sampler for them to share.

"I'll have to bring you here more often. It's much easier to order with someone who speaks the language." He had sat by while Lian had an extended conversation with their waitress in Mandarin. He often forgot when he was talking to her that English was more of a second language. Then he had just sat there indulgently when the owner had come over to chat.

"They're very nice. Our waitress was born in the U.S., but her parents are from Shanghai. She came to Virginia to go to school. Her parents moved back to China last year." Lian took a bite of another dish.

"And the owner?" Jonas scooped a few more bites onto his plate. Lian had devoured most of it.

"He is from a small village a few miles outside of Beijing. Very small. He and his wife moved here thirty years ago. She passed last year, and he's thinking of going home."

Jonas just shook his head. "You should have been an FBI agent. It's all about getting people to talk."

Lian shook her head. "I can't shoot a gun to save my life. The bullets just won't go where I want them to."

Jonas was amused by her admission. "Not all agents carry guns, though most do. I could teach you."

Lian had a vision of Jonas behind her, his body braced against hers as he helped her aim the gun. Her blood heated from the thought. From the look on his face, Jonas had the same thought. "I'll pass. It's not exactly a skill that an interpreter needs."

"Why did you try to learn?"

Lian set her fork down for a moment. "It was my first job with the FBI. I met a woman who offered to teach me. Said every woman should know how to defend herself. I took her up on the offer. After a few lessons, she told me to buy a whistle."

"I failed my first firearms exam if that makes you feel better." Jonas lifted a hand to the waitress for the check.

"A little. It's definitely harder than it looks." Lian thanked the waitress, telling her to let the chef know everything was wonderful. She took the to-go container from Jonas, who held it out to her.

Lian waited until Jonas was in the car before she spoke. "You can take me back to my hotel. I drove in with Dex."

"Where are you staying?" He headed out of the parking lot when Lian gave him the name.

"Dex told me you asked if he and I had been more than friends."

Jonas flicked on the turn signal. "He talks too

much. But I had to ask."

"You could have asked me." Lian settled deeper into the seat.

"Then I'd be obvious."

Lian erupted in laughter. "Really? We'd already shared dinner and a kiss by the time you asked."

Jonas glanced over, then back at the road. "Okay, so I didn't want to ask you. I wasn't tired after our date, so I went over to Dex's. We occasionally share a beer and a game on television. It just came out."

"He's been smitten with Mindy since he met her. I met Dex at the same time, so there was never a chance of us being a couple. Plus, I don't date Americans."

Jonas pulled into the parking lot of the hotel. "You are an American."

"I know. I just never saw myself settling down here, so I don't date when I'm in the States."

Jonas realized he'd never asked her if there was someone else. "What about in China? Have a boyfriend there?"

Lian crossed her arms over her chest. "If I had a boyfriend back home, I wouldn't be here with you."

Jonas took hold of one of her arms and turned her to face him. She looked ticked off at him. "Sorry."

Lian tried to pull her arm away, but he held onto it. "Good night, Jonas."

"I'll walk you up."

"It's not necessary." Lian tugged her arm again; this time he let it go.

"I think it is." Jonas got out of the car and took her

arm once again.

"I'm not sleeping with you."

"So you've said."

Lian pouted a bit at his attitude but let him lead her to the elevators. She pressed the button for her floor.

"I had a nice time."

Lian relented. "I did too."

"Invite me in for a drink?" Jonas took the key card from her hand.

"I don't have anything to offer you."

"Okay, so invite me in so I can kiss you without an audience."

Lian let Jonas open her door and guide her inside. She went to the fridge and put the food inside. When she turned, she found herself in Jonas's arms.

Jonas didn't kiss her first. First, he tugged off her gloves and tossed them on the dresser. His fingers then went to the buttons of her coat and undid them one by one. He slid it off her shoulders and tossed it onto the nearby chair.

Lian knew she should protest, but she stood silently as he pulled his coat off and tossed it on top of hers. His fingers found the pulse in her wrist as he pulled her against him. He took her mouth with his. There was no hesitation on either of their parts when his tongue opened her mouth to his. Jonas needed a taste of her as much as he needed his next breath.

Lian kissed Jonas back, her tongue dancing with his. Her fingers opened up his suit jacket so she could feel the muscles on his chest through the fabric of his shirt. When that wasn't enough, she tugged the shirt from his waistband, then tugged the undershirt out until she found skin.

Jonas returned the favor. He tugged the blouse from her skirt and found the skin of her back with his fingers. Her skin was incredibly soft, and the scent of her skin tickled his nostrils. He lifted her and pressed her against the wall, his body anchoring hers. He could feel her soft hands on his skin, and he shrugged out of his dress shirt to give her better access.

Lian immediately took the invitation to remove his undershirt and touched him as she longed to do. The muscles on his chest were well defined. He didn't have the overblown muscles of a bodybuilder, but the long, thick, ropey muscles of an athlete. Her fingers trailed over his chest, then down his biceps. The muscles flexed under her hands as his hands fisted on her braid. When he used it to tug her mouth back to his, she obeyed.

Jonas took her mouth again but made no further move to undress either of them. Breathing heavily, Jonas finally pulled back.

"Jonas?" Lian felt her feet hit the floor. At some point, she lost a shoe, and she was unbalanced on one heel.

"I promised." Jonas kissed her again, then bent to pull off her other shoe. In her bare feet, she barely hit his shoulder.

Lian remained braced against the wall while Jonas

bent again, this time to grab his shirts. He pulled the undershirt on, then buttoned up his dress shirt.

Lian realized he was leaving. Then his words came to her. He had promised her. Her knees were unsteady, her pulse was hammering, and her body was on fire, but she made no move to stop him.

"Tomorrow?" Jonas's voice was harsh in the quiet of the room.

"Tomorrow." Lian watched as Jonas left the room.

Lian flipped the extra lock on the door once she was able to move again. She stripped out of her clothes and fell on the bed. Tomorrow. She shouldn't have agreed, but her body had other ideas. She had no resistance when it came to Jonas. Had he not stopped, they would now be in her bed making love. Despite all the warnings she had given him and herself, she was falling for him. Hard. Jonas wasn't like other men she knew. He was confident, intelligent, and determined. She had watched him spar with Dex, and she had become enamored with his body. Sitting with him over a couple of meals and working with him for the past few weeks, she had become enamored with his mind.

Lian rolled onto her stomach and punched the pillow under her head. Jonas had the CIA file on Biao, so it was only a matter of time before finding Kang and neutralizing Biao became Jonas's number one priority. Her contact called him dangerous. Lian had read the file, and vicious, violent, and evil were the adjectives that came to mind. Lian was out of her league, so she'd done the only sensible thing. She'd turned the file over to Jonas.

One good thing was that Mindy was now out. Lian had smashed the phone and dumped it in the river. She had melted the memory card so the data on it would never be recoverable and dumped it, too, in the river. Other than their association, nothing Lian had done could be tied to Mindy. And she knew Dex would keep her safe should anyone suspect Mindy's involvement.

Lian wished she could trust Jonas with her secrets. But one thing she knew for sure was that Jonas was dedicated to his job and to his country. He would never betray either of those things. Once upon a time, Lian had known what was right and what was wrong. Then she had fallen into the gray, shadowy world where nothing was what it seemed. Like she had told Mindy, the good guys were not always good, and the bad guys were not always bad.

Lian could see her laptop and phone from where she lay. She had sent all the files to her contact at the CIA. She needed to dump the laptop and her phone. Once she had done that, the files she had downloaded from Jonas's computer would be permanently destroyed, all emails and phone calls she had made erased, and any trace of her involvement in an investigation of Jonas would be destroyed.

Her investigation into Bo would not cease. She was now confident Jonas knew nothing of his brother, that he had no knowledge of what had happened in Hong Kong last year. Now she just had to wait until her job was done with the FBI; then she could go back to China. Once back in China, she would tell Jonas about what she had done. She would tell him why she had done it, and who she had done it for. Then her debt would be repaid, and perhaps she could finally settle down and climb out of the shadow world she had lived in for the past two years.

* * *

Lian woke to a loud knock on her door. Glancing at the clock, she saw it was after ten. Still groggy, she walked to the door and saw Jonas on the other side. Keeping the chain on the door, she opened it enough to speak.

"What are you doing here?"

"It's tomorrow. Were you still sleeping?" Jonas's tone was not apologetic.

Lian laid her head against the door. "Yes, I was still sleeping. Give me a minute."

Jonas waited patiently until she finally opened the door. She was wearing a thick, white robe, compliments of the hotel. Her hair was a mess, despite the braid she still wore.

"I brought you coffee." Jonas handed her a cup and a bag.

Lian set the coffee down and opened the bag. Sugar and creamer were inside. She doctored up the brew and took an appreciative sip. "When you said tomorrow, I thought you meant tonight."

"I've got my men working on the breach. I have the files you sent me yesterday and have Dex running searches on Biao. I knew Kang was dirty, but this guy Biao might be pulling his strings. In which case, I need to shift my focus to Biao."

"But Biao is in Hong Kong, not Los Angeles."

"True. But if we track Kang's activities, it may lead us to Biao. And given the nature of the business, it may only be a matter of time before Biao visits his investments."

Lian crossed her legs and quickly covered them when the robe slipped. She saw Jonas's appreciative look. "Okay. I buy that. So you wait for Biao to show. Then you arrest them both?"

"We gather more evidence, and then yes, we arrest both men. An anonymous source sent me some heavy evidence against Biao. The government will arrest him and hold him. He'll never see daylight again. I owe you for that. You're the one who found Biao."

Lian clutched the lapels of her robe. "Any linguist could have found him, but I'm glad. People like him prey on innocents and destroy lives."

"Yes, he does." Jonas' eyes narrowed. "What do you know of it?"

Lian set the coffee to the side. "I'm not convinced they are selling guns, Jonas. I think they're selling people."

Jonas rose and loomed over her. "That's not the first time you've hinted at it. What makes you so sure?"

Lian stood quickly and went to the window. She pulled the curtains open and kept her eyes on the view outside instead of Jonas's suspicious ones. "People are sold and tracked just like any other commodity. You forget I worked with the FBI before, and I helped find that boy in Chicago. People disappear and are sold into slavery all over the world. Those serial numbers could have been people."

Jonas turned her to face him. "The cops found guns. We know Kang is selling them all over the west coast. What makes you think it's people? Nothing in the files suggests it."

"The transcripts and the money trail. The so-called guns that were sold were sold pretty cheaply given their quality and quantity. The serial numbers didn't match the guns the cops found. Kang uses the Mandarin word for 'cattle' quite a few times in his conversations with Biao. Kang might have started with guns, but I think he moved on to something bigger and more lucrative."

"Get dressed. We're going into the office."

Lian nodded. "I need a shower. Give me a few."

Jonas simply waved her away and pulled his cell phone from his pocket.

Lian unbraided her hair and stepped into the shower. She took a hurried shower and didn't spend a lot of time messing with her hair and face. She left her hair loose so it would dry, and simply moisturized her face and used a little powder to lessen the shine.

She pulled the robe back on and left the bathroom to grab a change of clothes.

Jonas was sitting near the window, his gaze on the view below. He turned when he saw her emerge. He rose and came to where she stood. He took a few loose strands of her wet hair in his hands. "You do tempt a man."

"And you a woman."

Jonas shook his head to clear it, then turned his back to her. "Get dressed before I forget my promise."

Lian's palms were sweating, and she felt the strength in her thighs go lax. There would be retribution in the future for her actions in some form. Her time with Jonas was growing short. She was already guilty of lying to him. And allowing him into her heart and into her body would make her lies so much worse when he learned of them. In this moment, she was beyond caring.

"Wéibèi nǐ de chéngnuò." Lian stood across the room from him.

Jonas turned to her. "What does that mean?"

"Break your promise."

Jonas remained where he was for a moment. He could see Lian trembling under the robe. "I like it better in Mandarin."

She said it again but in a softer voice. "Wéibèi nǐ de chéngnuò."

Jonas closed the curtains and crossed to where she stood. He took the sash of her robe and untied it.

Lian didn't move, didn't protest. He opened the robe and pushed it from her shoulders. It fell in a white pool at her feet. Her body was slender but fit. Her breasts were small but fit her frame. Her thighs were slightly rounded, and despite her small stature, her legs were long and lean. He lifted a hand and stroked her from shoulder to breast.

"Shì." Lian stood there, letting Jonas look.

"I need to learn Mandarin." Jonas lifted her and set her on the bed.

"It means yes."

"What's the Mandarin word for lovely?"

"Kě'ài."

"Kě'ài." Jonas repeated the phrase.

Lian smiled when Jonas tried to say it. "Close enough."

Jonas stripped off his shirt and his jeans. He pulled his wallet from his jeans and pulled out the condom he had stashed there. He finally stripped off his briefs and climbed onto the bed, covering Lian with his body.

Lian's hands went to his shoulders, looking over his body as he had hers. She had seen his chest last night, and the rest of him didn't disappoint. Her hands stroked over his chest and back. She pushed her hands against his chest, and he obeyed by rolling onto his back. He let her explore his body until he was trembling beneath her.

Smiling, she straddled him. Her long hair fell over her shoulders, across his chest. She used the strands to tease his body. She felt his hands snake over her skin, his fingers finding her breasts. They were covered by her hair, but that didn't deter him. Needing to taste, she bent to kiss him. She placed soft kisses on his forehead, cheek, and chin before seeking his mouth.

Jonas let her continue her exploration of his mouth and body until he couldn't stand anymore. "Lian, there's only so much a man can take."

Lian muttered something in Mandarin and slid down his body to place soft kisses on his chest. She found a nipple with her teeth and was rewarded with a slow moan.

"I don't think I want to know what that means." Jonas lifted her and settled her on her back. Her thighs parted for him, and he accepted the invitation.

Lian lay still as Jonas's mouth found her breasts, his fingers stroking her hair from her body. He kissed and nibbled her breasts as his fingers found the soft core of her body. Her hips reared up from the bed, her body seeking more of him.

Jonas grabbed the condom and quickly donned it. With a thick, muttered oath, he entered her body in one slow, easy stroke. She was panting under him, her body once again still, her eyes closed. He heard her mutter again in Mandarin, but it was a desperate sound, a plea, so he grasped her hips tighter against his.

Making love with Jonas was more than she had ever experienced. His body fit hers perfectly, the hardness of his body exactly what she needed to ease the ache in hers. He lifted her hips to deepen his penetration, and she begged him for more in a combination of Mandarin and English, the tone of her words—not the actual words—conveying her need to him.

Jonas tried to slow the pace, wanting this moment to last. Lian's breathless cries beneath him, however, made that impossible. His pace quickened, sweat dampening both of their bodies. Their breathless cries mingled in the darkness of the room. Jonas felt Lian's body go still beneath him before succumbing to the climax he had driven her to. Jonas soon followed, barely aware of anything else but the feeling of climaxing inside a now limp Lian.

Lian lay still beneath Jonas, her fingers in his hair, holding his head to her shoulder. She heard him mutter something, but she didn't understand the words. It was another few minutes before he moved. He rose up on his elbows, then slowly eased his body from her. He rolled onto his back beside her. She rolled over and rested her chest on his, her chin on his shoulder.

They were both quiet for a time. Lian thought she might have dozed off, but when she stirred, not much time had passed.

"What changed your mind?" Jonas stroked a hand over her loose hair. It lay across her back like a blanket.

Lian sat up. She looked at Jonas and felt a little

sad. She gave him a small smile. "Wǒ chàndǒuzhe. I trembled."

Jonas sat up and stroked her cheek with the back of his hand. "I think that might be the sexiest reason any woman has ever had for letting me take her to bed."

She laughed, banishing the sadness. The time for retribution would come later. "You were a first. I like to think of myself as imminently practical. You don't make me feel practical. You make me forget the rules."

Jonas rose. He tugged Lian up beside him. "You're the type of woman who makes a man want to break the rules."

Jonas tugged her back into the shower. Lian stopped him for a moment to tie up her hair. She then followed him inside. She picked up the rag she had used earlier and soaped it up. She took her time washing him, her fingers lingering over various parts of his body.

Jonas took the rag from her and returned the favor, his mouth following the water as it rained over her skin. He found her breasts with his mouth, making a feast of the firm flesh. His fingers lingered between her thighs. "Ever made love in the shower?"

Lian's fingers clenched in his hair as he kissed his way down her body. "Most of the places I've lived haven't had much in the way of running water."

"Then your education has been sorely lacking." Jonas kissed his way back up her body, this time lifting her thigh and pinning her body against the wall of the shower. His fingers teased her until she was begging him. He didn't have another condom with him, and he silently cursed himself for the oversight. He should have known that once wasn't going to be enough with Lian.

Lian was panting, her thigh clenched around Jonas's waist. "What's wrong?"

Jonas could have cursed but didn't. Instead, he used his hands and mouth on her until her cries echoed off the shower walls.

Lian went limp in his arms, but Jonas held her upright. Still holding her leg, he grabbed a towel and started to dry them both off. Lian realized that Jonas was still hard against her. She looked up at him, the unspoken question in her eyes as he released her and set her on her feet.

"Next time we do this at my place. I have a whole box at home."

Lian realized what he meant. She reached out to him, but he turned away before she could touch him.

"I hate to be the voice of reason, but we should head to the office. I want to hear the tapes and see the evidence that makes you think we're talking about people and not guns." Jonas briskly dried his hair, his eyes on Lian's in the mirror.

She simply nodded. The man had gotten what he wanted, and the agent was now fully in control. She couldn't blame him. She had sent him the file on Biao, hoping he would put two and two together on his own. Lian had no doubt he would, but the thought of the people Biao and Kang had sold kept her from waiting for him to figure it out on his own. If they could spare even one person the horror of what human trafficking did to people, she would consider their mission a success.

Lian went to the closet and pulled out a fresh pair of wool slacks and a sweater. The weather was still freezing outside. She went to the bath and took the time to mostly dry her hair before plaiting it.

Jonas was once again near her window, the curtains open. He was dressed and holding his coat. "Ready?"

Lian nodded. She locked the door behind them.

Chapter Seven

Jonas swore, his voice loud in the quiet bullpen. "How did I not see this?"

Lian set a hand on his shoulder. "To be fair, you've been tied up trying to figure out who hacked your computer. And I just finished translating the last of the audio that mentions Biao."

"I'll need to call the detective in charge in Los Angeles. The local police have been trying to nail Kang for months. They've had no more luck than I've had up until now. They need to know what they might be dealing with."

Lian tried to be the voice of reason. "Men like him don't get where they are by making mistakes. If you hadn't realized he was running guns, you might never have gotten permission to tap his phones. The Los Angeles Police Department doesn't have the resources you have, and it would have taken them months to gather enough evidence against him to even get a search warrant. And there's no guarantee they would have found anything more than the guns."

It was the idea that Kang was running people that made him sick to his stomach. He couldn't fathom what was broken in a man's brain that would have him do such a heinous thing. People were not commodities. He had been involved in an investigation into a human trafficking ring when he'd first graduated from the academy. The team had ended up rescuing a dozen refugees who had been sold. Eight of them had been young children. The fear in them was tangible and made his stomach clench. They had witnessed and been victims of unimaginable crimes. The refugees hadn't spoken English, and it had taken hours to get an interpreter to the scene. All twelve of them had sat in the truck, watching the goings-on around them with fear and confusion in their eyes. It had been a long time since he had thought of them, but the memory was as fresh today as it had been the night it happened.

Jonas swore again as he continued reading the transcripts. The words were vague, but he had a feeling Lian was right. He would need definitive proof that Kang was trafficking people, but at least now he was on the right trail. "If my superiors agree, I'll need to go to Los Angeles."

Lian took a seat next to Jonas. "It's been a pleasure working with you, Agent Cole."

Jonas barely registered her words. "I imagine I'll get the team I asked for. I'll need you to stay and translate whatever else we record."

Lian slid over so Jonas would look at her. "My assignment is over. I translated what there was, and you now have your proof."

"You can't leave now. We haven't caught him."

Lian shook her head. "There will always be a bad guy. There will always be one more recording, one more file."

Jonas rose and paced. Then he turned on her. "How can you even think about leaving? If this man is trafficking people, then he's the worst type of criminal. Don't you want to help catch him?"

Lian tried to calm him. "That is your job. Mine was to translate. I've done that. I told you I couldn't stay."

"You're not done yet. We're not done yet." Jonas crossed to her and pulled her to her feet. His lips were bruising against hers, but she opened her mouth to the invasion, not resisting him.

"Give me two weeks, Lian. I just need a little more time." Jonas released her.

"I'm serious, Jonas. I can't stay. I can translate from anywhere in the world."

"What is so important that you have to go?" Jonas wrapped her in his arms.

"A promise. One that cannot be broken." Lian touched her fingers to his lips.

"So what was today? Goodbye?" Jonas took hold of the fingers that touched him.

"Today was a mistake, one I made with my eyes wide open. I didn't lie to you, Jonas. I told you I didn't want to get involved."

"Then don't do it for me, do it for the people they've stolen. I'm sure that whoever you made your promise to will understand."

Lian knew he had the right of it. The woman she owed the promise to would agree that helping Jonas put Kang behind bars was the most important thing. But she was already on thin ice. The FBI was not stupid. They would eventually figure out she was the one who stole the files. Jonas might want to bed her, but he wouldn't trust her when it came to the security and integrity of the position he held. She, and every other person at the FBI, would be under scrutiny until they had their hacker.

"I'll stay until you leave for Los Angeles. From there, you can send me encrypted files to translate for you."

Jonas nodded. "All right. I'm going to send these files to my superior. If you're right about this, we need to move fast. And with several seasoned agents tracking Kang, we'll find him. And if we're lucky, he'll turn on his pal Biao."

Lian doubted it, but she wasn't going to argue. She took a seat and waited for Jonas to finish sending his report.

It was hours before Jonas finished for the day. He'd gotten approval to put a team together. He would take Dex and a few other agents from his team. He also had a few people in the cybercrime unit he wanted to take. He and his men would track Kang on the ground. The cyber unit would track him through cyberspace.

"It's late. I should take you home."

Lian nodded. "Will you stay?"

Jonas didn't hide his surprise very well. "I'll need to make a stop at the drugstore first."

"There's one in the hotel." Lian grabbed her coat and put it on.

"Even better." Jonas grabbed his coat and led Lian out of the building.

* * *

Jonas's phone buzzed around three a.m. He and Lian had just gone to sleep an hour before. His body ached a bit, but it was a pleasant feeling. It had been a long time since he'd spent a couple of hours making love to a woman. Even with his fiancée, he rarely had the energy for more than a quick round before passing out. Lian's body was the type that a man savored.

Lian stirred beside him, her fingers reaching out to touch him. "What is it?"

Jonas leaned over and grabbed the phone he'd left on the nightstand. "Not sure. Only someone from work would text at this hour."

Lian watched as Jonas walked naked to the desk. He dialed a number. She sat up, holding the sheet to her naked breasts.

"Agent Cole. Yes." Jonas listened to the words on the other end, barely able to believe what he was hearing. "You're absolutely sure?"

Lian saw Jonas tense. She couldn't make out the words, but his eyes went cold as he looked at her.

"I'll take care of it. We don't need a team for one woman." Jonas set his phone down on the desk.

"What is it?" Lian climbed out of bed, taking the sheet with her.

"You're good. I never would have suspected you were the one who hacked my computer."

Lian paled. "What makes you think I did?"

"How about the fact that you're not denying it? Or how about the fact that you all of a sudden have the desire to go to bed with me? I never pegged you for the type to sell your body, but I'm sure you've fooled more than one man over the years."

"Jonas, I can explain." Lian dropped the sheet and grabbed the nearby robe.

"The only thing you're going to do is get dressed and come with me."

"I can't do that." Lian belted the robe, her fingers trembling.

"I can make you, and we both know it." Jonas grabbed his underwear and slacks. He was buttoning his pants when he saw Lian take a step toward the dresser where his jacket was. His gun and holster lay beneath it.

"Do you really think you can get past me?" Jonas quickly grabbed the weapon and trained it on Lian.

"Desperate times, and all that. You won't shoot me." Lian took another step toward him.

Jonas's arm was steady as he held the weapon on her. "Don't bet on it, sweetheart. I'd rather take you in unharmed, but I'm not picky."

Lian circled him, keeping just enough distance between them to not concern him. She knew the chances of getting him to relax were slim, but she just needed to catch him off guard. And she'd only have one chance.

"Why did you do it? Are you working for Kang?" Jonas kept the gun trained on her. She had stopped a few feet in front of him.

"No. I'm not a criminal." Lian balanced her weight on her right foot.

"Get dressed." Jonas took a step forward.

Lian spun on her right foot, kicking out towards the hand that held the gun with her left. He lost his grip, sending the gun flying across the room. She pivoted again, using the bed as a spring to vault over to where the gun lay. She had the gun in her hand and pointed it at Jonas before he could take a step.

Jonas stopped in his tracks. Lian had the gun pointed right at his heart. She had moved with lightning speed and with the skill of a martial arts master.

Lian was breathing hard as she held the gun on Jonas. "Take a step back."

Jonas took a step back, but only one. "Want to know how we caught you?"

Lian kept the gun on Jonas while she stripped out of the robe. She found her underwear and tugged it on one-handed. The bra wasn't going on with only one hand, so she ignored it. She went to the closet and pulled a one-piece dress out instead. "One should always learn from one's mistakes. How?"

Jonas ignored the quick surge of lust at seeing Lian

strip off the robe. "Two phones. No one has two phones. Friday night I saw it lying on the desk. While we were at the office today, two FBI agents made a visit to this room. Guess what they found."

Lian swore in Mandarin but didn't take her eyes off Jonas. She went for his jacket and found his cuffs. "Put on your shirt."

Jonas obeyed, but his eyes never left hers. "So now what? You can't get away."

"Yes, I can. With you as a hostage." Lian tossed him the cuffs. "Cuff your wrists in front."

Jonas's eyes went glacial, but he obeyed. Her hand didn't waver while she held the gun. "So much for not knowing how to use a gun."

Lian came close enough to pinch the cuffs a little tighter. "I said I couldn't aim a gun; I didn't say I couldn't shoot one. At this distance, I couldn't miss."

Jonas stood still while Lian draped his suit jacket over the cuffs. She then went and packed a small bag. She tossed both of her cell phones inside it, along with the laptop. She tossed a few undergarments and clothing items inside, then fetched a few items from the bathroom.

Jonas thought about trying to rush her when she went into the bath, but the risk was too great. He needed Lian alive. He wanted to know what she knew. In close quarters, the gun was likely to go off, killing one of them.

"Now we're going to walk out of here and go to my car. Shout for help and I'll shoot you. I know there are no FBI agents waiting outside. You wouldn't want them to see you leave my hotel room."

The hallway was quiet. Lian pointed to the stairs, and Jonas took them slowly. Lian was keeping enough distance between them to prevent him from making a move on her. She then directed him to where her car was parked.

"Backseat, passenger side." Lian opened the door. Jonas got in. Lian took the sash of her robe that she had fashioned into a loop and used it to anchor Jonas's arms to the overhead handle used to hold onto when climbing in and out of the car. It wouldn't hold for long should Jonas pull hard enough, but this way she could see his hands while she drove.

Lian started the car and quickly made her way toward the highway. Jonas was glaring at her in the mirror that she turned so she could watch him. Digging into her overnight bag, she pulled out a cell phone and dialed her contact at the CIA.

"Things just got a lot more complicated." Lian flipped her turn signal and headed onto the on-ramp that would take them north, making sure not to exceed the speed limit.

"No. Not that. I just kidnapped Agent Jonas Cole. He figured out I was the one who hacked his files."

Jonas sat still, trying to hear the voice on the line. Other than the voice being male, he couldn't make out any other words or sounds.

"I don't suppose you have any bright ideas. I could drive to your place, but it will take a few hours."

Jonas tugged his arms, but Lian raised a brow at him. He settled back into the seat for now. She didn't seem inclined to shoot him. He supposed he was more valuable alive.

"All right. I will. And yes, I have enough cash. I'm not totally green. I'll talk to you later."

"Who's your friend? Kang? Biao?" Jonas tugged at the cuffs again, but they weren't coming off. She had cinched them tightly.

"Just a friend. Your men won't find his name on my laptop or phone."

"So what's the grand plan? You've kidnapped a federal agent. You've hacked the FBI. When I bring you in, you'll be charged with an act of terrorism. You're dealing with gun runners, drug runners, and you've done so outside U.S. borders with Biao. It makes the charges that much heavier."

Lian dug her other phone out of her bag and dialed another number. "Hi, Dex, it's Lian."

Jonas yanked hard on the cuffs, but the handle didn't budge. He growled at her from the back seat.

Lian just shook her head. "I wanted to let you know that I have Jonas. I'm not going to hurt him. I'm going to make a pit stop soon, and I'll tell you where I leave him."

Lian hung up the phone before Dex could respond. "Dex would no more betray his country than you would. Relax."

"People are going to notice a man tied up in your backseat once dawn comes."

Lian changed lanes and continued north. "Lucky for me, it's winter. I've got at least three hours before that happens."

Jonas was quiet for a while, his mind running through the possible scenarios of how this would end. Finally, he spoke. "Why did you do it?"

Lian yawned. "If I thought there was even a remote chance you'd believe me, I'd tell you. It's all part of the promise I made."

"To your male mystery friend?"

"No. To Naiwen Lee."

Jonas grunted. "Is that name supposed to mean something to me?"

"Not yet. But one day it will. And one day you'll forgive me for this."

"Not likely. I look forward to slamming you behind bars."

Lian dropped quiet for a moment. "How about I tell you a story?"

Jonas glared at her in the mirror.

"There was a woman who had taken an assignment overseas for the American government. The assignment was supposed to be a simple one. She'd done assignments similar to this one, though for a different government agency. She was asked to act as an interpreter for a government agent. But the agency lied about what it was they wanted her to do, and she ended up with a different assignment. One day while on that assignment, she stumbled into something she shouldn't have. She was taken captive by a man, an American man. This man was involved in many illegal activities. When he attacked the interpreter, a woman named Naiwen Lee came out of hiding in the large room and struck him in the back of the head with a heavy statue. Naiwen took care of the other woman, cleaned her up, and fed her."

"Get to the good part." Jonas's arms and wrists were starting to ache.

"Be patient. Naiwen had been bought by the American when she was barely a teenager. She bore him two sons. The first she sent off to escape his father. The second was born to replace the one she had sent away. Her first son she hadn't seen since he was four. The second she had seen but hadn't spoken to since she'd given birth to him."

Lian took a deep breath and continued her story. "It was only a few short hours after Naiwen had struck the American that the women realized that Naiwen had killed the American. Naiwen said she could not just watch as he killed the interpreter. The interpreter promised to help Naiwen find her first son. But the second son told the police that Naiwen had murdered his father, and Naiwen and the interpreter had to go into hiding. The two women spent months in hiding before the interpreter left, promising Naiwen she'd return. She also promised to do what she could to stop the second son, who immediately stepped in to take over his father's business."

"So why did the interpreter use the FBI and take

an agent as a lover? For Kang or Biao?"

Lian shook her head again. "One of them will lead her to the man she's really looking for. I never believed in coincidences, but this case has been one big one. Kang was not on my radar, or on Naiwen's. But much to my surprise, she recognized Biao's picture."

"How do you have Biao's picture?"

Lian smiled at him in the mirror. "I'm the one who sent you the CIA file."

"I don't even want to know how you got that file." Jonas turned away from her gaze in the mirror.

"I asked nicely." Lian took the right ramp and headed east.

Jonas clenched his fists at the thought of Lian giving herself to some unknown CIA agent. It was irrational, but he still wanted her, and jealousy seared through him at the thought of another man touching her. Whatever magic she held over him, it was powerful.

Lian kept driving until she hit a small town. She left Jonas in the car, taking her bag and the gun with her. She paid cash for a hotel room. She requested a ground-floor room in the back.

"Ready for a nap?" Lian drove the car and parked. There were no other cars.

Jonas held still while she undid the sash. He rubbed his wrists as best he could. Lian handed him the key card and made him open the door, keeping close enough that he couldn't slam the door in her face.

Jonas went and sat on the bed. "Kidnap a lot of men? You seem good at it."

Lian set the gun on the dresser opposite Jonas. He'd have to get past her to get to it. "You're my first."

Jonas gauged the distance between Lian and the gun, and him from Lian. When Lian simply raised her brow at him, he leaned back against the headboard.

Lian took the sash and looped it again. "So few hotels have old-fashioned headboards anymore. Lift your wrists over your head."

Jonas did, and he cursed when she quickly fastened him to the top of the headboard that was screwed into the wall.

Lian leaned over and massaged his arms. "They must be aching."

Jonas would have protested, but she was right; his arms hurt. The massage helped with some of the pain.

Lian dug her other phone from her bag. "I'll leave my phone with you. There is nothing on it that I can't replace."

He watched as she set the phone on the bed next to his leg. "So now what?"

"Now I get some sleep, and so do you."

Jonas sat in disbelief as Lian pushed some pillows behind his neck and backed up. She curled up in the second bed and promptly fell asleep, or at least appeared to.

Jonas tugged at the restraints, but he wasn't going anywhere. Figuring it couldn't hurt, he slept as well.

It was almost one in the afternoon when Lian woke. When she stirred, she looked over at Jonas. Tears welled up in her eyes. She didn't know how things had gotten this far. She was supposed to be back home when he found out what she had done. The American government wasn't going to lose sleep tracking her in China. She wasn't a threat.

But she had known that taking Jonas as a lover was a mistake. She had known that when she left him, it would hurt more than leaving any other man. Losing him was almost as bad as losing her parents had been.

"Going to try tears next?" Jonas tried to stretch, but it was impossible tied up the way he was.

Lian wiped the tears away. She made a quick trip to the bathroom. She bet he needed the bathroom, too, but she didn't dare risk setting him free yet.

Lian washed her face and stared at her reflection in the mirror. She had dark circles under her eyes, and they were red from the tears. She quickly tied her hair back and went back into the main room. She dug into her bag and pulled out a knife. She went to the desk and picked up the gun. She unloaded it and set it back down.

Lian went to Jonas. She opened the blade and set it on the bed. She then turned on her cell phone. She had shut it off right after her call to Dex so it couldn't be traced. "I really am sorry, Jonas. This is not how it was supposed to happen."

Jonas looked into her bright blue eyes. The secrets he remembered seeing in them the first time they met were still there.

Lian kissed him lightly on the mouth and stepped back. She picked up the knife. She saw Jonas tense and looked away from him. She tucked the knife into his hand. "It should take you less than a minute to untie yourself. The keys to the cuffs are on the dresser next to your gun. Goodbye, Jonas."

Jonas watched as she picked up her bag and the keys to her car. By the time he got the sash cut and freed from the bed, she was out of the parking lot, headed back to the highway. It looked like she was headed west.

Jonas didn't bother to uncuff himself. He grabbed the phone and dialed Dex. "I'm in a hotel off Highway 95. Lian's car is on it headed west. Get a BOLO out on her car now."

Dex sighed in relief. "Thank goodness you're all right. What is going on? Where are you? I'll get the BOLO out and send someone to get you."

Jonas gave Dex the name of the hotel and the town they were in. Lian hadn't bothered to blindfold him, so he knew where he was. He just wished he knew where Lian was headed.

Three hours later, there were no hits on his BOLO. Jonas was in the back of a car, headed toward the hotel where his car was. The agents had the good sense not to ask him any questions. He knew he'd have a lot of explaining to do when he got to the office, but for now, his mind was in full flight, trying to remember if Lian had at any time given away anything that might hint at where she'd gone.

When he got to the office, Dex was there. "All right, boss?"

"I'm fine. No word on Lian?"

Dex shook his head. "No. I brought Mindy in for questioning, but so far all she is saying is that she knows nothing about what Lian was doing."

Jonas clapped a hand on Dex's shoulder. "I can go talk to her."

Dex nodded. Mindy had been spitting fire since he picked her up. But she was the only person besides him and Jonas who had any sort of relationship with her. And Mindy being here with Lian made her a suspect. Thankfully nothing in the files he'd copied from Lian's computer or cell phone mentioned Mindy. And the only calls on Mindy's phone were from Lian's phone, and nothing incriminating was on Mindy's phone.

Two hours later, Jonas came back to the bullpen. "Take Mindy home. She doesn't know anything. And if she does, she's not going to give it up."

"I didn't find anything on her phone or laptop. She might really have just followed a friend. They really are friends."

Jonas rubbed his face with both hands. "You're friends with her, too. Did you think she was capable of something like this?"

Dex dropped into his seat. "Honestly? If someone

had asked me before if she was capable of what she did, I would have said yes. But I also would have said she would never do something like this. There has to be a good reason."

Jonas gave a harsh laugh. "She said something similar. Said I'd forgive her one day."

"So now what?"

"Now we do what we can to find her. And I'll head the team up to Los Angeles to find Kang, assuming I still have a job in the morning. You go take Mindy home. You're going to have some serious groveling to do to get back in her good graces."

Dex nodded. "Thank you for trusting me, Jonas. I know what this must look like."

"I'm the one who got duped. Go home and get some rest. You're going to need it."

Dex left, heading to where Mindy was waiting.

Jonas went to his office. He rubbed his face again. For Dex's sake, he hoped Mindy was innocent. As for himself, his heart ached with loss, and it ticked him off. He would find Lian, and he'd make her hurt the way she'd hurt him.

Chapter Eight

Lian stood on the balcony looking out at the ocean. The waves were whipping against the shore today, a sure sign that a storm was headed in. She had stood in this exact spot every morning for the past two weeks.

"Kang got away. My sources tell me he got on a plane, but no one is sure where he went. Jonas is on his way home."

Lian looked over her shoulder at Griffith Dunn. The older man was a retired CIA agent, but he hadn't gone soft. He was a little over six feet and two hundred twenty pounds of sheer muscle. His hair had gone steel gray, and it suited his chiseled features.

"Any word from your contacts on Biao?" Lian leaned against the railing.

"Not yet. They believe he's still in Hong Kong but underground. Naiwen sends her love."

Lian scooted over so Griffith could join her. This situation wasn't easy on either of them. Griffith was trying to get asylum for Naiwen. The Hong Kong police were still looking to bring her in for the murder of Alexander Howard. As far as the Hong Kong police were concerned, she had murdered an upstanding member of the Hong Kong business community. Lian knew the police wouldn't listen to her and Naiwen's version of the night Howard died without some serious proof of Howard's and, in turn, Bo's guilt.

"How is it going with getting Naiwen asylum?"

Griffith leaned against the railing. "Slow. The people I've reached out to don't want to hear the story. And since my only witness to the death is wanted by the FBI at the moment, it's not looking good."

Lian leaned her head on Griffith's shoulder. "I really screwed this up."

"Nah, you just made it a little harder. I've got a meeting with my old director. With a little convincing, he'll get your name cleared. He'll be ticked, and probably never hire you again, but he knows what happened to you. He knows it was his fault; he owes you for that. You were trying to help the CIA nail Howard, and Naiwen saved you from him."

The night Naiwen killed Howard would be forever etched in her memory. He would have raped her had Naiwen not intervened. She remembered the feel of his calloused fingers on her breasts and between her legs. Just thinking about it made her want to vomit. Then she remembered Jonas's fingers on her, and it made the memory bearable.

But that night a year ago, it had taken more courage than Lian thought Naiwen had to take that antique statue and bash Howard with it. He had bled out on the floor while Lian and Naiwen huddled in the corner. They had been locked inside that room with Howard's body for more than a day. Bo had come looking for his father when he hadn't shown up for a meeting, and when Bo couldn't find him, he had the house searched from top to bottom. But Bo hadn't known of his father's secret room. Howard didn't even trust his own son. It was Griffith, who had illegally gained entry to the home, that rescued them. Bo had seen them leaving the house with CIA escorts, but if Bo had recognized the woman as his mother, he hadn't given a hint of it away. Naiwen knew who stood before them, as she had seen pictures of her second son. But there was nothing of her in him; he was his father's son.

For a good hour, other agents forcefully kept Bo from the house. Bo had immediately called the police upon seeing his father's body being removed from the home. Griffith had not hesitated to take the two of them into protective custody. The warrant for Naiwen's arrest had reached Griffith the next morning, and he had put both women into hiding where even the CIA couldn't find them.

During the months they had spent in hiding, Naiwen had found comfort in her newfound freedom. Lian had been worried that she would have been longing for captivity again. People who had been held captive their entire lives didn't know how to live in the outside world. But the woman who had the courage to set her first son free found her way out once more. She had even found that she could love.

Griffith pushed away from the balcony. "I will bring her home. And once she's here, I won't let her go."

Lian heard the vow and let Griffith go. He and Naiwen had spent many hours together. It had taken almost a month for Naiwen to even look at Griffith. It took two months before she would speak to him. But once she looked, really looked at him, the two had become inseparable. Lian hoped Griffith got his happy ending. Lian had very little such hope for herself.

Lian headed back inside and had a shower. She touched the shorter strands of her hair, hair that now barely hung below her shoulders. Her hair had been a defining characteristic, and Griffith told her it had to go. People might recognize her from the pictures the FBI had sent to police stations around the country. She rarely went out, but Griffith was right. The more she could do to disguise her appearance, the better. She still had a box of brunette hair color sitting in the bathroom, but as of yet, she had not had the courage to use it.

Lian went downstairs and found Griffith in his office. "So what is the grand plan? I know you have one."

"I've been thinking about Agent Cole. You seem to have a high opinion of him. It seems like an extreme coincidence that the man he's hunting is tied to a man that is tied to the man we're hunting."

Lian went to the window and looked out at the

rolling waves. "When I took the job with Jonas, it never occurred to me that our cases would cross. But nothing about this case has been easy, so I suppose it was bìrán."

"I suppose it was inevitable. Though I lean more towards a cosmic joke on us mere mortals. Nothing about investigating Bo has been simple. How much did you tell Jonas?" Griffith hadn't pressed her since she came, but the time for treading lightly had now passed.

"I told him I was doing someone a favor. I didn't tell him much more than that. He's not ready to hear the truth. I know he's not guilty of any crimes. He's a good agent. He's dedicated to his country and would never betray it."

Griffith rested his chin on steepled fingers. "Perhaps he can help us."

Lian turned her gaze to Griffith for a moment, then turned back to the water. "Even if he believed you, he'd be obligated to arrest me. I kidnapped a federal agent."

"True. But you did it for a good reason."

"Something tells me he won't see it that way." Lian turned her stormy blue eyes to him. "But you will approach him anyway."

"I'm not CIA anymore. You're not an agent. Dallin is willing to give us some autonomy, especially if it brings Bo down. But we need someone on our side who has the authority to actually arrest him."

Lian shook her head. "I trust you, Griffith.

Naiwen trusts you. I wish you luck in convincing Jonas. Kang led us to Biao. Biao may or may not lead us to Bo. You know that."

Griffith nodded. "But Naiwen recognized him. The only people she would have come in contact with were people working for Howard. With Bo in charge, Biao won't be far away."

Lian growled in frustration. "You're assuming that Biao will pledge allegiance to Bo. Naiwen might have killed Howard, but Bo was not exactly a model son. Bo has his own agenda. And it was likely only a matter of time before he turned on his father. Howard was getting old, and his power was fading."

Lian came to Griffith. "He smiled."

"What?" Griffith turned to see her face.

"Bo. He smiled when he saw his father dead on that gurney as the police wheeled him out. That smile haunts my dreams. Howard was evil. Bo is his son."

Griffith patted her hand. "But Jonas is not. Bo probably knows he has a brother. It might be psychologically harder for him to confront a brother. With Jonas on his trail, he may make a mistake."

"Except Jonas doesn't know Bo is his brother. He doesn't even know he has a brother. And after what happened, he won't believe a word I tell him."

"Perhaps. Either way, I think it's time I pay him a visit. Like I said, Dallin is willing to give us some leeway."

"Unless he can get the federal charges against me waived, I'm not sure how this is going to help. You can't just bring Jonas here and hold him prisoner, you know. And if he sees me, I'm going to jail."

Griffith smiled. "I think you underestimate your power, my dear."

Lian blushed. In a moment of stupidity, she admitted to her affair with Jonas. But secrets had ways of making their way to the light. Jonas probably wouldn't be too quick to tell everyone about their brief affair, but neither would he forget. He was convinced she had betrayed him, used him. He was not a man to forgive.

Griffith rose, leaving Lian beside his desk. "I'm going to pay another visit to Dallin. Then I'll make a trip to meet Jonas. If I think he can be trusted, I'll bring him back. If not, I'll leave, and we'll figure this out on our own."

"Except you'll leave Jonas with a new trail to follow. You run the risk of him finding out who you really are."

Griffith wasn't worried. "My file doesn't exist. I was never with the CIA. He'll be chasing a ghost."

Lian took a deep breath and let it out slowly. Sometimes she felt like a ghost. She'd been living in the shadows for the past two years, and she wasn't sure she was ever going to escape.

* * *

He'd hit a wall. Kang was still missing. Jonas was unable to locate any more information on Biao, and he hadn't been able to trace Lian. It was as if all three of them had fallen off the face of the earth. He had plenty of other cases to work on, but it still ticked him off that he'd lost his chance to capture Kang.

Jonas shut down the screen when a knock sounded on his door. He'd gotten a message from a man who only called himself Griffith about information he had on Biao. He claimed to be ex-CIA. Jonas wasn't too proud to take help wherever he could get it. He didn't necessarily want to work with an ex-agent but was willing to listen to what he knew.

Instead of replying through the door, Jonas went and opened it. The man who stood before him was probably a good twenty years older than he was. His hair was steel gray and was about his height. Yes, this guy definitely could be ex-CIA.

"Agent Cole? I'm Griffith." He held out a hand.

Jonas shook the man's hand and gestured for him to enter the room, closing the door behind them. "Have a seat. Your message said you might have some information pertinent to my case on Kang. Though that begs the question: how do you know I'm investigating him?"

"I always did like a man who got to the point. I'm the one who pulled the file on him for Lian."

The mention of Lian had him sitting upright and rigid in his seat. "Do you know where she is?"

Griffith just smiled and leaned back in the chair. "I'm aware that she is wanted for kidnapping you. I can't say I haven't been taken in by a pretty face once or twice in my time. But in this case, you can forget whatever it is you think you know about her."

"If you know where she is and don't tell me, you can be arrested for obstruction."

Griffith waved a hand at that. "I'm not here to talk about Lian. I'm here to talk about Kang, Biao, and a man named Bo."

"All right, I'll bite. What do you know and how do you know it? You said you pulled the CIA file. Are you really CIA?"

"I was. You can look me up, but you won't find a record of me." Griffith dug into his pocket and pulled out a folded piece of paper.

Jonas took it from him, and on it were numbers. "What are these?"

"The first number is my file number at the CIA. The second number is the access code to get clearance to my files. My name was erased from the files when I retired last year. I have your file; I figure it's only fair you have mine."

"So what about Kang, Biao, and a guy named Bo?"

Griffith shook his head. "I'll meet you at the bar across the street. I'm not interested in having our conversation on the record."

Jonas grabbed his coat and led Griffith out of the building. They settled at a table in the corner of the bar across the street.

Griffith ordered a beer and smiled when Jonas ordered a lemonade. "I don't know a lot about Kang. He's a low-level guy, but he's interested in moving up.

Now, Biao, he has power and is probably using Kang either for his American contacts or as a possible fall guy. I lean more towards the second. Biao is a powerful man in Hong Kong. He got his power by working for a man named Alexander Howard. Howard was killed about a year ago. His son, Bo, took over his father's business."

"What business?" Jonas thanked the waitress for their drinks.

"Mostly import/export and some manufacturing. The Chinese government, and the Hong Kong local government especially, loved him. The Hong Kong police are still hunting his killer. The CIA had been watching Howard for years. He bought off so many people over the years to mask his illegal activities. None of them ever were documented outside CIA investigations. The CIA was not quite ready to take him down when he was killed. His son, Bo, took over where his father left off. I'm pretty sure he and Biao struck a deal. Bo heads a large branch of one of the largest triads in the world."

"So why didn't the CIA take Bo down if they have evidence that he took over his father's business and heads a triad?"

Griffith leaned forward. "You know how it is. The CIA thought they might be able to use Howard, and in turn, his son. He was a U.S. citizen with a lucrative business in China. He had contacts and knew people the U.S. government would love to exploit."

Jonas nodded. It wasn't ideal, but sometimes you had to strike a deal with those you couldn't trust in hopes of getting what you needed. "So why doesn't the CIA approach Bo?"

"He is more radical in his beliefs than his father. Bo hated the fact that he was half-American. And quite frankly, he hated his father. We're pretty sure Bo was more upset that he wasn't the one to off his father than he was about his death. He is still helping the Hong Kong police hunt his father's killer down, but it's for show. It makes him look like a good citizen and keeps suspicion off him."

"So who killed him?"

"A woman named Naiwen Lee."

The name got Jonas's immediate attention. That was the name from Lian's story. "Are you going to continue to sit here and lie to me about Lian's whereabouts?"

"I assume Lian told you that Naiwen saved her life. Lian was working for the CIA when she met Howard. She overheard him making some illegal deals. Howard's favorite pastime was human trafficking. Lian was helping the CIA gather intel against Howard. Howard spied Lian when he was talking to a contact, so he took her captive. He tried to rape her, and Naiwen slammed a heavy statue on the back of his head. Saved Lian's life. In return, Lian promised to help her get free. That led her to take on a case with the FBI."

Jonas's hand made a fist. "So she targeted me.

Why me? What do I know that the two of you don't?"

"That was the question Lian set out to answer. The answer was nothing."

"That's bull, and you know it."

Griffith held up a hand. "Kang is tied to Biao. Biao is tied to Howard. Howard is tied to you."

"How?" Jonas was tired of the games.

"That I can't tell you. That's Lian's story to tell. I promised her. She thinks I'm insensitive."

Jonas got to his feet, angry with the older man. "I've had enough of her stories. Either turn over what you know and turn over Lian, or I'll make sure you're arrested for obstruction."

"Obstruction for what? Lian isn't wanted for any crimes."

Jonas picked up his coat. "I'd say kidnapping a federal agent is a good enough charge to get the ball rolling when I find her. Then I'll add hacking FBI files and go from there."

Griffith pulled a business card from his pocket. "When you get back to your office, you're going to find that a woman named Lian Albright is no longer wanted for any crimes. Neither kidnapping nor hacking FBI files."

"And why is that?"

"Because as of last night she is officially working for the CIA, albeit in a minor capacity. All the things she did fell under the rights of her position. Your section chief has already agreed to drop all charges at the request of the FBI Director. And it makes my life much easier."

Jonas heard enough. He snatched the card from Griffith instead of punching the smile off his face. "Easier how?"

"On the back of that card is my home address. Come for a visit and you'll get the rest of your answers."

"And if I don't?"

"Then you won't get the answers you want. Trust me. Come."

Jonas watched the older man walk out of the restaurant and head back down the street.

As soon as Jonas arrived back at his office, he pulled up the file on Lian. He slammed his fist on his desk. All charges had been dropped.

Instead of calling his section chief, he pulled up a government database and typed in the data Griffith had given him. The files showed that Griffith had been a decorated CIA agent. His last case had been in China, where he had been trying to bring down one Alexander Howard, who was killed by one Naiwen Lee. It seemed Naiwen had been put into protective custody, and no one knew where she was today. Jonas had a feeling Griffith knew exactly where she was.

Nothing in the file mentioned Lian or her working on the case. When he tried to pull up her name, he was blocked. At least now he knew where she had been the past year. Further digging had convinced him she hadn't been in Maryland. It seemed she had no ties there, or ties to anyone here in the U.S. outside of Mindy and Dex, and apparently this Griffith character.

Jonas was tempted to put a BOLO out on Griffith and find out where he was headed, but it seemed pointless since the man had given him his home address. He most likely was headed there. It was more than possible that that was where Lian was. And it was just as possible that she was on a plane headed back to China. Jonas wasn't too sure how much of what Griffith said was true. He figured he had two choices. He could stay here and spin his wheels, or he could go find out what Griffith was hiding.

Jonas left his office and headed to his boss's office.

Section Chief Jacquelyn Montgomery looked up when Jonas stepped into her office. "It's already done, Jonas."

"So we just drop the charges against Ms. Albright? What kind of leverage did the CIA have?" Jonas didn't take a seat when his superior waved him to one.

"A deal was cut higher up than me. It seems she's a key witness to a case an Agent Griffith Dunn had been working on before he retired. His superior, a man named Dallin, said arresting Lian would compromise their case." Jacquelyn waved to the chair again.

"Agent Dunn was in my office less than an hour ago." Jonas took a seat.

There was no expression on his superior's face as

she leaned back in her seat. "Yes, I know. Dallin thinks you can help with their case. He's asking for you to be temporarily assigned to their investigation."

Jonas gritted his teeth. "And what did you tell him?"

Jacquelyn pulled up a picture of Jonas kissing Lian in the parking lot outside headquarters and turned her screen so he could see it. "That's going to depend on you."

Jonas cursed. "You think I can't be objective?"

Jacquelyn turned her screen. "Depends. I received a copy of the files Dallin had on Lian. She consulted with them on a case about a human trafficking ring. She was a consultant, not an official CIA agent. Dallin said she saw and heard things that could clinch their case. Apparently, she's been in protective custody for the past year, but no one seems to know where she is, except Agent Dunn."

"And he was retired. That makes no sense. And the person of interest in their case is dead."

"Apparently, the retirement was strictly to protect Lian and a second asset. And Lian is the only witness besides the person who killed their man who knows what happened in that room. Dallin said this second asset won't come out of hiding until the man's successor is behind bars and the murder charges are dropped."

Jonas cursed again. "The second asset has a name."

Jacquelyn nodded. "Yes, she does. And I think there's more to Dallin's story than he's letting on. But they are tracking people much higher up on the triad food chain than you are. Kang is small potatoes in comparison to this Biao character, but he's small potatoes in comparison to whom the CIA is tracking. I think it's worth a shot to have you help with the investigation. CIA doesn't have authority here, but we do."

That got Jonas's attention. "The CIA is willing to turn the case over to us?"

"That's right. Dunn is retired, Lian is only a consultant with the CIA, and she's been on our payroll for the last month. I'd like you to meet with Dunn and see what else he has to say. He might be willing to help us find Lian if we pull her into the case instead of arresting her. Once you get the rest of the details, we can get a task force together that includes Lian and take down Kang and Biao."

"So you're going to trust me to do this?"

Jacquelyn stepped from behind her desk. "I know you, Jonas. You're a good agent. One day you'll sit in this seat and others above it. Whatever your feelings are for Lian, I trust that you'll get the job done. If you think you can put your feelings aside and work with Dunn and Lian, then you've got the assignment."

"I'll head up the coast tomorrow. See what I can learn."

"Good. And good luck."

Jonas nodded and closed the door behind him. He left to go home and pack a bag.

Chapter Nine

The house was a monstrosity sitting near the ocean. Through the dark lenses of his sunglasses, Jonas took in his surroundings. Besides the wreck of a house, there was a pier that looked in disrepair and a path that led to the beach. Other than that, the house was isolated, considering it was near the water. There were homes on either side, but they were a good distance away.

Jonas slammed the door closed on his SUV and headed toward the front door. The front porch looked to have been fixed up recently, the new wood a bright contrast to the worn boards. He wasn't surprised when the front door opened with a loud creak.

"Glad you could make it, Agent Cole." Griffith held the door and gestured for him to come inside.

The inside was as bad as the outside. The old wood floors needed refinishing, and the wallpaper was peeling off the walls.

"I can't say the same." Jonas took off his sunglasses and tucked them into his jacket pocket. "Nice house."

Griffith chuckled. "It's a work in progress. When I retired, I needed a project."

"You got one. Where's Lian?"

"Like I said, I like a man who gets to the point.

She's not here." Griffith headed toward the back of the house, knowing Jonas would follow.

Jonas stepped into a finished, gourmet kitchen. The dark wood cabinets and dark counters were contrasted by a lighter backsplash and flooring.

"This was the first room I redid. I like to cook." Griffith went to the double side by side refrigerator. He pulled out a couple of beers, twisted off the caps, and handed one to Jonas.

"I wouldn't know where to begin." Jonas took a large swallow of the beer without looking at the label.

"I spent too many years in the field. Swore when I had my own house I'd eat home-cooked meals every day."

Jonas could understand that. In the field, you ate whatever was handy. "I was surprised to hear the CIA had turned the case over to the FBI."

Griffith took a swallow. "They turned the case over stateside. We still have men on the ground watching for Bo in Hong Kong, but we think he might be here in the States or will be soon."

Jonas followed Griffith into a room off the kitchen. Inside was a home office that had some fancy equipment, fancier than a retired CIA agent would need. "All right, I'll bite. Tell me more about this Bo character."

Griffith booted up the computer and put the data on the large screens that lined one of the walls. "On paper, Bo is as honest as his father. He's playing the grieving son, swearing he'll stop at nothing until justice is served. It's been the same song and dance for the past year."

Jonas leaned against the desk and kept his eyes on the screen. "Justice for his father's murder? The files say you put his killer in protective custody."

Griffith pulled up an image of Bo. "I did. I put Naiwen and Lian in protective custody. I didn't trust Bo not to buy off the local police, and I was operating alone. The Hong Kong police were furious but had no proof I knew where they were. They brought me in for questioning when I surfaced after hiding them. As soon as they were forced to release me, I resigned, and the three of us disappeared."

Jonas set his empty beer bottle down. "When did you and Lian come out of hiding?"

Griffith tossed his own empty bottle in a nearby recycle bin. "I came out eight months ago. I bought this house and settled in. Lian came out two months ago. She heard rumors Bo was headed to the U.S. She thought you might be involved, so she came here and followed you."

Jonas's jaw clenched as he tried to control his anger. "That's the problem. I don't understand why the two of you thought I might know anything about this Bo character. I was hunting Kang. And if Lian is to be believed, she had no idea that my case and hers would cross."

"She was quite shocked. She had me pull all the files I could on Biao when Naiwen recognized him after his name kept popping up in your recordings."

Jonas turned on Griffith. "All right, cut the crap. Why was she following me, and why did she hack my files?"

Griffith didn't answer the question but pulled up a new file. He remained silent until Jonas turned back to the monitors.

Jonas couldn't help his low growl. The pictures on the screen were of Lian, but instead of her beautiful, smiling face, her face was marred by large bruises, a few cuts, and swelling. Someone had beaten her badly.

"That was how I found her. The two women were locked in a room in Howard's compound and had been for over a day. Intel had come in that Lian had gone missing. I knew Howard had her. I infiltrated the house, and I knew from a blueprint of the house where Howard kept his núlì."

"What does that mean?" Jonas took a step closer to the monitor.

"Slave."

Jonas turned to look at Griffith. The man had murder in his eyes. "What is your relationship with Naiwen?"

Griffith got his emotions back under control. "We spent eight months together. It took two months before she would even speak to me. She had been living under Howard's tyranny since she was sixteen. She had his first son at seventeen and his second at twenty-two. If he weren't dead, I'd hunt him down and kill him."

Jonas swore loudly. "You fell in love with her."

Griffith could only nod. "I did. Of all the women in all the countries I've been to, this small woman worked her way in. I'm fighting to get her asylum. Lian can testify that Howard's death was self-defense. Naiwen is refusing to come out of hiding until I have Bo in custody. I'm not sorry, Jonas, and I'll do whatever I have to do to protect Naiwen and get her into this country."

Jonas crossed back to the desk. "And Lian is your key."

"She is. Besides, once she explains everything to you, you'll be glad the charges were dropped."

"I noticed you didn't say I'd forgive her." Jonas closed the picture of Lian on the computer.

"She did kidnap you. Must have been quite a blow to the ego." Griffith laughed and shut the rest of the screens down.

"She disarmed me with a spin kick and practically flipped over the bed. She had my gun before I could blink."

"She's fast. Her parents let her learn martial arts from a teacher in the village they lived in. She was an American living in a foreign country. Not all the places her parents went were safe. They wanted her to be able to protect herself. When she came to the U.S., it was the one thing she insisted her uncle let her do. If nothing else, it was cathartic."

Jonas could believe that. She was a teenager who lost her parents. Exercise was a great way to work off stress. "So now what?"

"Now we eat. Kang, Biao, and Bo are underground for the moment. We need one of them to resurface. I've got people gathering intel and feeding it to me. We'll need to translate most of it."

Jonas followed Griffith out of his office. "I don't suppose you speak Mandarin?"

"I know some. I can mostly keep up with Lian when she gets on a roll. But I can't read and write it, though. But then again, that's what fancy translation programs are for."

Jonas took the second beer Griffith offered him. "So that's another reason you need Lian? Are you feeding the recordings to her in hiding?"

"Yes. So far, nothing."

Jonas relaxed while the other man made dinner. Jonas hated to admit it, but he was beginning to like Griffith.   Dinner conversation drifted among different topics, but mostly to places and cases.

"I should head to a hotel." Jonas shook his head at the offer of a third beer.

"No need. I've got an extra room. After the kitchen and my office, I fixed up the bedrooms."

Jonas figured staying close might be a smart move. He excused himself and got his suitcase from the car. An hour later, he was showered and standing in the dark by the bedroom window facing the water. The dark waves and the sound of them pounding the shore were soothing.

Jonas wasn't ready for sleep. Instead of climbing

into bed and getting the rest he knew he needed, he left the room. Griffith's room was down the hall, so Jonas headed the other way. He checked the other bedrooms, but they were unoccupied. The ground floor was equally quiet. The office door was locked, but that didn't surprise Jonas. Only a careless man would keep the door unlocked to the room that held all his secrets.

The living room was empty except for a few pieces of furniture, as was the dining room. There was a den, but it, too, was empty. Jonas went to the large picture window in the living room and peeked out. All he saw were shadows.

Twenty minutes later, Jonas climbed into bed and willed himself to sleep. It seemed the rest of his answers would have to wait until Lian made an appearance. He had a feeling he wouldn't have to wait long.

* * *

Jonas poured himself a second cup of coffee and tried to clear his head. He'd slept well enough. He'd learned to sleep anywhere and at will over the years. The only problem was he hadn't been able to control his dreams. Like so many nights since he'd met Lian, she had invaded them. And when he wasn't asleep, he kept thinking about what Griffith had said. He just couldn't imagine what Lian would tell him when she finally surfaced.

Griffith joined Jonas in the kitchen, wearing nothing but a pair of sweatpants. "Still trying to figure it all out?"

"Where is she?"

Griffith glanced over at the clock on the microwave. "Right now? On a plane. I sent her to Los Angeles to talk to a contact of mine. My friend isn't big on phones or computers. It was a bust, but at least he'll know to keep his eyes open."

"And where is the plane taking her now?"

Griffith downed a cup of black coffee and poured a second. "Here. You'll see her soon enough. She figures the longer she puts it off, the worse it will be. She's unsure of your reaction."

"It's not as if I can arrest her. You saw to that." Jonas rinsed the cup and set it in the dishwasher.

"We both know that's not what has her nervous. For now, we'll have breakfast, and you can work off some of your tension. I've got a gym in the basement."

Two hours later, Jonas was standing under the hot spray of the shower. His muscles were sore from the heavy workout. Griffith hadn't skimped on the gym, and the older man was in great shape. After working out for a while, the two men had sparred. Griffith said he was having Lian teach him martial arts. Said it helped keep his mind and body centered. Mostly Griffith's mind was on Naiwen, and Jonas knew when a man had a woman on his mind, he was a man distracted.

After he got out of the shower and dressed, he wandered towards the front of the house. Just as he suspected, Griffith had left. The man's black SUV was no longer parked out front. He was no doubt picking up Lian from the airport. Not content to wait, Jonas went back to his appointed bedroom and pulled out his laptop. According to the airport's website, there was a flight that would land in twenty minutes coming from Los Angeles. That gave him a couple of hours before the pair returned.

Jonas keyed in his password and logged into his files. He had a team working on tracking Kang and Biao. Bo was another story. He wanted more information on the man. An hour later of digging, the information he found was much as Griffith had said. Bo was playing the grieving son, demanding justice for his father's death. On paper, the man looked clean. His business dealings seemed on the up and up, and business was looking good. The man had contacts with businesses all over the world, including the U.S. It looked as if the man had a major contract in the works, one with a large conglomerate in Los Angeles. Jonas didn't believe in coincidences and had no doubt Bo had dealings with Kang or Biao or both through the Los Angeles corporation.

Jonas dug further and found several pictures of Bo and Alexander Howard. Bo was just five years younger than he was and had a similar height and build. The man had dark hair about the same shade as his own that was tied back in a ponytail that hung down his back but had a darker complexion than his own. Bo's father had light hair and lighter skin. Bo was an interesting mix of both his parents. He had not seen a picture of Naiwen, but Bo seemed to favor his Chinese heritage in looks more than that of his American father. Jonas saved the pictures and added them to his file.

Jonas glanced out the window when he heard a vehicle pull into the drive. He watched as first Griffith, then Lian, exited the SUV. Part of him half-expected the pair to disappear. He wasn't happy with his immediate reaction, both physical and emotional, to the sight of her. He had hoped he would be able to look at her dispassionately as if she were a stranger. And in some ways, after what had transpired between them, they were. But his body had different ideas. He cursed and turned away from the window and headed downstairs to confront her.

Lian stopped on the bottom step of the porch when the front door opened. Jonas was standing there, his eyes cold as he looked at her. He wore black jeans, black boots, and a black pullover, which added to the dark look.

Lian climbed the rest of the steps. "Zǎoshang hǎo, Jonas."

Griffith took Lian's arm and led her past Jonas into the house. "She said, 'good morning,' by the way."

Jonas closed the door behind him. "I think I got that one."

Lian shrugged out of her coat and hung it on the

coat rack by the front door. She pulled off her red hat and fluffed out her hair. "Seemed like an appropriate greeting, under the circumstances."

Jonas stopped what he was going to say when he saw her hair. The previously waist-length braid was gone, and her hair hung in short waves just past her shoulders. Unwillingly, his fingers reached out and touched the ends of the strands.

Lian turned tired eyes to Jonas. He dropped his hand when her eyes met his. "I need a shower and a nap. I've been running all over L.A. for the last few days. I promise we will talk later."

Griffith put his hand on Jonas's shoulder when he would have followed her up the stairs. "I can give you a status report, then the two of you can talk later."

Jonas didn't take his eyes off Lian's retreating back until she was out of his sight. "What status report?"

"Actually, it's more of a negative report. Sources say Kang is not in Los Angeles. But my other sources say that Bo is not in Hong Kong."

"And you're more interested in where Bo is so you can get your girlfriend asylum." Jonas walked to the back of the house to look at the view of the water.

A soft sound came from the doorway. Jonas and Griffith turned to see Lian standing in the doorway.

Lian looked at Griffith. "I changed my mind. I need to borrow your office."

"Are you sure you want to do this now?"

Lian nodded. "It's best to tell him now. Then maybe I can sleep."

Lian walked past the two men into Griffith's office. She plugged the laptop she was carrying into the monitors.

Jonas followed Lian into the office and didn't move an inch when Griffith closed the two of them in the office alone.

"I was in Hong Kong on a surveillance mission for the CIA. It was believed that an American businessman named Alexander Howard was using his import/export business as a cover for human trafficking. At first, the CIA thought he was running drugs and guns. I'm guessing at one point he did, and probably still was, but people are more lucrative. But as more and more evidence was gathered, a sickening pattern developed. I got a job at Howard's headquarters, but everything seemed legitimate. A specific agent wanted to dig further and wanted me to get as close to Howard as possible."

Jonas took a step into the room to get a better look at the documents Lian was pulling up on the screens. "Let me guess, Griffith wanted you to pretend to be interested in Howard to get him to open up and talk."

Lian shook her head. "Not Griffith. Someone else. Problem was, I wasn't a trained agent, and I didn't understand what was going to happen. I suppose that was naïve of me. At first, I spent time talking to different people, people who would never dare repeat what they told me to the police. Rumors were that he liked teenage girls. And rumors were that he would pay for them. I thought that there was no way I was getting close to him. I wasn't young enough. But I was wrong."

Jonas came to stand beside Lian. "So what did you do next?"

"I talked to different staff members and found out about a woman who had fathered him two sons. He wasn't married to her, but she lived in his house. She wasn't allowed to leave. I remember wondering why he kept her around. She was no longer young, as his two sons were grown. I decided to take a chance and get myself hired to get closer to Howard. I pretended to be his new interpreter. It was too easy to get close to him."

Jonas's hands fisted at his sides. "He found out who you were and who you were working for."

Lian shook her head. "I don't think he realized who I worked for. He just knew I heard too much to be left free. I had no warning, and neither did Dallin, the man I was working for. But I was wired and managed to get a distress message out before the wire was removed. I ended up tossed into a room inside Howard's mansion, and the door locked behind me. That's when I met Naiwen, the woman who bore him two children."

"Griffith told me what almost happened and showed me the pictures." Jonas turned to face her. Tears were in her eyes, but they didn't fall.

"I didn't think I was going to make it out of that house alive. Naiwen saved my life. Had Howard…" Lian broke off, her throat constricting.

"So what do I have to do with his son Bo? Why were you spying on me?"

Lian got control of herself. "When the police showed up, I told them what happened, but they didn't believe me. Naiwen couldn't speak. She had spent too many years living in servitude. Bo was screaming that we murdered his father. The local Hong Kong police believed Howard to be a valuable member of the community. He brought in a lot of business and a lot of money. And he pumped a lot of money back into the local economy. People loved him. Griffith managed to get Naiwen and me out before we were taken into police custody, and he put us in hiding."

Jonas tried to ignore the tears in her eyes but found it difficult. He turned back to the screens. "So then what?"

Lian took a seat at the desk and pulled up a series of files. "Naiwen wouldn't talk to Griffith, but she would talk to me. She told me how she had found a way to send her firstborn son to America to be adopted. The people who helped her were part of an organization that helped victims of trafficking. Naiwen refused to consider leaving. She thought that if she stayed behind, her son would have a better chance of getting out. Howard didn't take much interest in his son, so she thought that if she stayed, it would be some time before anyone noticed the boy was gone. She was right. It was almost a week before Howard noticed."

Jonas stopped and looked at the picture Lian had pulled up of Naiwen. Though she was now in her late fifties, she was still very lovely. Her dark hair was hardly streaked with gray and fell down her back. Her dark eyes stared out from the face of a woman who looked a dozen years younger.

Lian continued her tale. "Naiwen refused to tell Howard where the boy went. He promised retribution. She eventually conceived a second son, and he was removed from her at birth. He was shipped off to boarding school as soon as he was old enough. It wasn't until he was grown that she saw him, and by that time he was every inch his father's son."

Jonas took another step towards the screens, his eyes still on the woman. "Did Howard find his oldest son?"

"No. I started digging into the birth records and contacted the organization that relocated her son. I found out that his birth name was Jiao Lee. It took some time, but I eventually was able to find his adoption records." Lian pulled up a few more files and arranged them side by side.

Jonas looked at the other screens. His stomach clenched. "What is this?"

"I found her son. He had been adopted and had become an FBI agent. Shortly after I found these records, Bo disappeared from Hong Kong. Griffith and I couldn't help but wonder if somehow Howard or Bo had already found him. And we couldn't help but wonder what type of man Howard's eldest son had become. So I took an assignment that brought me into contact with one Supervisory Special Agent Jonas Cole, born Jiao Lee."

Jonas spun on his heel, grabbing Lian's arms and bringing her nose to nose with him. "You expect me to believe that I'm Alexander Howard's son?"

Lian didn't struggle in his grasp. "DNA doesn't lie. Your DNA is on file with the FBI, and Griffith had Howard's DNA tested after his death. Naiwen offered a sample of her own. You're Naiwen's son."

Jonas released her, his breath coming in short bursts. "I think I need to sit."

Lian crossed to the cabinet and poured Jonas a drink. She handed it to him as he remained standing and staring at the evidence in front of him. "I staked you out for a few days, seeing where you went and who you met with. Nothing came of it. Then I went to work for the FBI. I hacked your files to see if there was anything incriminating against you. I knew the chances of finding anything were slim. But if nothing else, I had found Naiwen's son. I promised her I would find you, and I did. But though you were a dead end to finding Bo, suddenly there were ties between Kang and Biao, who in turn has ties to Bo. It was a long shot, but it paid off."

Jonas knocked the drink back and went to Lian's laptop. He started to read all the files she had pulled up.

Lian took a seat next to him and pulled back up

Naiwen's picture. "I told her I found you, and she wept when I sent her your picture. She wishes you well and is very happy you grew up to be such a fine man."

"What did you tell her about me?" Jonas was still in shock, struggling to find the right words, the right questions to ask.

"I did some searches and pulled up what I could find about you. I told her about the various awards you've earned during your time as an FBI agent. I told her what you do there and what your future most likely is there. Mostly she is just happy you found a loving adoptive family and grew up well."

"You must know about my childhood before I was adopted. Did you tell her about it?" Jonas stared at the picture of his birth mother.

"No. No one's life is perfect, but I'd like to maintain the illusion for her. It would only hurt her to know what your childhood was like. I have the story on paper, but I'm sure it doesn't do it justice."

Jonas pulled his eyes away and focused on Lian. "Don't think I'm about to spill my guts to you."

Lian stood, not surprised by his anger. "Wouldn't dream of it. Naiwen is happy that you are happy. But her story on paper wouldn't do justice to the horrors she lived through. She spared you her fate. If nothing else, you should thank her for it."

"I need some air." Jonas left the room and went out to the back deck.

Chapter Ten

Griffith came into the office. "How did he take it?"

Lian wrapped her arms around her waist. "Better than I thought. But he'll have questions once he processes it."

Griffith hugged her briefly. "He'll come around."

Lian shrugged. "It doesn't matter. I told him. Your contacts are all on the lookout for Bo, or Biao, or Kang. One should lead to the others. For Naiwen's sake, I hope it's Bo. I should rest and then pack up the rest of my stuff. I can be on a flight back to China in a day or two."

Griffith went back into the kitchen and looked out the glass doors. Jonas was leaning against the railing. "Do you think leaving now is a good idea?"

"I'm not a CIA agent, nor am I an FBI agent. Jonas is good. If I've learned nothing else over the course of the last few weeks, it's that. If you weren't hiding me, no doubt he would have found me. You turned it over to him, at least stateside. Let him do his job."

"I can't help but wonder if his knowing Bo is his brother will make it harder for him to take him down." Griffith pulled a beer out of the fridge and handed it to Lian.

She rolled the ice-cold bottle between her palms.

"Given the evidence that supports the fact that Bo took over his father's business, and probably even now has young women and children being shipped all over the world to be sold, I don't think he'll have a problem. Just keep feeding me your recordings, and I'll get them back to you. I can do that from home as well as from here."

Griffith sighed when Lian handed him back the unopened beer and went upstairs. He looked back at Jonas, who was staring out at the ocean. He took the beer outside and handed it to Jonas.

Jonas took it but didn't open it.

"I'm sure it's hard to wrap your mind around it."

Jonas rocked back on his heels. "I haven't thought about where I came from for years. When you're a kid, everything is confusing. And I was a difficult kid. I made sure no one wanted to adopt me. After I was adopted, and my parents straightened me out, I didn't think about it anymore. All I can think is that I don't look Chinese."

Griffith laughed. "That you don't. But the hair and eye color are your mother's. Lian's hope was that you had inherited your mother's temperament instead of your father's."

"How did she find me?"

Griffith leaned on the railing. "It took her six months and a lot of dead ends. Even when she finally found you, she wanted DNA confirmation first. Once she had that, she told Naiwen. Naiwen must have cried for a good hour. She had always hoped you found a good life, but part of her always feared something terrible had happened to you. She had put her trust in strangers to get you to safety. As you can imagine, trust doesn't come easily for her."

"You fell in love with her. What made you?" Jonas couldn't look the man in the eye.

"She was barely sixteen when she was taken from her family. Her family are vague memories for her now. But buried deep inside her is a strong woman. She saved Lian from Howard. She sent her son away to save him. Howard broke her, but with time she'll heal, though she'll always bear the scars of what she's lived through. But just knowing what she does about you went a long way toward healing her broken spirit. As we got to know one another, and as she learned she could trust me, she revealed more of the soft, loving woman that is inside her, too."

"I suppose she wants to meet me."

Griffith clamped a hand on Jonas's shoulder. "She does. But she doesn't want to interfere in your life. She simply sends her love and hopes one day you might want to meet her. And if you don't, she says she understands."

"I suppose I'd have to be a real bastard not to want to meet her." Jonas ignored the hand on his shoulder.

"Not really. You have parents. You have a life. You're very far removed from your roots in Hong Kong. She would understand if you don't want to see her. But regardless, I need your help getting her to the U.S. I have to find Bo and prove him guilty. You can do that for her. And you can do that for every person who's been exploited by Alexander Howard and Bo Lee."

Jonas rubbed his eyes. "So what about Lian? Where does she fit into your grand plan?"

"First and foremost, she's a victim and a witness against Howard. Lian, if I can prove Naiwen's innocence, she can testify that Naiwen did what she did to save Lian. But outside of that, Lian knows the language and the culture. She was involved from the first day she signed on to help the CIA with surveillance. And I'm hoping you can convince her to stay."

Jonas turned to Griffith. "Where is she going now?"

"Home."

Jonas watched Griffith head back inside. By home, he meant China. Jonas turned back to the water. He wasn't sure what he was feeling. He was still angry with Lian for lying to him. If he could, he would haul her in. But he wasn't so angry that he didn't realize Lian could be an asset. And it would be better if she were here and not thousands of miles away. Cursing under his breath, he went back inside to look at Lian's files in more detail. It wasn't every day that an orphan found his birth parents. And it wasn't every day that you found out that you were the biological child of the worst type of criminal on the planet.

The first file he pulled up was the picture of Naiwen. It was surreal. And part of him couldn't believe what Lian had told him. The second file he pulled up was the DNA comparisons. The report was very clear that Naiwen's sample proved she was his mother. Part of him didn't want to believe it. Griffith was right about one thing. He had a family, and it wasn't this woman whose face belonged to that of a stranger.

He was startled back to reality when a flash drive dropped next to his hand. He looked up to see Lian watching him. "What's this?"

She gestured to the laptop. "It has a copy of all my files on it."

"How do I know that the drive has all of them?"

Lian's mouth tightened, but she didn't give in to his obvious provocation. "How do you know that laptop has them all? You're going to have to trust me."

Jonas surged to his feet. "Trust you? You lied to me. You stole files from me. You pulled my own gun on me. You tied me up and kidnapped me."

Lian took a step back when he would have grabbed her shoulders. "I did what I had to do. And you want to talk about trust? You spied on me, hacked my computer, and had me watched. That was not exactly an act of trust."

"Except I was right not to trust you. Did you think just because we had sex that I would believe everything you said?"

Lian paled but stood her ground. "I told you it was a bad idea. I told you to leave me alone, but you kept after me. I'm not proud of what I did, but in the same situation, I would do it again. I made a promise and kept it. But for what it's worth, I knew you weren't involved with Bo before I went to bed with you. But I couldn't let you arrest me. The truth would have remained buried forever."

Jonas took a step towards her but didn't touch her. "And you couldn't trust me with the truth. If you knew I wasn't involved with Bo, you should have come to me with the truth."

Lian shook her head. "I didn't know how. You barely know me, and I hold the answers to some of the biggest secrets in your life. Griffith wanted to take charge, come to you with what we knew, and get you on Bo's trail. I wasn't sure how you would take the knowledge of who your parents are. I thought if I could earn your trust, you would sit and listen to what I had to say. Instead, I had to come at you with it this way."

"Because you're such a sweet, trusting soul, you kept your secrets and lied instead."

Lian came at him, shoving him until he hit the wall. "I would give anything to have my parents back. I would say or do anything. Can you understand that? But you, you would have kept on the rest of your life perfectly happy in your ignorance of where you came from, of who you are. There are times I wish I had never known my parents because then losing them wouldn't have hurt so much. They would have been a vague memory instead, like yours were to you. And here I am anyway. I got to be the lucky one to find out the truth about your parents. I got to be the lucky one to tell you that your father was a sadistic bastard and your mother a victim. That sat like acid in my belly every time I was near you."

Jonas kicked away from the wall. "Yeah, right. So you lied to me and kidnapped me because the truth was just too painful."

"I could punch that smirk off your face." But instead of coming closer, she spun on her heel and crossed the room.

Jonas picked up the flash drive from the desk and tossed it from hand to hand. "Any more secrets you'd like to share? Or any more sob stories designed to make me feel sorry for you?"

She stopped but kept her back to him. "Your father and brother are human traffickers. Your mother a victim. You come from the country I was born into, the one I call home, a place you don't remember. When you're done processing all that I've told you, come find me. I will answer your questions and help you if I can."

"You want to help me? Then stay." Jonas heard the words come out of his mouth before he realized his intention.

Surprised, she turned back to him. "Want to try that again?"

Jonas dropped back into the chair he had vacated. "Griffith said you were going back to China. But I want you here. I don't trust you, but I need your skills. You want to help? Then stay and help. In return, I will do what I can to help Griffith get Naiwen asylum.”

It didn't get past Lian's attention that he hadn't mentioned meeting her. Now wasn't the time to push him, not about his mother or anything else. And because he asked, she gave him the answer he wanted. “I'll stay.”

Jonas didn't try to stop Lian as she left the room. Unable to sit still any longer, he tucked the flash drive in his pocket and left the house. He spent the next couple of hours walking the beach, trying to wrap his head around what Lian had told him. Despite his desire to believe otherwise, he believed what Lian had told him. His biological father was dead, and his birth mother was still alive. And he had a brother, one who was tied to a major criminal organization, and it was now his job to find him.

Jonas dropped to the sand, his eyes burning.

* * *

Griffith kicked out with his left foot and was blocked by Lian's left arm. “I can't believe you agreed to stay.”

Lian feinted to the right, swung her left leg into a sweep that took Griffith to the floor. “It's not like he can arrest me now.”

Griffith took the hand Lian offered him and got to his feet. He took two paces back and got back into position. "True. But I thought you had pretty much decided you'd had enough."

Lian swung with her left arm, spun, and struck Griffith on the side before he could block. "I just gave the man the shock of his life. It didn't seem right to leave when he asked me to stay. Once he's calm and thinking rationally, he's going to have questions that only I can answer."

Griffith managed to get a strike past Lian's defense, and she hit the ground. He quickly stepped back, knowing she would be quick to get back to her feet and retaliate. "Maybe we've both lost our minds. I'm too old to play these games, and I thought you wanted a normal life."

Lian flipped back to her feet, dropping her arms to her side. "I do want a normal life. I just am not sure I know what that looks like anymore."

Griffith dropped his defensive pose. "The director said he has enough information to get asylum for Naiwen."

Lian grabbed a bottle of water she had lying nearby. "That's great. Another reason to stick around. I imagine I'll be called in for the hearing."

Griffith nodded while trying to catch his breath, irritated that Lian was hardly breathing harder than she had before their sparring match. "The director has your recorded testimony from last year. I don't know if you'll be called or not, but yes, being here would make an appearance easier."

Lian was about to take a swallow of her water

when she saw Jonas enter the room. "Good morning, Jonas. I won't bother to ask how you slept."

Jonas nodded at her, then at Griffith. "No, I don't suppose you will."

Lian tossed the bottle on her gym bag. She then grabbed and tossed Jonas a pair of sparring gloves. She went back to the mat and waited, her eyes never leaving Jonas's.

Griffith circled the mat so he could watch. "She has a nasty left hook."

"Don't help him." Lian tightened her gloves.

Jonas looked at Lian but didn't put the gloves on. "I'm not going to fight you."

Lian shrugged her shoulders. "It's the only satisfaction you're going to get out of this fiasco. You might as well take a shot."

Jonas tossed the gloves at Griffith. "I'm not going to fight you."

Lian nodded, then she shot across the mat, quickly taking Jonas down. She went to kick again, but he quickly rolled out of her reach. She watched with satisfaction as Jonas quickly got to his feet and came at her. She blocked several of his swings before getting a few hits in and once again swept her foot out and took him down.

Jonas rolled to his feet, this time accepting the gloves Griffith tossed at him. He quickly donned them. He then went on the offensive. He managed to get a few hits in past Lian's guard but was careful not to hit her too hard or in the face.

The match between them didn't last very long. Lian had known from watching him fight before that she would have to be quick but didn't stand much chance of winning the match. She got a few more good hits in and blocked several attacks before Jonas had her down and pinned. She lay beneath him, her breath heaving.

Jonas's eyes were fixed on Lian's, his hands pinning her arms and his legs pinning hers. When he felt his body react involuntarily to the closeness of her body pressed against his, he released her and shot to his feet.

Lian took a moment to catch her breath before getting to her feet. She glanced back at Griffith, who simply nodded at her and left the room.

Jonas took a few more steps back. "I've been in contact with my team. There still has not been any movement from Biao or Kang."

Lian peeled off the sparring gloves. "No doubt they've gone underground. I figure I'll let you worry about them. I'll worry about Bo."

"Don't think I can be objective? Don't think I can take him out?"

Lian shook her head at his defensive tone. "No, I think you can. It's not as if you know him. What I think is that you'll run yourself ragged trying to split your priorities."

Jonas supposed she had a point. "We'll have to head back to Virginia. It will be easier for me to track these men from home base."

"Except you're supposed to visit your family for your birthday. I read your file, so I know it's next week."

Jonas swore. "I forgot."

"You might as well go. Biao, Kang, and Bo know people are looking for them. There is no way it was kept secret when you went to Los Angeles last month. And they are men with connections. They'll all lie low for a while. You should take the trip. It might convince them that you're not close to finding them."

Jonas wiped the sweat from his brow. "They'd be right. You have no hard evidence against Bo, so there really isn't much you can do there until you have Naiwen here to corroborate your and Griffith's story that Bo is a criminal."

"I have a feeling the CIA is still gathering evidence. But maybe if we can catch Biao, we can tie him back to Bo."

Jonas disagreed. "Don't get your hopes up that he'll turn on Bo. Bo would simply have him killed."

Lian tossed a bottle of water to Jonas. "So I say you should make the trip to Chicago."

"Only if you come with. I don't trust you not to run."

"How long, Jonas?"

"How long, what?" Jonas drained the bottle and crushed it.

"Until you trust me again."

Jonas's hand fisted at his side. "Don't think I'll ever trust you again."

Lian let the ache in her heart sweep through her as she watched Jonas leave the room. She was afraid that it would be his final answer.

Griffith stepped back into the gym. He spoke Mandarin as he approached her. "He needs time."

Lian answered back in Mandarin. "Time is not something we'll have a lot of. There will come a time when he may have no choice but to trust me. And if he doesn't, things could get ugly."

Griffith looked out the back window to see Jonas heading off down the beach at a run. "I'll do my best to talk some sense into him."

Lian took the hand Griffith had balled into a fist and kissed his knuckles. "I am not sure that beating him up is the best way to get him to listen."

"I'd say your little sparring match today went a long way toward softening him up."

"Perhaps. Time will tell."

Lian left the room and headed to the shower. Right now, the only thing she could do was to do her best to help find the evidence they needed to get Bo convicted and do what she could for Naiwen.

Chapter Eleven

The flight to Chicago was uneventful and spent in silence. Lian had tried to get Jonas to talk about something, anything, but he was resistant. He had spent the past couple of days going over the files she had given him. He had read through detailed reports on Howard and what he was suspected of. His face had been unreadable as he'd stared at the picture of the man who'd sired him.

Once he had finished going through the files on his father, he had spent even more time poring over the files on Bo. Lian wasn't sure what she would have done in his position. The man he was looking at on the screen was his own brother. But the two men couldn't be more different. Jonas stood up for the law; Bo broke it. Jonas stood for those who couldn't stand up for themselves; Bo knocked them down.

So now Jonas was simply brooding over everything he had learned. Lian knew it was a lot to take in. Her parents might be gone, but her legacy was one she could be proud of.

Lian exited the plane and headed toward the car rental counter. She hitched her carry-on higher on her shoulder. She knew Jonas was right behind her. She could feel his eyes boring into her back.

"Great." Jonas grabbed Lian's arm to halt her.

Lian looked up at him. "What?"

"My parents are here."

Lian looked across the terminal where an older couple stood with big smiles on their faces. The sheer happiness on the woman's face gave her away as Jonas's mother.

"Jonas!" Abby Cole rushed over to hug her son. "Happy birthday! We are so glad you could come."

Jonas hugged his mother back, just as tightly as she was hugging him. "Me, too. I wasn't sure I was going to be able to make it."

Jonas's father, Henry, followed behind. "Good to see you, son."

Jonas hugged his dad. "Same here. I told you guys I would rent a car. You didn't need to brave rush hour."

Henry grabbed the bag Jonas was carrying. "You know your mother. She didn't want to wait any longer than necessary to see you."

Jonas laughed, well aware that his mother wasn't known for her patient nature.

Lian came up behind Jonas. She smiled at the older couple when their questioning eyes turned her way.

"This is the first time you've brought a lady home." Henry wrapped his free arm around his wife's waist.

Jonas, who had not forgotten Lian was behind him but wished he could, gestured to Lian. "This is Lian Albright. She's a colleague. We're working on a case together.   After my visit, we're headed off on assignment."

"It's nice to meet you anyway." Abby held a hand out to Lian.

Lian shook the woman's hand. "It's nice to meet you, Mrs. Cole. I have some friends in the city, so accompanying Jonas gives me the perfect excuse to visit."

Henry held a hand out. "Where are you staying?"

Lian glanced at Jonas, then back at Henry. "I haven't booked a room yet, but there's a place near Chinatown that I'm fond of."

"Nonsense. You should stay with us." Henry held out a hand to take the bag Lian was holding.

Lian hesitated. "I appreciate the offer, but I'm sure you'd like to spend some time alone with your son."

Abby seconded the invitation. "It will be nice to have a woman to chat with. My daughter is at home, waiting on her baby. I've been going over there every couple of days, but her in-laws are visiting, so I'm trying not to go over there so they can enjoy their visit."

Jonas shook his head. "You might as well say yes. They'll stand here all night until they convince you. There's a spare room, so you'll have privacy."

Abby took Henry's hand and started walking toward the baggage area. "Wonderful. Let's go get your bags so we can get home. I've got dinner in the crockpot. There's plenty for all."

Lian couldn't help but notice Jonas was scowling at his parents as they headed for their luggage. She dropped back so that his parents wouldn't hear them. "For the record, this was not my idea, and I'd appreciate it if you'd stop looking at me like I'm a criminal. It might tip your parents off that something is wrong."

"As far as I'm concerned, you are. But like I said, they would have stood there all night convincing you. It's easier to give in to their demands."

Lian had to quicken her steps to catch up with Jonas as he strode away. This time, she was the one scowling.

* * *

Lian sat across from Jonas at the dinner table. Abby had served up the simple meal on her best China. She knew, because Jonas had made a comment about his short visit, that it wasn't worth the effort, even if it was his birthday. Abby had simply waved that away.

"I hope your meal is okay. You haven't eaten much." Abby took a bite of the stew she had prepared for her son's arrival.

Lian glanced up from her bowl. She realized she had been staring at it instead of eating it. "It's delicious. I'm just very tired, and I'm afraid I am not doing it justice."

"I imagine whatever it is you do with the FBI, it's probably quite tiring. Every time Jonas comes home, he spends a couple of days catching up on his sleep."

Lian glanced at Jonas. She doubted he had told them much about the details of his work. "I'm a linguist. I promise my work is not nearly as hard as your son's, but the assignment we are working on together has entailed a lot of long hours."

"Linguist?" Henry broke a biscuit in half and slathered it with butter.

"Yes. Mandarin. I've done a few assignments with the FBI. One was right here in Chicago a couple of years ago. It was sort of a coming home for me."

That got Abby's attention. "Are you from Chicago?"

Lian glanced up at Jonas again, but she couldn't tell anything from his expression. Figuring it wasn't going to hurt anything, she answered his mother truthfully. "Not exactly. I was born in Beijing. My parents were missionaries there. When they passed away, I came to Chicago and lived with my uncle for a short time. I finished high school here."

Abby patted Lian's hand. "I'm very sorry to hear about your parents. Does your uncle still live here?"

Lian shook her head. "No. He did what a lot of Midwesterners do and retired to Florida. Last I heard from him, he was living it up on the beach with a lady he met there."

"You said you were going to meet some friends?" Abby set her spoon aside.

Lian picked up her spoon and took a bite. It was obvious Abby wasn't going to eat if her guest wasn't. "I made some friends when I lived here years ago. I haven't called them yet to tell them I'm in town, but I was planning to pop in on them tomorrow for lunch."

Abby picked her spoon back up and took a bite of her own. "I'm sure they'll be super excited to see you."

Lian dropped her gaze. "Yes."

Jonas picked up the conversation when Lian suddenly dropped silent. "Her friend owns a Chinese restaurant. She claims they have the best Chinese food you'll ever eat."

That got Henry's attention. "Chinese? Where?"

Abby smiled at her husband. "Henry loves Chinese food. I've tried to cook it myself, but it never turns out nearly as good as in the restaurants."

Lian glanced back up. She'd been thinking about how she'd ended up in Chicago and remembering her first visit to the restaurant. Despite the pain she'd been feeling when she'd walked into the restaurant, she had fond memories of the time she'd spent there.

Lian took another bite and cleared her throat. "You should come with me. I know they'd love to have you. I was planning to go at lunch when it's not so busy. I'll call them tonight and let them know."

Abby was quick to reply. "Oh, we wouldn't want to intrude."

Lian smiled at her, a genuine one. "Trust me when I say they won't mind. Everyone is jiā, or family."

Henry answered for his wife. "We'd love to go. And if the food is as good as you say, then they'll have new customers. Our favorite place closed down earlier this year when the owner passed away. His daughter ended up selling the place, and now it's a deli."

"You won't be disappointed. That I can guarantee."

They finished the meal, and Lian excused herself. She went to the bedroom and found her phone. She called the restaurant and told Quan to expect her and a few guests tomorrow. They chatted for a few minutes before she hung up. She had to wipe away a few tears after their chat.

"I was checking to make sure you didn't need anything before you went to bed." Abby's voice was soft, and the look in her eyes was sympathetic.

Lian looked over from where she sat on the bed. She had left the bedroom door open. "I'm fine."

Abby didn't bother to pretend she hadn't seen her tears. "I always cry when I know Jonas is coming home. My other two children live so close. My oldest son, now I worry about him. Being a cop in Chicago is not an easy job. My daughter, she has a normal job, but with the baby coming, I worry. But Jonas, he doesn't talk about what he does much. I know what he does is important, but also dangerous."

Lian brushed away the last of her tears. "I haven't known Jonas long, but I do know the work he does is important. But if it makes you feel better, the job he does now is probably less dangerous than the one he had before. All the work we've been doing has been at the home office, not in the field."

Abby entered the room and took a seat on the bed next to Lian. "That's what he tells me. We were so excited when he was promoted. He said it would be more regular hours. He did say he would be spending less time in the field. It was a huge relief for me and his father."

"Grilling my coworkers, Mom?" Jonas leaned in the doorway, smiling at his mother.

"Just confirming what you told me. You always tell me that one should always verify the facts for oneself."

Jonas held a hand out. "That I did. You should let Lian get some sleep."

Abby bid Lian good night and kissed her son on the cheek before heading to her own room.

"Are you going to tell them?" Lian set her cell phone on the bedside table.

"Yes. But not tonight. I'm not sure how to broach the subject with them. I'd appreciate it if you kept quiet." Jonas glanced down the hall to make sure his mother was still in her room.

"It's your story to tell." Lian wanted to say so much more but kept quiet.

"Yes, it is. Good night."

Lian remained seated while Jonas closed the bedroom door behind him as he left. Forgiveness was not going to be easily earned. Lian didn't need to ask herself why it mattered. He mattered to her, and his pain mattered to her. And though he probably wouldn't admit it, learning what he did about his parents was a big blow, one that he couldn't have been prepared for. She had wanted to ease him into the truth, but fate hadn't been on her side. Now she had lost whatever trust she had gained, and that, probably more than his forgiveness, was going to be almost impossible to get back.

Lian undressed and pulled on her favorite nightgown. Part of her knew she should have resisted his request and gone home. But home wasn't going to ease the ache in her heart. Only Jonas could do that, and she wasn't sure what her next step should be.

Lian lay down, with visions of kidnapping Jonas again until he forgave her. The idea had some appeal but certainly was not practical. Time was what she needed, but she wasn't sure time was on her side.

* * *

Jonas stood with his parents while listening to a flurry of Chinese. The moment Lian had set foot in the restaurant, she'd been embraced by a woman around her age, then by a man about her age, then a much older man, whom he assumed was the owner who had given Lian a job so many years ago. There were tears in the woman's eyes, and he was pretty sure there were tears in the eyes of the older man as well. These people were not her blood, but they were her family.

Lian turned, her eyes full of happiness, as she gestured for them to join her. "Quan, this is Jonas and his parents, Henry and Abby."

Quan, the older man, bowed to them. "Nice to meet friends of Lian."

Lian wrapped an arm around Quan while she introduced the younger couple. "And this is his daughter, Yisa, and her husband, Chon."

"We were glad to hear Lian was in for a visit, and it was nice of her to bring guests. Please, come sit." Yisa led them to a small room off the back of the restaurant. There was a large table set up in honor of Lian's visit.

Quan held a chair for Lian and gestured for everyone else to come in and sit. "I have a special meal planned."

The pair started up again in Mandarin.

Yisa set a couple of pots of tea on the table. "You have to forgive them. They have a tendency to be rude when they get together. My father so rarely hears news from home, and Lian always comes with tall tales to share."

Lian smiled at Jonas's parents. "Sorry. Yisa will call us out when we've gone on too long. It's been two years since my last visit, but it always feels longer."

Quan patted her hand. "We are glad to have our daughter in for a visit."

The meal was massive, and the conversation lively. Lian taught Abby a few words in Mandarin, while Henry made sure to taste at least one or two bites of every dish laid out before them.

"You really went above and beyond." Lian stood and set about cleaning up the dishes.

Quan simply nodded at Abby, Henry, and Jonas. "It is not often you bring guests. I keep hoping one day you will bring with you a man worthy of marrying you."

Lian ignored the comment and stacked up a few more plates. "We should get some boxes and let Henry take some of this feast home."

Henry seconded that idea and helped himself to the containers that Chon brought in for them.

Abby rose and started helping Lian clean up the dishes. "All I can say is that we'll be back. We've eaten at a lot of different restaurants in town, but this place is by far the best."

That kicked off a conversation about other restaurants and other styles of food. Abby thought it was funny when Quan started listing his favorite places to eat, and the top of the list was a pizza place not too far from his restaurant.

"We should go and let you enjoy some alone time with your family. We can't thank you enough for inviting us." Abby hugged Yisa and surprised everyone by giving Quan a hug as well.

Lian stopped and noticed Jonas staring at her. In the midst of the gathering, she could almost forget he was watching her. Right now she wasn't sure what was in his eyes, but for the first time in days, it wasn't anger she saw. "I'll catch a cab back to your parents' house later tonight. I'm going to stay for a while."

Jonas nodded. "We'll keep the door unlocked."

Thank yous and containers of food were passed around for a final time, and Lian watched the trio leave.

"He watches you." Quan came and picked up the last of the dishes.

"He's angry with me."

"Why?"

Lian turned troubled eyes his way. As she spoke, she naturally slipped back into Mandarin. "It is a bit complicated. I did not tell you because I did not want to worry you, but I was in Hong Kong two years ago. I took an assignment. It was supposed to be easy, but things turned dangerous. I met a woman, and I made a promise to help her find her son."

Quan handed the dishes to Yisa when she came back through the doors. His eyes stayed on Lian's. "Did you find him?"

"Yes. He and his parents were here tonight. I was the messenger who told him about his real mother, his real father, and that he has a brother. His father was a bad man. He died, and his other son has stepped into his shoes. Jonas is with the FBI. I think the legacy of where he came from is difficult for him to accept."

Quan knew her better than that and could tell she was keeping secrets. "What I saw in him was not a man who was upset by a messenger. Why the anger?"

Lian brushed at a stray tear. "I lied to him. We were becoming close, though I knew it was a mistake.

I knew he would be angry with me for the things I had done behind his back, but I could not tell him the truth. I had to know I could trust him first. I was going to tell him the truth, but I did not get the chance before he found out. And now he is angry."

Quan knew not to press her for too many answers. He knew some of the work she had done for both the American and Chinese governments. "I see love in your eyes when you look at him."

Lian broke. "I cannot undo what I did. And it hurts so much when he looks at me, knowing he would love to see me punished for my lies. But I did the right thing."

Quan held her while she cried. He was not surprised that the tears were short-lived. Lian had gone through much in her life, but she was a fighter. "I see more than you do. Yes, I see anger. But I see fascination. I see desire."

Lian poured them both a fresh cup of tea. "But do you see love? Because I cannot think of a single thing other than love that could make him forgive me."

"Perhaps, buried under the rest. You fight for what you want. You know as well as anyone that time does heal wounds."

Lian hugged Quan and rose. "We should find something a little stronger to drink."

Quan smiled and headed back to the bar. Under the counter, he pulled out a bottle of mijiu.

Lian took the bottle from him while he grabbed a couple of wine glasses. "It's been so long since I've had a real glass of rice wine, but I see it is not one that you made yourself."

"Getting too old. There is a new Chinese market open down the road. There is nothing she cannot get for you."

Lian savored her first sip and settled into a booth in the back of the restaurant. It was busy tonight, but Yisa and Chon looked like they didn't need their father's help. "Are you going to retire soon? You have talked about going back to China."

"Mmm. I think I will stay here. Yisa and Chon are talking about starting a family. I want to see my grandchildren grow up. But you. You still have not decided."

"I swore I was going to go back to China and stay there, but I get restless." Lian finished her glass and poured another.

"You have never had a home. The village you grew up in was the closest thing to one you had, and even then you traveled more than you stayed. You have been to parts of China that tourists will never see. And even here in America, you do not stay in one place."

"I do not belong. I do not belong here. I do not belong there." Lian leaned back and closed her eyes.

Quan patted her hand. "You do not stay in one place long enough to learn to belong. I think your man, Jonas, may be the answer to your loneliness."

Lian knew loneliness was probably a better word for what ailed her. She had Quan and his daughter, but as much as she loved them, they had their own lives to live. She had Mindy and Dex, and she hoped that their relationship worked out. She had Naiwen in China, though Griffith would have her in the U.S. soon, of that she was sure. She had friends in China, but none nearly as close as those she had here in the U.S.

"Maybe I am trying to force something that is not right for me. I grew up in China, and that is where my memories of my parents are, but maybe that is not where I am meant to be. Everyone I care about is here in the U.S."

Quan poured them both another glass. "It is amazing how clear one's thinking can become when one has a few glasses of mijiu in one's belly."

Lian laughed and saluted him. "To mijiu."

Quan raised his glass. "To mijiu."

Chapter Twelve

Lian was grateful that the door was unlocked when she arrived back at Jonas's parents' house. She and Quan had finished the bottle and shared a second with Yisa and Chon. It was now about two in the morning. She probably should have stayed the night there but thought it might be rude to her hostess if she didn't come back. Though she was very tempted during the cab ride to simply have the cab driver keep driving.

Sighing, held by her promise to stay and help Jonas, she closed the front door behind her, remembering to lock it. Lian found her way to the stairs and tried to avoid the creaks. She made her way up and tiptoed down the hall.

"I was wondering if you had disappeared." Jonas flicked the light on in his bedroom, which was enough to illuminate the hallway.

Lian held a hand over her eyes. "Please shut that off."

Jonas took a step into the hall and watched as Lian staggered a bit toward her bedroom door. "You're drunk."

Lian turned and pointed a finger at him. "Yes, and I'm in no mood to have you kill my buzz. I had a wonderful evening, and I'm not letting you ruin it."

Jonas watched as she carefully opened her bedroom door and held the knob until she was inside the room. "How much did you drink?"

Lian didn't bother to answer his question. She fell onto the bed. "Can we talk tomorrow?"

Jonas came into the bedroom and pulled off her boots. "It is tomorrow."

"Then can we talk when the sun comes up?" Lian managed to sit up, get her coat off, and get herself under the covers.

Jonas tossed her coat over a nearby chair. "So how close did you come?"

Lian pushed her hair out of her face and sat up. "How close did I come to what?"

Jonas leaned against the wall, carefully studying her face. "Not coming back."

"Probably closer than I thought, but not as close as you did."

Jonas nodded. He had seen a different side to Lian tonight. Tonight, she was the loving daughter come home. She had been relaxed in a way he had never seen her. Looking at her, laughing and crying with people she loved, it was hard to remember that this was the woman who hacked his files and kidnapped him at gunpoint.

"You shouldn't be looking at me like that." Lian slipped out from under the covers and swung her legs over the side of the bed.

"And why is that? I was attracted to you before."

Lian crossed her arms over her chest. "Trust a

man to be able to compartmentalize his feelings. You'd toss me in jail the first chance you got, but you'd take me to bed first."

Jonas crossed to her and pulled her into his arms. Yes, there was anger still. Part of him understood why she had done it, but she could have chosen some other way to approach him. She had opted to lie. It was hard to forgive that. And if he were being honest, his pride still hadn't recovered from the blow of being kidnapped by this woman.

"I've got this theory that I can work you out of my system." Jonas's mouth hovered over hers.

It was oh so tempting, but she knew it would be a mistake. "And maybe you'll just find yourself in even deeper. Either way, I'm not testing that theory right now. I have to go to the bathroom, and I'm tired."

Jonas took her arm when she would have brushed past him.

Lian didn't give him a chance to speak. "Don't make me hurt you."

The corner of Jonas's mouth kicked up. "I think you might mean that. All right, for now. Go to bed."

Lian glared at him but left to go to the bathroom first.

Jonas left her room and went back to his own. He waited until he heard her bedroom door close before he lay down on his own bed. He doubted he'd get much sleep, but it was too early, or perhaps too late, to wander the house.

He slept a little, but by five a.m. he was throwing

the covers back and heading downstairs for coffee. He hadn't slept much since Lian had told him about his family. In truth, he'd probably not slept well since the night he'd learned of her betrayal. Work had been consuming him during the day, but thoughts of Lian had filled his nights.

"It's too early for such heavy thoughts." Henry yawned as he came into the kitchen.

Jonas looked up from where he had been staring blindly into his empty coffee cup. "I'm not sure there is ever a good time. Want some coffee?"

Henry nodded and took a seat at the kitchen table. "You and your brother carry a heavy burden. Both of you have seen and done things that most people can't imagine. But these days you carry an extra burden. Being part of the counterintelligence unit in the FBI can't be easy."

Jonas set a cup in front of his father and took a seat across from him. "It was supposed to be more regular hours than anything else. And I'm not in the field so much. It's not easier, but I wouldn't say it's harder. Just different."

"Then what has your mind so full?" Henry took a sip and watched as his son glanced up at the ceiling.

"It's complicated."

"Women do have a tendency to complicate things. That woman upstairs certainly has your attention, but there's something else I see when you look at her."

Jonas knew his father was right. "It's not just her that's a complication. It's what she brought with her.

I want to talk to you and Mom about it at one time. What I have to tell you might be hard for you to hear."

"Okay. But while your mother is not in the room, what is the status of your relationship with that young woman?"

Jonas drained his cup. "She's not so young. But then neither am I. Long story short, I slept with her; then I learned she had betrayed me."

Henry knew his son wasn't one to exaggerate or be overly dramatic. If his son said she betrayed him, then he had no doubt she did. "And yet she's here with you."

"That's where it gets complicated. She took an assignment at the FBI so she could spy on me. She stole my files and went through them. She said she was trying to find any connection I might have to a man she and a friend of hers were looking for. When I found out she was the one who stole my files, she kidnapped me at gunpoint to avoid arrest."

Henry once again looked at the ceiling. "That slip of a woman kidnapped you?"

"Don't let her fool you. She had me disarmed and held me at gunpoint in what I would consider, under any other circumstances, quite amazing. Lian has been studying martial arts since she was a small girl."

Henry's face was serious, but there was a glimmer in his eyes. "I'd like to have seen that. I suppose the fact that she bested you is part of your current problem. That and wanting her back."

Jonas didn't miss the humor in his father's eyes but

chose to ignore it. "I would have arrested her the next time I saw her, except her friend has a lot of pull with some very important people and got the charges against her dropped. Instead, I ended up deciding I needed her help."

Henry was used to getting bare-bones stories from his son and didn't press for more details. "That doesn't sound quite so complicated."

"It gets better. But that part is the part I need Mom for."

Abby came into the kitchen, tying the sash to her robe. "What do you need Mom for? You two having a heart-to-heart without me?"

Henry kissed his wife's cheek when she bent down to him. "We wouldn't dream of it. Our son says he wants to talk to us about something and wanted to do it when we were together."

"I don't suppose you're going to tell us you're finally getting married. After Sylvia left, I had pretty much given up hope."

Jonas found he could smile at that. "If Sylvia and I had married, we'd probably be divorced by now. It was for the best."

Abby made a sound in her throat that told them what she thought about that. "Of course, it was for the best. She was nowhere near good enough for you. Does what you have to tell us have anything to do with Lian?"

Jonas nodded but waited until his mom had settled into the seat next to his father before speaking. "As I was telling Dad, Lian came to work for the FBI because she wanted to spy on me. When I finally realized something was wrong, I confronted her. She's been looking for a man named Bo. He's a very shady character from Hong Kong. She thought that if she could find Bo's brother, then perhaps he might lead her to Bo."

"So who is this Bo's brother? An agent of yours?" Henry didn't like the feeling that was settling in his stomach.

Jonas looked at his father but couldn't look his mother in the eye. "I am."

Two coffee cups thudded onto the table in unison. It was his mother who spoke first. "Lian knows your birth family?"

Jonas turned eyes filled with turmoil on the only mother he'd ever known. "She met my birth mother. Her name is Naiwen. Lian took what Naiwen said and used the information to trace me. At the time, Lian was working for our government and had access to some very sophisticated technology. All the evidence she had pointed to me. She then took a DNA sample from Naiwen and had it compared to mine. There is no mistake. This Naiwen woman is my biological mother."

The room was silent for a few moments as his parents digested what he'd told them.

Henry took his wife's hand. "What of your father and brother?"

"His name was Alexander Howard. Naiwen killed

him accidentally when she tried to stop him from attacking Lian. His son Bo wanted to press charges against Naiwen, but a government agent put both of them into protective custody. It was during that time that Lian found me. She wasn't sure she could trust me, given that Howard was suspected of several heinous crimes, and his son followed in his footsteps."

"Naiwen wasn't part of their crimes?"

Jonas felt the need to be completely honest. "She was not his wife. She was his property. She bore him two sons against her will, and he kept her prisoner in his house. Lian says that Howard had bought her when Naiwen was very young."

Everyone turned in unison when Lian made a soft sound in the doorway.

Lian's voice was flat when she spoke. "China has a very high rate of human trafficking. But like so many other countries, including America, it's not something that is often discussed. People like to pretend it doesn't happen."

Jonas couldn't take his gaze off Lian. Her short hair was tumbled around her face, and she was still wearing her clothes from yesterday. He could see a sheen of tears in her eyes, and he could tell she was struggling not to shed them.

Henry, knowing more of the story than his wife, jumped in. "So you suspected my son would be part of such a heinous crime? My son is a decorated FBI agent. He has devoted himself to his country."

Lian took a slight step back at the animosity in

Henry's voice. "I couldn't be sure. Both Howard and Bo were able to hide their activities from the authorities. I was gathering intel through an embassy in Hong Kong when all of this began. By the time the dust settled over Howard's death, I was being indicted, as was Naiwen, on conspiracy to commit murder. I've no doubt that the men had high-end officials in their pockets. Fortunately, earlier this year, the charges against me were dropped. I was free to come out of hiding."

"And my son?" Abby leaned against her husband for support.

"I had nothing to go on that Jonas was innocent or guilty. I had two choices. I chose to find Jonas on my own and see if I could find proof one way or the other. Had I not pursued this on my own, chances are that a full-blown investigation would have ensued, and all of this would have been made public. If Jonas were innocent, my investigation would keep Bo from knowing who his brother is. It could stay between me and Jonas. Bo's contacts are many, and they are everywhere. If Jonas were guilty, I would have made the phone call I didn't make before and had a full investigation started. Then it wouldn't matter because Bo would already know Jonas was his brother because they would have been in on it together."

Jonas had to swallow a lump in his throat. He hadn't thought of that before. If Bo had the contacts Lian believed he had, then if the CIA had found him,

Bo would have found out eventually. It was possible Bo might try to use him to lure Naiwen out. A long-lost son would be quite the lure.

Abby broke the silence. "It's a fantastic story. Are you sure Jonas is this Naiwen woman's son?"

"I was very thorough before I came back to the U.S. I wouldn't have come if I hadn't been absolutely sure." Lian gave the trio a small smile. "You'll have to have Jonas give you the rest of the details. I should go."

Neither Henry nor Abby protested.

Lian looked at Jonas before turning away and heading back to the stairs.

"It's like something from a movie. Are you going to meet her? You have to be dying of curiosity." Abby took Jonas's hand.

"I don't know that I can, even if I wanted to. I mean, I suppose every orphan wants to believe that their mother didn't want to give them away. They want to believe their mom hadn't a choice, and that she thought of them every day. I have a very vague memory of my birth mother, but I can't be sure if the memory is real or one I made up when I was young."

Henry laid his hand over his wife's that held Jonas's. "But she did what she had to do. If Lian is to be believed, it sounds like she never forgot you. She asked a stranger to take on the task of finding you, all these years later."

Jonas rubbed his brow with his free hand. "Lian said Naiwen wants to meet me but understands if I don't feel the same. She said Naiwen was just happy I was raised by a loving family and that I turned out so well."

Henry got up from his seat. "I don't imagine there is much you can do right now about Naiwen. What are you going to do about Lian? It's obvious to both me and your mother that you care for her."

"Lian says the only thing she sees in my eyes is anger."

Abby rose to stand next to her husband. "She needs to look deeper than that. I see hurt. I'd be angry about it on your behalf, but I see hurt in her eyes, too. The kind that lies deep. You two can either keep hurting one another, or you can try to fix your relationship. You might deny there is one, but your father and I know better. We can worry about Naiwen later. But I think it's wonderful that Lian was able to give you the gift of your birth mother. It sounds like Naiwen is a brave, selfless woman, and I can see those traits in you. It's a wonderful foundation she gave you."

Jonas kissed his mother's cheek. "And you two raised me into the man I am. I suppose I should go talk to Lian."

When Jonas got upstairs, Lian's bedroom door was open. She was packing up what little she had unpacked. "Running away?"

"I'm pretty sure I've worn out my welcome. I'm going to stay with Quan. I'll meet you at the airport when we're ready to fly to L.A."

Jonas closed the door and leaned against it. "I hadn't thought about what the repercussions of a full investigation would be when I was found innocent. So, when did you think I was innocent?"

"There's a loaded question. Would you really believe my answer?"

"And if I said yes?"

Lian zipped up her suitcase and looked at him. "All right. I'll play. Like I told you before, I went to bed with you after I figured out you were innocent. I had the proof I needed only a few days after I hacked your files. If you will remember, I told you getting involved was a bad idea because guilty or innocent, I knew things about you that you didn't. And I wasn't going to tell you what I knew about you until I was far away. I knew in my gut you weren't guilty, but believing something isn't the same as proof. You should know that better than anyone."

Jonas kicked away from the door. "I was investigating you when I took you to bed. I didn't believe you were guilty, but I had no proof. I was wrong; you were. I remember thinking how untrusting I'd become over the years, but I kept digging anyway. So I guess that makes my crime a little worse than yours."

"What did your parents say that made you change your tune?"

Jonas came over to her and cupped her chin. "Can you imagine what I must be feeling? I've had a lot to absorb. I haven't quite forgiven you yet. I'm still willing to test my theory that I can work you out of my system. Either way it turns out, I'd be the winner."

"So either you'd succeed in working me out of your system, or you'd be in deeper? You figure either of those is a win for you? That's cold." Lian jerked away from him.

Jonas pulled Lian into his arms, jerking her body back against his. "You might be right."

Lian could have fought him. She knew she could break the hold he had on her, but her traitorous body was melting against his. She hadn't been able to fight him before she'd gone to bed with him, and she was pretty sure any battle she waged now would be pointless.

Feeling her surrender, Jonas backed her up against the wall. His mouth ravaged hers as he pulled at the hem of her blouse. She lifted her arms to help him. He grasped her thighs, and she wrapped them around his waist. Her arms came around his neck, her mouth as avid on his as his was on hers.

He unhooked her bra and feasted on her breasts. He wanted nothing more than to lay her down on that bed and take what she was offering. But it didn't get past his consciousness that his parents were downstairs, and they would no doubt know what he was doing with Lian in her bedroom.

Lian stumbled when Jonas suddenly set her on her feet and released her. He was still dressed while she was half undressed. Embarrassed at how quickly she succumbed to him, she grabbed her blouse and tugged it into place.

"I think it's a good idea if you go to Quan's until we leave. I need to think, and I can't do that with you around." Jonas quickly left the room.

Lian's knees shook, and she took a seat on the edge of the bed while she tried to catch her breath. Her heart was pounding, and her body was edgy with unfulfilled desire. She would have thrown something at the door behind him, but she held her temper. It wouldn't do to lose it in front of his parents.

Lian came downstairs a short while later and was going to say goodbye to Jonas's parents, but she only found his mother. Feeling awkward, she set her suitcase down. "I just wanted to thank you for letting me stay."

"Jonas said you're going to spend the rest of your visit with your friends." Abby kept her back to Lian.

"Under the circumstances, I feel I should go. I never meant to hurt your son, but my first allegiance is to Naiwen, not to him."

Abby turned, wiping her wet hands on a towel. "Does he make your list?"

Lian didn't pretend to misunderstand. "Yes. I care for your son. I knew the first time we went out that I was making a mistake. I knew he wasn't going to thank me for the message I was bringing him, assuming he was innocent. I had planned to be safely back in China before he found out. Things didn't quite work out how I planned. But either way,

Naiwen knows he's grown into a fine man, and I've repaid the debt I owed her."

"Jonas is a fine man. He's a good man. A kind one, when it suits him. But he grew up rough, and it took a long time for him to build trust and become a real member of this family. He needs someone to love him unconditionally. Nothing else is going to get past his defenses."

"I know of his childhood. He may not realize how much. I had to trace him from Hong Kong to America, and through several agencies to follow his records. I know everywhere he's been except for when he disappeared from the system. No records were on him until the adoption, but I have a very good imagination."

"In this case, I think being the messenger might have been harder on you than on Jonas being the receiver of that news. He now has proof that his mother loved him. He may not know what he wants to do, but I have no doubt once he gets past his hurt and confusion, he'll be curious about the woman who gave birth to him. I can't imagine you knowing what you knew and having to keep it to yourself while you investigated him was easy."

"As soon as I got to know him, I knew he wasn't a traitor. But knowing isn't proof, which is what I told your son. And yes, it was not easy knowing what I knew. It wasn't easy telling him, either. We were at odds by the time I was able to share the truth with him, that he wasn't as receptive to the truth as he might have been. I don't know what he told you, but I doubt he'll ever trust me again."

"Like I said, he needs unconditional love."

"And I know that if I tried to offer it to him, he wouldn't trust it. I've burned my bridge with your son. Now all I can do is help him catch a criminal. Once that is done, I'll be out of his life."

Abby watched as Lian left the kitchen. There was already a cab waiting outside, so she must have ordered one the moment she went upstairs. Abby felt bad for Lian, but she felt worse for her son. Her son was going to have a hard time breaking down the walls that Lian had erected against him, but Abby wasn't sure he would even know how.

Chapter Thirteen

Jonas entered the kitchen shortly after Lian left. He knew the moment she had closed the front door behind her.

"Go ahead and sit down and have breakfast. Your father is upstairs having a shower." Abby started pulling ingredients from the refrigerator.

Instead of sitting down, he went and poured himself and his mom another cup of coffee. His mother had always been able to help him straighten out his thoughts. Right now, he could use her advice.

Abby took the cup but set it down. She took a moment to lift a hand to her son's cheek. "Finding out about your mom was difficult for you. I can see it in your eyes."

Jonas kissed his mother's cheek and pulled away. "You're my mother. I don't know this other woman. But you don't seem upset."

Abby went back to fixing breakfast. "Her loss was my gain. But I can't help but pity her. If Lian's story is true, this woman has had a very difficult, very lonely life. I imagine knowing you're here, that you grew up to be a fine man, must ease some of the guilt that lies in her heart."

Jonas popped some bread in the toaster. "You always see things from a different perspective. Some women might be jealous. Some women might be resentful. But you feel compassion. It's what makes you so special. It's what allowed you to take a young, troubled boy and bring him into your heart."

Abby waved that off. "Don't make me into some kind of saint. If you were still a young boy and she showed up trying to take you back, you can bet I would have fought her with everything in me to keep you. But you're a grown man, not a child. And she's lost so much. Are you going to give her a chance to know you?"

"She doesn't plan to force herself into my life, but she's such an abstract in my mind. I've seen her picture, but I don't know her voice. When I look at her, I don't feel any recognition. Shouldn't I feel something? Some sort of tie?"

Abby handed Jonas a plate with a large omelet on it. "I think that the recognition you're talking about is fiction. I don't see how you can look at a picture and feel something like that."

Jonas took a seat and a large bite. His mother always cooked for him when he visited. She claimed it made her feel like she used to feel when he was young. And looking up into her face, seeing age where it hadn't been before, he still saw the younger woman she'd been when she'd brought him home with her for the first time. He was forty-two now, a grown man, but she had the uncanny ability to make him feel like the young boy he'd once been.

"I suppose it would be unfair to refuse to see her.

But there's time. I'm in the middle of a case, and the completion of this case just might allow Naiwen the freedom she's never had." Jonas's thoughts went to his unknown brother. Thinking of the unknown man, there were no ambiguous feelings. If he found him, he'd do what he could to bring the man to justice.

"Take it one day at a time. I imagine any relationship you might have with this woman will take time. But you can't do that with Lian. She'll lose patience and disappear."

Jonas couldn't help the small smile that played on his lips while listening to his mother talk about Lian. Despite the tense conversation earlier that caused Lian to leave, he knew his mother liked her. They had talked and laughed at dinner like two old friends. And his mother had seemed quite taken with Lian's family. "Still holding out for me to get married?"

Abby set a plate on the table with a much smaller omelet on it, along with the toast. "I'm your mother. I want more grandchildren. You're my only holdout. But Quan said something at dinner last night that stuck with me. I think that if you don't tie Lian down, she'll be gone before you know it."

"What did he say?" Jonas asked, sipping his coffee.

"At first, he said something about wandering feet. It wasn't easy to understand him. He said that Lian has been searching for what she lost when her parents died."

"What's that?"

"Belonging. He called it China blue, though I think he meant 'blues'. He said a piece of her heart was buried with her parents back in China and that part of her still aches. He said every time she comes back, he wonders if it will be the last time."

Jonas already knew Lian had not had a close relationship with her uncle. Even if she hadn't told him, he would have known after seeing her with those she was close to. "You think I should let Lian off the hook because she's sad?"

Abby patted his hand and dug into her breakfast. "It's more than sad. I think she needs someone in her life, someone that is hers that can't be taken away. And I'm not as naïve as you and your father think. Even though you're upset with her, I can see intimacy between you. You've already been to bed with her. Part of your heart already belongs to her, or you wouldn't be so angry with her."

Jonas certainly wasn't going to discount his mother's opinion. Though he loved his father, his mother had always understood the parts of him that were hidden. "Lian told me that she didn't think I could work her out of my system."

"That's because she's a wise woman. You should be really sure of what you want before you take another step in either direction. If you pull further away, you'll lose her. And if you take a step forward and it's not what you want, you'll break her heart. She's already in love with you. Not that I can blame her, of course. Who wouldn't love my son?"

Jonas buttered his mother's toast. "You're biased."

"You got that right. Now eat your omelet. You can't chase bad guys on an empty stomach."

Jonas gave her a small salute and ate his breakfast.

* * *

Lian felt like she would spend the rest of what was left of her time with Jonas sitting beside him, but with him being miles away from her mentally. He had been even more contemplative since they'd boarded a plane bound for L.A. that morning. It was late now, and Lian was looking out the window of her hotel room, wondering what would come next.

She had contacted Griffith, but he didn't have anything new, at least not where Bo was concerned. He was starting to feel optimistic that he could get Naiwen asylum. He said he'd finally gotten some of the right people to agree to review her case. At this point, Lian had a feeling that if Griffith didn't get his way soon, he was going to pack a bag and head back to China and grab Naiwen from where he'd stashed her. Lian had no doubt Griffith had the right contacts to get Naiwen into the country through less than legal means. The trick would be getting Naiwen to agree. She'd lived so long on the outskirts of society, Lian knew the woman didn't want to spend what was left of her life living in fear of being found out.

Lian moved away from the window when her second phone buzzed. As she moved toward the table, there was a knock on her door. Lian picked up her phone before heading to the door. Naiwen was checking in on their progress, and Lian took a moment to answer her. The only person who could be behind her door was Jonas, and Lian wasn't sure she was up to dealing with him right now.

A second knock had Lian sighing and tucking the phone into the pocket of her robe that she wore over her clothes. Though warm outside, Lian had a chill since Chicago that she couldn't seem to shake.

Because it was an ingrained habit, she took a peek through the peephole before opening the door. Jonas stood before her, a large white bag of takeout in his hands. Without saying a word, she took a step back so he could enter her room.

"I brought sandwiches. I contemplated Chinese, but after the food we had at Quan's, I don't think I could find anything that comes close." Jonas headed to the seating area that held a table and two chairs.

"Animosity is bad for the digestion." Lian closed the door and leaned against it, crossing her arms across her chest. She was not yet willing to sit.

"One thing an FBI agent has to be good at is putting themself in the mindset of their quarry. If you understand them, you can begin to think like them and understand what motivates them. It's not always a pleasant experience, but it's necessary."

Lian dropped her arms but didn't move from the door. "I suppose it's easier to catch the bad guy if you can think like him. What does that have to do with me and sandwiches?"

"The sandwiches were an excuse to come knocking on your door. I've been trying to put myself in your shoes. I think I've come to some new conclusions." Jonas pushed the chair out for her to take a seat with his foot.

Lian, figuring that if a confrontation was going to ensue, she might as well sit down and get it over with now instead of letting it fester for later. She unwrapped the sandwich Jonas set in front of her. "I don't suppose this is the part where you forgive me."

Jonas took a bite of his sandwich and contemplated her. He swallowed and paused a moment before he spoke. "Not sure I'm there yet. I can understand why you did what you did, but I still have a problem with how you did it. But it did occur to me that I might owe you an apology."

Lian swallowed the lump of sandwich in her mouth. "And when did you come to that conclusion?"

"Sitting with my mom. She's always been able to level set me when I get off track. She feels sorry for you. And I was pretty harsh with you. For that, I'm sorry."

"Just that?" Lian set the sandwich aside, unable to eat it.

"And maybe for getting a little too much pleasure from our sparring match at Griffith's house."

Lian almost smiled at that. "You won that match, but then I knew you would if we went toe to toe."

"That kick and flip in your hotel room was pretty

slick. I've never been disarmed by a suspect before."

Lian shrugged. "Disarming your opponent is easy when they're caught off guard. You weren't exactly prepared for a confrontation that night."

Jonas tipped his head slightly to the side as he tried to figure out what she was thinking. "I had just climbed out of the warm bed we'd been sharing. Good food and great sex had me relaxed."

Lian heard the words and blushed a bit. It hadn't been even an hour since he'd rolled off of her when he'd received that phone call telling him that she'd been the one who'd betrayed him. He'd gone from satisfied lover to federal agent in a breath. Disarming him had been sheer luck. Had she been any slower, or even slightly off her mark, she'd currently be behind bars.

Still contemplating her, he spoke again. "I have something else to apologize for."

"I can't imagine what." Lian gripped the neckline of her robe and held it closed.

"Even while I was asking you out, I was investigating you. You have to be able to trust the people closest to you. I'd learned the hard way that you couldn't always; that you can't just sit around and hope for the best. I was calling myself an untrusting bastard while I was searching your files. My first hint of suspicion came from your so-called assignment at the university. There were paychecks, but no other evidence that you worked there. Even after we'd gone to bed together, I still kept digging."

Lian wasn't worried about that. "I'm not exactly the most trusting soul either. I know just about everything there is to know about you, and it's not because we had met and gotten to know one another. I was investigating you up until the night before our first night together. I knew you were innocent, but I had to prove it. And going out with you was one way to keep an eye on you. But I think you know that wasn't the only reason. Or I hope at least. And it wasn't why I let you into my bed."

"I know."

Lian heard the sincerity in his voice, and some of the chill she'd been feeling eased. "So now what?"

"Maybe we can start over. We've got a while yet before we nail this Biao character. And I may be just the man to lure Bo out of hiding."

Lian shook her head. "Griffith will take care of Bo. His only goal is to find Bo, arrest Bo, and get your mother out of hiding. But falling short of that goal, I think Griffith is running out of patience. He may do something drastic."

"Such as?"

"Such as going back to China and smuggling Naiwen into the States."

Jonas had a feeling Lian might be right. He hadn't spent much time with Griffith, but Griffith was likely to go outside the law to get what he wanted. With his CIA contacts, there was no doubt in Jonas's mind that Griffith could succeed should he put his plan into action. "Then I guess we need to move a little faster than he does."

"Except we've nowhere to start. I found nothing. You found nothing. These men are smart. They've been evading the police for years. What are the chances that we'll succeed where so many others have failed?"

Jonas finished his sandwich and tossed the wrapper in the nearby trash can. "I've been busy while you've been in hiding. We found something the CIA missed. So much time was spent following the triad members and Biao's and Bo's movements. They had family histories on each person, but in the past year, Biao got married."

Lian was glad she didn't have food in her mouth. She would have choked on it. "Married?"

"Yes. He got married to an American woman named Maryanne McKinnon a year ago. It was a fairly short jump from meeting to marriage. We found out that Biao has a daughter. Her name is Fan. We found them because adoption papers were filed. Biao's wife filed adoption papers so she could be Fan's legal parent. Maryanne used to live here in L.A."

"How old is Fan?"

"Records state she was born in Hong Kong five years ago. Biao is listed as her father. Her mother is listed as a woman named Gua Yu. We found her death certificate. She died just about a year ago. That is when Biao married Maryanne, not even a week after Gua's death."

"Do you think he killed her so he could marry the

American woman?" Lian couldn't help but feel sorry for the unknown woman. She could only imagine how Biao had treated Gua. Lian was doubtful that the relationship was consensual.

"We're fairly certain. Biao may find it easier to get in and out of the country with an American wife."

"We're certainly not going to find him tonight. We should both get some sleep."

Jonas admonished her. "And you changed the subject."

"What subject?"

Jonas took her hand. "The one where we start over."

"You think you can do that? Because I'm not sure I can."

Jonas rose and tugged Lian to her feet. When she didn't resist, Jonas kissed her. His fingers slid up the nape of her neck, cupping her head to hold her still for his kiss. He lifted his head when she didn't kiss him back.

Lian felt tears gathering. "At your parents' house, I got caught up in the moment. I would have let you have me right there in your parents' guest room. But I've had a lot of time to think. I can't do this. I can't be with you when you can't trust me. If I didn't have any feelings for you, maybe I could. I care about you Jonas. Given time, I could love you. But I don't think you can get beyond what I did to you."

Instead of letting her go, he walked backward until the back of his knees hit the oversized chair that sat near the windows. He pulled Lian onto his lap. "There was a woman once. She said I trusted no one. She said I had no passion. And then she told me she hated my job and had found someone else."

Lian snorted, then realized what she'd done. When Jonas looked at her questioningly, she spoke. "No passion, my fanny."

Jonas laughed; he couldn't help it. "To be fair, I wasn't around much."

Lian twisted in his lap until she sat astride him. She wanted to see his eyes. "Would you have forgiven her for cheating?"

"No, but I think I can forgive you. Her motives were selfish. They were those of a woman who didn't care who she hurt. You hurt me more than I thought any woman could, but you didn't do it maliciously. You did it to help a friend. To help two friends. Taking down Bo would do the world a great service. But if you ever kidnap me again, I will return the favor."

Lian smiled at him. She couldn't help it. The ache that had settled in her heart eased. The chill she had faded completely. She leaned back and stripped off the robe. "I don't really want to start over, Jonas."

Jonas's eyes darkened as he watched her start to unbutton her blouse. His hands went to her waist so he could help pull the blouse off. Staring at her breasts, his hands felt empty. Slowly his arms came around her and he undid the hooks of her bra. The white lace material fell away. She made no protest when his fingers closed over the hardened peaks of her breasts.

Lian came up on her knees and leaned over Jonas so she could kiss him. Her much shorter locks fell forward, and she tried fruitlessly to push them out of the way.

Jonas's fingers left her breasts to tuck the strands behind her ears. "I don't think I told you I like your hair."

Lian leaned back, her chest flushed with heat. "Yeah? I cried when I cut it off. Griffith said it was too recognizable. I'm glad you like it. Had you not shown up, it would have been an awful brown color."

"I do. I'm sorry I was the reason you did, and I'm glad it's not brown. Griffith was right. It would have been hard to miss."

Lian sighed and leaned over and kissed his neck. Her fingers went to his chest so she could unbutton his shirt. When he worked, he always had a dress shirt on, along with an undershirt. She found it extremely sexy, peeling his sedate shirts from his bronzed, muscled skin. She trailed kisses up his chest as she went.

Jonas lifted both of them to their feet. He quickly stripped away his pants and underwear while Lian finished with his shirts. Just as quickly, he removed the rest of her clothing. But instead of taking her to the bed, he paused to pull a condom out of his pants' pocket before he sat back down and pulled Lian once again astride his lap.

Lian couldn't help but feel exposed. After donning the condom, his fingers strayed to her back, stroking the skin. She shuddered when his fingers drifted lower, opening her up further to his touch. Unable to resist him for even a moment, she shifted until she could take him inside. The relief of having him once again inside her was almost painful, and the harsh sound he made in the back of his throat told her he felt the same. Lian simply sat there for a time, relishing the feel of him.

"I don't think I could have gone the rest of my life without having you again." Jonas's voice was harsh in Lian's ear. He lightly bit her earlobe before turning her head so he could kiss her once again. The smell of her, the taste of her, was intoxicating, and he lost what little control he had left. Despite his prone position in the chair, he lifted his hips and surged further inside. He grasped her hips and moved her on him the way he wanted her to.

Lian, though on top, let him take control. She was helpless to stop him, even if she had the desire to try. Their tongues mated in time with the rhythm of their bodies. She cried out into his mouth, the sudden pleasure of the moment taking her beyond anything she'd experienced before. She was his; she would always be his. Her last coherent thought before she succumbed was a prayer that he would always be hers.

Chapter Fourteen

"I think we need to go back and focus on Kang. Kang is the one I was tracking first, and the one I think will lead us where we want to go." Jonas sat in front of his laptop watching data come across his screen. He had found more names to go along with Kang's. He was slowly putting the pieces together. Once he had the entire picture assembled, he would move in.

Lian came up behind him, yawning but interested. "Low life scum number one. If he's transporting people, he would need bigger vehicles than if he were running guns. Of course, he's probably doing both. He may have temporarily dropped off your radar, but his cronies should still be around. If he has shipments coming in regularly, then it's due any day."

Jonas pulled up another window. "My men were able to find some of his men. I've got a dozen names. We've been tracking them. They all speak English, so I haven't needed anyone to translate. They've mostly been partying, probably because the big boss is away. But I am pretty sure you're right. Kang is the bottom feeder, but he wants to move up in the organization. He isn't going to just let these men take care of it. And since we're talking about people, most likely women and children, Kang isn't going to entrust them to a bunch of drug-addicted thugs."

Lian shuddered. "He wouldn't want them damaging the merchandise. So that's it? We wait for Kang to resurface?"

"Yes. We get Kang. Kang gives us Biao. Biao gives us Bo."

"I'm glad you have faith because I don't. If Kang turns on Biao, Bo would be just as likely to take Biao out first before the connection can be made. Howard was slick. Bo is more so. He's not above killing his own men to protect himself."

Jonas knew she was right. The more he learned about Bo, the more he wanted to nail him and put an end to his business. He knew he'd have to act fast. People's lives were depending on him and his team. Jonas had men already on the way, along with the team of men he'd left behind. But Jonas figured a criminal was a criminal, no matter where they were from. It was only a matter of time before they got bold and resurfaced. And with Lian here, she could easily translate without him having to wait for computer programs to run. As great as the technology was, he preferred people to do the interpreting rather than machines.

"For now, there is nothing we can do. I've got a couple of drone operators watching the men we've got tagged from above. I've got men on the ground. If things weren't so urgent, I'd try to get a man inside, but there isn't time for that. And these men wouldn't trust an outsider easily."

"Especially if the man weren't Chinese. Kang would be more suspect of a Chinese newcomer, but he'd be likely to trust him faster. If you sent in a Caucasian male, he'd probably be dead before you could blink." Lian knew the triads didn't trust outsiders, especially ones that weren't of Chinese descent. Griffith had hired Chinese operatives to infiltrate Howard's teams. Howard was American, but he didn't trust anyone, especially a Caucasian, regardless of their country of origin. Lian had stood out like a sore thumb, garnering too much attention. She'd learned the hard way that men in the triads attacked first and asked questions second. Her cover had been airtight, and as far as she knew it hadn't been breached. Howard had simply not trusted her and had her grabbed at the first opportunity.

As if Jonas could hear her thoughts, she heard him ask how she'd gotten involved with the CIA.

"Lian, I want to know. How did you get involved with the CIA?"

"About the same way I got involved with the FBI. Griffith speaks Mandarin, so he had been assigned the case. There were others as well, though most of them were of Chinese descent. I had worked in the U.S. Embassy, and my name had gotten around. I had left the embassy and was working in Beijing for a small business when I was approached. I hadn't thought much of it at the time, though now knowing what I know, I should have been more cautious."

"Did Griffith approach you?" Jonas turned in his

seat to focus his attention completely on Lian.

"No, it wasn't Griffith. He would never have asked a Caucasian civilian to interpret for him. And Griffith never would have picked a female. It was Griffith's boss, a man named Dallin. He's the one Griffith contacted to get the FBI to drop the charges against me. He's also the man Griffith is using to get Naiwen asylum. As far as Griffith is concerned, Dallin is responsible for what happened not only to me but also to Naiwen."

"I've heard of him, though what I've heard isn't much. Mostly I hear he's ruthless and will do whatever he has to do to get the job done."

Lian turned toward the windows. "You've got that right. I played right into his hands. At first, I thought I was simply playing interpreter for Dallin. He knows some Mandarin, but he didn't want anyone else to know that. But mostly what he wanted was someone he thought might appeal to Howard. And I did. Dallin had researched Howard's taste in women. And while he seemed to prefer Chinese women, he liked to pick up an occasional American female. Dallin then said the best way to find out what he needed to know was to infiltrate Howard's business. First, he had me at the embassy to establish my cover and ask questions of people who knew Howard, either by working with him or for him. Next Dallin pulled some strings, and I got signed on as an interpreter for Howard's business. I then became the person Howard wanted by his side interpreting for him.

Howard's Mandarin was mediocre at best, but Dallin was right, and Howard took an immediate interest in me when we met."

Jonas nodded and kept quiet.

Lian continued. "At first, I just followed Howard to his business meetings. Then he started getting more personal in his comments and started asking me out. He said I made him less homesick, seeing and hearing a pretty lady speaking English. The man gave me the creeps, and I told Dallin I wasn't interested in his games. But Howard was already hooked, and since I was the bait that had hooked him, Dallin wasn't going to let me go."

Jonas came up behind her and pulled her against him. She was trembling, and he doubted she realized it. "How did you end up trapped in Howard's home?"

Lian relaxed against him. "We went out to dinner. The place catered to foreigners. Howard said he liked to go there from time to time, again to not feel quite so homesick. But he had arranged a meeting. I didn't know what he was up to; I thought we were just having dinner. Partway through, he excused himself, supposedly to go to the restroom, but I had seen the way he had been scoping out the room and had seen the man he'd been looking for arrive. The look of satisfaction on his face was unmistakable. I hope the man never played poker. He'd have lost."

Taking another deep breath, letting her weight rest on Jonas, she continued her story. "I was feeling confident in myself that night. Don't ask me what made me decide to play hero. Dallin had been feeding me all kinds of garbage about how I was serving not only my country but China's people as well. He said I needed to do whatever it took to help him take Howard down. So I followed. If I had any sense, I'd have recorded the conversation and fed it to Dallin, but my heart was pounding, and my mind wasn't quite working. I heard him make a deal with the man he'd come to meet. It was then I realized Howard was dealing in people. Dallin hadn't told me, and from listening and interpreting the conversations going on around me, I assumed it was drugs or guns."

"Howard caught you?"

Lian nodded. "He caught me. And I was dumb; I tried to run. It would have been better if I had gone back into the restaurant where I might have found safety in numbers. Instead, I fled into the alley. I fought his men, but there were too many of them. I took out a couple, but that was it. Martial arts is fine when it's just a few, but I was outnumbered and outmuscled. I was taken to Howard's home. It was the first time I'd been there, but I recognized it from the pictures I'd seen on Dallin's computer."

Jonas turned Lian to face him. "I saw the pictures. I saw what he did once he had you inside his house. What I want to know is if he raped you."

Lian kept her eyes down, but in this, she could tell him the truth. "No, but he would have. His men, after taking a few shots of their own in retaliation, dumped me in his private space. He kept a bedroom and office that could be secured. I found out later it also had an escape route. I was in there probably close to an hour, terrified of what was going to happen. Dallin knew I was with Howard that night, but no one had come to my rescue. Howard came into the room and locked the door behind him. There was no way out of that room. Only Howard and one of his men had the access code. He hit me, and he hurt me. I know I was screaming, but it didn't matter. I figured when it was all over, I'd be dead."

Jonas pulled her against him once again. "But Naiwen struck Howard on the back of the head."

Lian clasped her arms around Jonas, letting his presence comfort her. "I didn't know she was there. She had stayed hidden. And Howard never expected Naiwen would turn on him. He probably didn't die right away. If we hadn't been locked in that room, and he had gotten medical help, he might have lived. But he was unconscious and never woke up. It was Griffith who rescued us. He had been watching the house, listening to what was going on inside. But Howard's rooms were impenetrable against the recording equipment. Griffith knew who I was, knew some of Dallin's plans, but he didn't know why I was there. It had been almost half a day before the men in the house realized their boss hadn't come out. And the only man who could access the room besides Howard still hadn't returned. Griffith disobeyed direct orders and broke into the house once he realized that I wasn't there voluntarily."

Lian took a short breath and continued. "I never did ask him how he knew the code to the room, but he did. Several team members entered the house and took down the guards. Griffith found me and Naiwen huddled in a corner on the opposite side of the room from where Howard lay dead. Griffith had a look of satisfaction on his face. He wasn't sorry Howard was dead. Then he saw us. Naiwen panicked and started praying in Mandarin that he would leave us alone. I just watched him. Then he said he was CIA, said Dallin had sent him, though that was a lie, and that he would get us out. I tried to calm Naiwen, but she was hysterical. Griffith managed to get both of us to our feet, but when we got outside, Bo was there. His father's body had been brought out before we had been, so Bo had seen his father's body. He called the Hong Kong police while we stood there. He started swearing he'd have both of us arrested for murder. Griffith decided that he'd played enough games, and he got the two of us out. Dallin was not far behind, but Griffith told him over the phone that he was disappearing and that he had me and Naiwen with him. Said it was the last time he'd go along with Dallin using innocent women as bait. He then dumped all his tracking devices and his phone and went off-grid."

Jonas could see Griffith doing exactly that. "Griffith is lucky Dallin didn't bring up charges against him."

"I got the feeling that Dallin wasn't at all surprised

by Griffith's actions, but the three of us stayed hidden. It's not hard to do in China. There are so many places that one can literally disappear to and never be found. We hid for months. It took Griffith almost that long to get Naiwen to even speak to him. But when she finally did, she fell for him as hard as he had for her. I won't tell you what went on between them. It's their business. But I can tell you that he'll do anything to protect her, and there is no way he will ever let Bo anywhere near her."

Jonas gently pushed her down to sit on the edge of the bed. "It's not his protecting her that concerns me. I got that impression, too. But he's letting you take some big risks. He's not that different from Dallin."

Lian defended him. "The difference is that I know now what is going on. I am not going in blind. Dallin lied to me, set me up as bait. Griffith wouldn't do that. He was not happy with me when I took that job with the FBI that would get me close to you. He told me it was a terrible idea and to let him sort it all out. But I had to do this for myself. I had to repay Naiwen for what she did for me. And I am happy to report I got to tell her that her eldest son grew up into a fine man, one with honor. If I'm lucky, I get to help put her second son away for good. I know that there will always be men like him out there, but at least I can help get rid of one man who would exploit those weaker than he is."

"It's a good attitude to have. There will always be another bad guy, but if you don't take out some, there will be so many more."

Lian stretched out on the bed and closed her eyes. "How long do you think we'll have to wait before Kang surfaces?"

Jonas rounded the bed and lay down beside her. He drew her against him. "I'm guessing only a day or two. Kang probably knows the Feds are watching him, but he can only wait so long. Biao is going to get impatient when his goods don't arrive on time, and I'm guessing Kang isn't going to want to upset the boss. My guess is that they'll try to create a diversion, something to get us off track. But I've got so many men watching them; it won't matter, because one way or the other, we'll catch them in the act."

Lian rolled over in Jonas's arms and toyed with the button of his shirt. "So do we just lie here until you hear something?"

It was tempting, but Jonas had other plans. The bed would come later. He gave her a rough kiss, then got to his feet. "Before everything goes crazy, I think we need to get out and get some fresh air. Act like normal people for a little while."

Lian was surprised when Jonas led them out of the hotel, and they started walking the city streets. Breakfast was the first thing on Jonas's agenda, followed by playing tourist and shopping. Lian, after about an hour or so, decided to go with the flow. Jonas was determined to enjoy the day, and she decided to enjoy his company. They didn't buy anything as they wandered the streets and peeked in store windows, but the weather was warm, and the only clouds were those on the horizon. It was a beautiful California day, and Lian let herself relax and enjoy it.

They were having a late lunch when Jonas's cell phone beeped. He pulled it out of his pocket and frowned.

Lian, who was feeling completely relaxed, tensed as she watched Jonas type in his response. She knew that face; he was angry. "What happened?"

Jonas finished his message and set his phone on the table. "Your room was tossed. Agent White was supposed to be watching it."

"What is that jerk doing here?" Lian didn't have much in her hotel room except for her clothes. Her laptop and her phones were in her backpack that she had taken with her this morning. She'd gotten paranoid about leaving her computer and phones behind since Jonas's men had raided her room looking for evidence of her being the one responsible for Jonas's data breach.

"Even jerks have their uses. I had put him on security detail at the hotel. He wasn't happy about it, but I expected him to do his job. He was watching our rooms in case someone came looking for me or you."

"I'm sure he'll have a great excuse. He usually does."

Jonas glanced at his phone when it beeped again. He swore. "His usefulness just ran out. He's dead."

Lian dropped her fork. Without asking, she got to her feet and hunted the waitress down. She handed the woman some cash and met Jonas at the door of the restaurant.

Jonas started walking away from where the hotel was. He kept Lian between him and the shops. Though someone inside the building could pose a threat, it was more likely that a threat would come from the street. "We'll rendezvous with a car up the street. I've got an agent picking us up."

Lian nodded. She might have disliked Agent White, but she could still feel sympathy for his family. She knew he had a wife and a son. "Where was he found?"

"Inside your hotel room. Agents are there now. What can be salvaged will be brought to you. You'll be moved to another location."

"And you?"

"It might be best if I'm not near you for the time being. Your room might have been tossed because the killer knew that's where I spent the night. Or it could be Bo's men, and they've found you. Until I'm sure who the target is, you're going into a safe house with agents guarding you."

Jonas saw a car pull up and recognized his agent. He nodded to the man and guided Lian to the backseat. He got in first, then pulled her in beside him. "Was anyone else hurt besides White?"

Agent Leon Tanner, a seasoned agent who'd worked with Jonas for many years, shook his head.

"White was the only casualty. Probably because he fought back. We have two civilians injured. Head injury to one and a stabbing to the second. Stabbing was to the arm. They weren't the target, just in the way."

Lian spoke from beside Jonas. "Any security footage? Was the attacker Chinese?"

"Yes, ma'am. We have footage, and the killer's voice recorded. After you and Agent Cole left, we turned on our listeners."

"Listeners? My room was bugged?"

Jonas took her hand. Her voice was trembling. "Mine, too. Just a precaution. They are turned on when we are not in the room. You're not being spied on."

"Probably a good thing since you were with me."

Jonas couldn't help but smile a bit. His agents would have gotten an earful had they been on last night. But the goal wasn't to spy on Lian but to make sure no one but authorized people entered her or his room.

Agent Tanner lightly cleared his throat and tried to pretend he didn't hear what was said. Everyone knew that Agent Cole and Lian Albright were having an affair, or at least everyone was pretty sure they were. "Agent White was killed by a knife wound to his throat. But he had several defensive wounds on his arms. Someone sliced him up."

Jonas didn't argue as Lian pulled her laptop from her bag. She had access to the FBI files since she was once again a consultant on this case. After a few minutes, she looked at him. He nodded.

Lian gave Jonas a rundown of what she just watched. "Kang. I'm sure of it. The man is wearing a mask, but your sources say he's deadly with a knife. Part of advanced weapons training. And we have Kang's voice on file. You'll find the attacker's voice is a match. The first footage file is from his attack on the man he stabbed. It was in the elevator. The man saw the face mask and confronted him. Mostly Kang just swore at him, telling him he should mind his own business right before stabbing him. In the second file, the footage shows the same masked man walking down the hallway to my room. Agent White went into the room a couple of minutes after Kang entered. When Kang left, there was blood on him."

Jonas was glad he didn't have cameras in the room. He didn't want Lian to witness Agent White's death. The audio was bad enough. "Did he say anything to Agent White?"

"Yes. He was feeling bold in the room. Probably thought it was safe. But it's a safe bet Kang was after you, not me. He asked White where you were. He said, did you think he was stupid. He knows he's being watched. He said he has eyes everywhere. You aren't the only one. My name didn't come up. And he doesn't mention Biao or Bo. He was very focused on his own mission. I'm guessing he was looking for anything that would give him an edge on you or to find you."

"Did he interrogate White?"

Lian bit her lip, hard. "Yes. You'll find the first wound Kang inflicted was enough to incapacitate White. If you hit the right spot, you can bleed out pretty fast. I would say White's wounds were not defensive. They were intentional and purposeful. White simply said you would catch him and put him in jail for life. Told him that a cute Chinese boy like him would be a prize in prison. Kang took offense and finished him."

Jonas rubbed his thumb over the spot where Lian had bitten her lip. "Once he tossed the room, he would have realized he had the wrong one. None of my things were there; everything in that room belonged to a woman. He probably ripped the room apart in a rage."

Lian had stopped the recording once she started hearing the room being trashed. Kang wasn't going to give anything else away without an audience to talk to.

Tanner turned on a side street and pulled into an alley. "White didn't call for backup when he went in. It was an hour before the other agents realized he was missing. No one saw Kang enter the hotel or leave. Agents are going through the footage to see how he got into the hotel, but it doesn't really matter. He knew what room he was looking for. Someone must have been watching you, Agent Cole."

"I went out last night, grabbed dinner, then went straight to Lian's room. I never went to mine. I agree that someone was watching, which means someone saw Lian when she opened the door."

Lian dropped silent. A Mandarin-speaking contractor for the FBI could be an asset to Kang, should he discover who she was. Agent White had held up to the torture. Of course, Agent White didn't know where Jonas was. She doubted she would hold up to what Agent White had endured. She shuddered as she leaned against Jonas.

Jonas's phone rang again, and he answered it. "Agent Cole."

Lian could hear a masculine voice on the other side of the line, but it was hard to hear the words. Right before Jonas hung up, she heard the name Bo and the words airport and American soil.

Chapter Fifteen

Jonas swore, his words loud and clear in the confines of the car. He opened the car door and helped Lian out. He took her backpack from her and ushered her ahead of him. He punched in the security code when they got to a locked metal door.

"Hi, Lian." Dex sat behind a computer but shut the screens down when they entered.

She crossed to where he was and accepted his hug. "Nice to see you. I wasn't sure what kind of reception I'd get when I saw you again."

Dex took a seat. "Hey, I wouldn't let a little espionage come between us. We've been friends too long."

"Plus, Mindy would have dropped you cold." Lian took the seat Jonas had pulled over to her.

"Mindy has been unusually quiet when your name comes up in conversation. But she has claimed your innocence from the beginning."

Lian knew that Mindy would have been interrogated when the warrant was issued for her arrest. She was glad to know that Mindy had survived it unscathed. She hadn't dared to reach out to her friend. Just because the charges were dropped against her didn't mean that Mindy wouldn't be arrested should anyone think that she was an accomplice.

"She's fine if you're wondering. She's staying at my place and job hunting." Dex stretched his back. He'd been at his computer most of the night and was going through security logs at the hotel to see if they could get any glimpse of the man who killed Agent White coming in or going out. White had been a jerk, but he was one of them.

"Wow. I didn't think you'd convince her quite so quickly, given how you two left it in Chicago."

"What can I say? I'm irresistible."

Jonas laid a hand on Dex's shoulder to get him back on track. "Of that, I have no doubt. Found anything else?"

"Not yet. Haven't determined his point of entry. It wasn't through the front doors. I half expected to see him stroll right on in. It's a nice hotel, but there isn't much in the way of security. He didn't shoot anyone, so I'm guessing he wasn't carrying. Gunfire would call too much attention to him, but you'll see for yourself at the morgue; he didn't need one."

Jonas would be headed there next. "I'm leaving Lian with you. Agent Tanner is going to gather her stuff and bring it over. Set her up in a room. I'm going to head over to the morgue first. Then I'm going to head over to the hotel and see what I can find. Kang might come back if he thinks I'm there. I don't want Lian anywhere near me in the meantime."

"Sure thing, boss. Let me go do that."

Lian shook her head as Dex left the room. "So

that's the plan? Lure him out?"

Jonas shrugged. "Sometimes the easiest plan is the best one. He came out in the open. He may again."

Lian stood and lightly kissed Jonas. She wasn't surprised when he pulled her closer, but instead of kissing her, he looked down into her eyes.

"Stay with Dex. I'm good if you want to see what else you can dig up, but this is the most secure place I can take you. I need you to promise me you won't leave. Wait for me."

"I can promise you I will stay with Dex. And thanks for not making me promise not to help."

Jonas stroked her cheek. "I know you better than that. You took a lot of risks to find me. You took a lot of risks stealing information from me. You took a lot of risks for Naiwen. I just need to know that any other risks you take will be supervised by me or my men."

Lian hugged Jonas to her, then let him go. "You should go before I get all mushy and emotional on you."

Jonas let her go, but he stopped and turned back to her when he reached the door. He shook his head lightly and crossed back to her. "Every day I go out into the field could be my last day. My mother thinks I'm in love with you."

Lian stood still, shocked. She never dreamed he would acknowledge he had any feelings for her after what she did. He hadn't exactly come out and said it, but it was a step in the right direction. "Your mother is a smart lady."

Jonas kissed her roughly and then once more. "I always thought so. I'll be back as soon as I can."

"Jonas?"

He opened the door but turned back. "Yeah?"

She smiled at him. "Your mother thinks the same thing about me."

He laughed. "Yeah, I know. I'll be back."

She watched as he closed the door behind him. "You can come out, Dex."

"You two are painful to watch, you know that? You two dancing around each other. You're so in love with him, you might as well tattoo it on your forehead."

"What about you and Mindy? You've been in love with her since Chicago, and yet you gave her up for your career."

"So I was an idiot. I didn't call it love, and neither did Mindy. She had her job, and I had mine. We agreed to end it. Now I know better. And though it took a couple of days of groveling after interrogating her, she finally admitted she loved me, too. But if she said she wanted to go back to Chicago, I would have to give up my job for her. Thankfully for me, she said her job has lost its luster and that she wants to stay."

"Everyone knows that social work can be brutal. Wears you down slowly. She's been ready for a change for a while. She just didn't want to admit it. I'm glad she came with me. And I'm glad you two worked it out."

"Give Jonas time. He told you about his fiancée yet?"

"His what?"

Dex shook his head. "Seriously, do you two even talk to each other?"

Lian thought back to some of their conversations. "Sure. It's just mostly work. You might have noticed we're in the middle of an investigation of a low-level triad member who's running guns and trafficking people."

Dex brought his screens back up. "There is that. Still, I'm surprised."

"So what about her? You can't drop a bombshell like that and then stop."

Dex kept his eyes on his screens. "It's not recent. They've been separated for a while, and they didn't get married. She cheated on him, and he took it hard. She left him the day he got promoted."

Lian remembered the story Jonas had told her about the last woman who betrayed him. But he had left out the part that they were engaged. "She was opposed to his promotion?"

"No. He never told her. Once she admitted she'd cheated, he didn't tell her. It was over as far as he was concerned. Even if she had apologized and come crawling back, he wouldn't have taken her back. She had completely violated his trust."

Lian pulled up the chair beside him and watched what he was doing. "Does this story have a point?"

"Yes, it does. My point is that Jonas still trusts you.

You might have stretched it to its limits, but you didn't break it."

Lian contemplated that for a moment. Then she nodded to herself. "Thanks, Dex. That helps."

"I do have a question for you, though."

"I think I'm afraid to let you ask."

"Will you stay for him? Since I met you, you've talked about going back to China. You said once before that you wanted to go back and stay for good. Raise a family there."

Lian closed her eyes for a moment. "I always imagined myself going home, and I always thought of China as home. Now I am not so sure where home is. For Jonas, for what we might have one day, I would stay."

"Good. Next time you two tap dance around the words, tell him you would stay for him."

Lian bumped her shoulder against his, and then pulled out her laptop. "Let's figure out how to end Kang so we can both go home."

Dex smiled at her and got back to work.

* * *

Agent White's face was barely recognizable. Kang had done a number on him. His body had several lacerations, but Kang had worked over White's face the most. The coroner confirmed all cuts were made prior to his death. Kang cut his throat, the final cut that killed him, but the coroner said he would have bled out either way. Jonas had made arrangements for an agent back home to inform Mrs. White of her husband's death. Jonas would normally have gone himself, but right now he had other priorities here.

Jonas was back at the hotel when Agent Tanner tracked him down. A private jet had flown in from Hong Kong. It was now confirmed that Bo Lee was on that jet. He was somewhere in Los Angeles. Twenty minutes later, it was confirmed that Ping Biao was also on American soil.

"Whatever is going down, it's big." Tanner handed the printed manifests from two different airports.

"Anyone with them?"

"Bo flew in with a woman. Employee records say she's his interpreter. Biao flew in with his wife and daughter. His wife is an American, but he and the child are not. They had to file papers to get into the country."

That surprised Jonas. "So both Bo and Biao flew in legally?"

"Yes. It's all on the up and up, or so says the paperwork. If there weren't evidence to the contrary coming in from the CIA, Bo wouldn't be on our radar at all. The man is squeaky clean on paper. Biao is another matter. I would guess his papers are forged. There is no way, with active terror alerts, that a man like Biao is getting into the country legally."

Jonas considered that. "Anyone tracking them?"

Tanner hated to be the bearer of bad news. "We had Biao under surveillance, but he managed to elude our people. We lost Bo as soon as he landed. He went into the hangar and never came out. Our drones didn't see him leave. When our agents raided it, there was no sign of him. Agents found underground tunnels. Agents are actively looking for him."

"All right. Our people will be listening for chatter. Kang probably reported to his superiors that the FBI was close."

Tanner set the papers down. "Which do you think is his superior? Bo or Biao?"

"Intel says Kang reports to Biao. CIA intel says Biao reports to Bo, but there isn't much proof. Like you said, Bo appears squeaky clean. He has enough money that he's probably bought off every official he could. It's cleaner that way."

Tanner checked his phone when it buzzed. "Either way, Kang's men are on the move. Dex just sent a text over. Agents are in place and ready to raid the warehouse the moment Kang shows up. Kang is smart, but his men were not so discreet."

"Good. We'll meet them. I want Kang, and I want him now."

Tanner followed Jonas to the car. It only took half an hour to get to the warehouse. Tanner had listened in on the raid. "Kang is in custody."

Jonas's smile was not a comforting one. "Good."

When they arrived, Jonas stood for a moment outside the warehouse as the agents finished securing the location. Several men were in custody, including Kang. He motioned to the agents. "I want him at FBI headquarters now. I want several men and the drones watching. He doesn't get away."

Several agents snapped to attention and escorted Kang to the waiting SUV. Jonas watched with satisfaction as they left. He entered the warehouse where several other agents were trying to sort out the chaos. Inside was a large semi-trailer. Several armed agents were standing outside the open doors, guarding the people inside.

"Lian was right." Tanner came to stand next to Jonas.

"She was. There must be close to a hundred people shoved in here. Do we have interpreters ready?"

Tanner shook his head. "The majority of the people are Chinese. A few are Caucasian, and a few are Hispanic. I hate to ask, but Lian would be the quickest person. Several of our agents speak Spanish, but none speak Chinese."

Jonas knew Agent Tanner was right. He made a quick call to Dex and asked him to escort Lian to the warehouse.

It was less than an hour when Lian arrived under armed escort. Dex and two other agents were with her. Jonas nodded approvingly to Dex. He took Lian's hand when she came to him.

"How many people?"

Jonas wrapped an arm around her waist. "Close to a hundred. We have moved the English-speaking people to the local precinct for processing. We also have immigration agents here speaking to the people who are Hispanic. But the majority of the people are Chinese, and immigration agents are still working on interpreters. We need to get these people calmed down and explain that they're safe."

Lian looked at the people in the truck. Some were crying, some were huddled together, and others were just sitting there waiting to see what awaited them next. "They were probably shipped by boat and then transported by truck with the rest. What do I say?"

Jonas guided her through the conversation. A few people in the truck came forward to speak to her and tell her their stories. He could see the sheen of tears in Lian's eyes as she relayed what they were telling her, but she stood her ground and did what needed to be done. It was hours before additional interpreters showed up and people were slowly taken away. Some were headed to the hospital. The rest were taken to a building the FBI had secured for processing the people they found. It would be a long night for many agents.

Jonas watched dispassionately as other agents unloaded crates of weapons from another truck. "We should head back. We have Kang, but I got confirmation that both Bo and Biao are stateside and here in Los Angeles."

"Both of them?" Lian rubbed her tired eyes, trying to absorb what that meant. Two triad leaders on American soil were not good.

Jonas led her toward the SUV. He left Tanner and Dex in charge. Two agents followed them to the vehicle. "Stay here. I'll escort Ms. Albright back to the safe house."

The two agents nodded and went back to their duties.

Jonas was halfway to the safe house when his phone rang. The number was unknown. "Hello?"

"Agent Cole, so glad you answered."

The voice was Chinese but not one he heard before. "Who is this?"

"Now, what fun would that be if I told you over the phone. I want to meet in person." The voice sounded almost friendly on the other end.

"So why don't you meet me at FBI headquarters, and we can have a chat?"

"There is no fun in that either. I am going to text you an address. You and Ms. Albright are both invited."

Jonas turned off the route he had been following onto another road. He didn't see anyone following them, but in this day and age, he could be watched from above just as easily as from the ground. "And if I decline your invitation?"

"What fun would that be? But I knew you would be difficult. Your Agent Tanner was careless. He left the vehicle unattended. In the chaos at the warehouse, your SUV was left unguarded. Underneath your vehicle is a bomb. A small one, but it would do the trick in eliminating you and your friend. I am fairly certain you will not want to risk blowing up your girlfriend, considering how valuable she is and all."

Jonas flipped on his lights and hit the gas. Assuming his caller was telling the truth, he needed to get out of the neighborhoods. "And I'm supposed to believe you?"

There was a sigh on the line. "But of course not. I figured you would be difficult. What if I promise not to hurt you?"

Jonas veered and got on the highway. It was late, and the roads were not as full of cars as they would have been during the day. "Promises from a man who won't tell me his name?"

"Jonas." Lian spoke. She held up her phone. On it was a picture of a device being planted on the vehicle they were driving. "He put a bomb under the car."

"I am sending the address, along with a picture from the live feed I have. I will see if you drop Ms. Albright off. You have thirty minutes. Either you and your friend show up, or I will blow your vehicle up. And I will not stop there. Agents Tanner and Bartlett will be next. And every agent you have at the warehouse will follow."

Jonas was tempted to throw the phone out the window, but he knew that his caller meant business.

"Biao or Bo?" Lian shut her phone off.

"Could be either, but it's one of them. It's no coincidence that they both showed up tonight."

Lian took Jonas's phone and punched the address into the GPS. "It's not far from here."

Jonas shook his head. "If we go, we play right into

his hands."

"And if we don't, he blows us up. He was serious about that."

Jonas's grip tightened on the steering wheel. "I know."

"I'd rather live to see what he wants than die not knowing."

Jonas glanced at her. Her eyes were dry, and her hands were steady. "You're serious."

"I've been playing dangerous games, Jonas. I'm betting the man on the other end of the phone is Bo. Biao wouldn't care about me, but Bo would."

"He didn't say anything about not telling anyone where we were headed."

Lian watched as Jonas called Dex. He tonelessly explained to him what had happened and where they were going. Lian listened, using calming breaths to slow the panic.

The address was a ranch-style home in a run-down neighborhood. Lian glanced around. "Not quite what I pictured Bo or Biao living in."

"In a neighborhood like this, people mind their own business. It's probably just a pit stop on a long road of various connections. Our sources have Bo staying at a five-star resort near the water. That is in keeping with his image."

"So now what?" Lian looked around to see if she could spot arriving FBI. So far, the street was quiet.

"I'm going to get out. Stay in the car." Jonas opened the car door and dropped silently to the ground so he could get a look at the device under the SUV. Sure enough, it was where the photo showed. He swore and stood.

"I had wondered if you would do the smart thing and show up." A voice came from the doorway of the house. In the man's hand was a gun. It was currently pointed at the ground.

"It's not as if you gave me much choice. Why don't you come out and greet us properly?"

The man laughed. "Toss your weapon on the front seat of the SUV. Then you and Ms. Albright can come in and join me."

Jonas gestured to Lian after he tossed his weapon on the floor to slide towards him and come out on the driver's side. She obeyed and kept behind him. "The FBI knows we're here. They are on their way."

"You do not disappoint." The man stepped back into the shadows.

Lian stayed directly behind Jonas. Not that she had much choice. He had a tight grip on her wrist to make sure she did. "It's Bo."

Jonas hadn't gotten a good look at the man but knew Lian was right. Biao was much shorter. Bo was about five-ten, whereas Biao was a few inches shorter than that. Jonas was a couple of inches taller than his brother. Part of him couldn't help but be curious about this man. He was a criminal, a man who bought and sold people, and Jonas knew him for what he was. But knowing that this man shared his blood left him with some feelings he couldn't sort out.

Jonas walked slowly towards the house. He couldn't see anyone else about. He did spot one of his men's drones perched on top of a nearby house. His men had eyes on him.

When Jonas and Lian entered the home, the door shut behind them, and the man flipped on a nearby lamp.

Bo Lee smiled at the pair, then his eyes went to Jonas. "Welcome, Brother."

Chapter Sixteen

"I suppose I should thank you, Ms. Albright, for locating my brother. Our father searched for him on and off for years without any luck. I was pretty sure he was dead. If the Howard fortune could not locate him, I was pretty sure no one could. One day I will have to ask you how you did it. It is a handy skill to have."

Lian took a step so she was next to Jonas. "Just have to know the right people."

Bo considered that. "I suppose. But then having the CIA on your side is a handy trick, even if it's an ex-agent like Griffith. How is Naiwen?"

"Fine. So long as she's safely tucked away and hidden from you."

Bo nodded. "Yes, but what about when Griffith gets her asylum. She will not be safely tucked away then. But no matter. I will worry about her later. Her asylum was granted, by the way. Came in late last night. Griffith should be informed anytime now."

"How do you..." She fell silent when Jonas squeezed her hand.

"What is the point of this family reunion, Bo?" Jonas was keeping one eye on Bo and one on the windows. He had seen a shadow go by.

"Let us take this to my office." Bo gestured with

the gun without pointing it at them.

Jonas reluctantly followed. "Kidnapping is a federal offense."

"I have not kidnapped anyone. You came here of your own free will."

Bo gestured for them to go ahead of him. He shut and locked the door from the inside. "Your FBI friends cannot see us or hear us. So let us have a nice chat. Take a seat."

Ping Biao rose from a chair in the corner. "I am tired of these games you play. A bullet will end this."

Bo shook his head, his words in Mandarin as he spoke to the other man. "You are already responsible for the death of one agent today. You are going to start a war with the FBI if you take him out. That is the last thing we need right now."

Biao responded in kind. "And maybe you are just soft because he is blood."

Bo's mouth tightened but did not respond to the taunt. "Ms. Albright speaks Mandarin, so you might as well speak English for Jonas's benefit."

Bo turned to Jonas. "My friend here thinks I should kill you. He ordered Kang to break into Ms. Albright's room in the hopes of finding where you were hiding. Agent White was an unfortunate casualty."

"We have Kang in custody. No matter what you do to me or Lian, he won't be going free."

Bo gestured for them to sit. "Kang was sloppy. My father never did like him, and neither do I. But he had his uses. Biao would rather I end this now, but I am not prepared to start a war on U.S. soil. At least not today. You have Kang's merchandise, and that is the bigger issue. Do you have any idea how long it takes to round up that many assets?"

"Why don't you just say it? You smuggled in almost a hundred people with the intent to sell."

Bo shook his head. "Did I? No, I think Kang did. And Kang does not work for me. He works for Biao."

"Who works for you." Jonas gritted his teeth. The man oozed charm. It was not hard to see why people were apt to believe him innocent.

"I fired you, did I not?" Bo turned to Biao.

"I am sick of these games. Do what your father would have done, and end this."

Bo switched to Mandarin. "My father is dead because of the way he did things. I am not my father. Remember that. You can go. Find out where the firearms are stashed. We cannot get the people back, but we can get the weapons at least. One more screw-up, and I will hold you responsible."

Biao spit at Bo, then at Jonas. He glared at Lian and left.

"You will have to forgive my associate. His temper gets the best of him. If I were you, I would watch out for him. He wants you dead. And he wants Kang back. If he sees an opportunity, he will seize it."

"And you?" Jonas couldn't figure out what Bo's angle was, or why he didn't simply put a bullet through their heads.

"I am a businessman, Jonas, and I cannot say I have ever considered fratricide. But more importantly, I have no plans to kill an FBI agent and bring the FBI's wrath down on me. What I have in mind is more of a compromise of sorts."

"What exactly do you want in return for Lian's and my life?"

"Straight to the point. What I want is Biao behind bars. He has proven dangerous since my father's death. He would take my place given the slightest opportunity. I could take him out myself, but that would hardly be in line with a man of my status. I think it much better if the FBI takes him out. Tonight, you will find him searching for the weapons you confiscated today. He is guilty of weapons running and human trafficking. I have proof. You take it, you arrest him, and then I am free to go back about my business."

"Which is weapon smuggling and human trafficking. Even if I put Biao behind bars, which I don't have a problem with, you would be next."

Bo shrugged. "You would need proof. Which you do not have. The CIA has been trying for years. Given what little information you might have from them, and even with Ms. Albright's help, you would not have enough evidence. Even Naiwen, your dear mother, would have nothing other than her words. And despite what some people think, words alone do not have power."

Lian spoke again. "I don't understand you. You

were on a full manhunt for Naiwen and me. Are you telling me you just gave it up?"

"Appearances, Ms. Albright, are very important. It is not the truth that matters, but what people perceive. I do not care one whit that Naiwen killed my father. She did me a favor. But I could not tell that to the Hong Kong police. I can promise you Naiwen's safety when she gets her asylum. She does not concern me. Nor does Griffith. Now you two, you do concern me. But for now, I am done. On the computer over on the desk, you will find the evidence against Biao I promised. And if your FBI friends can figure out how to get you out of this room, you can put it to good use."

Lian saw the lock from the inside that needed a code to open. It was the same setup that Howard had in his home. She watched numbly as Bo left the room, locking the door behind him.

Now that the man was gone, Lian relaxed slightly. She didn't like him, but even she could admit she could understand why he wielded so much power. Lian was a firm believer that criminals should look like criminals. Men like Bo should have yellow teeth, acne scars, and a large paunch. But Bo Lee wasn't any of those things. Bo Lee, by any measure, was a very attractive man. His black hair was long and thick, probably to the middle of his back, and the ponytail he wore it in didn't detract from his masculinity; it added to it. His skin was bronzed and flawless, not an imperfection to be found. His almond eyes shone an odd shade of brown and green, unique in a very Asian face. She had thought it before, and did again; he looked nothing like his father, unlike Jonas, who shared some of Howard's physical traits. But like Jonas, Bo was very fit and very dangerous. He had the sleek movements of an athlete, and knowing martial arts the way she did, and the way the body conformed to the muscle development of martial arts training, she knew he was not a novice.

But he also oozed charm. Had she not known who he was, she would have fallen for that charm. His smile seemed genuine, his eyes intelligent. His clothes were of the highest quality, but they were not at all ostentatious. The black slacks molded firm thighs, and the buff-colored shirt and slightly darker jacket fit his chest to perfection.

Lian looked back at Jonas, who had also been staring at the door, most likely with thoughts not so different from her own.

"I don't like this." Jonas pulled out his cell phone, but there was no signal. He went to the computer. On it was a file on the desktop, and the computer was hooked up to the internet. He copied the file to his email and sent it along with a note to Dex where they were.

Lian could only agree. "I don't like it, and I don't get it. He's not making it very hard for us to escape. And he doesn't seem inclined to kill us."

"It's like he's putting on a show for us. There is real evidence here against Biao. He could very well just want him arrested. He got my attention the quickest and easiest way he knew how."

"But can you use the evidence, considering where it came from?"

Jonas gave a harsh laugh. "The evidence is from the Hong Kong police department. It's all properly labeled. There is a clear chain of evidence. It's like Bo walked into the Hong Kong offices and copied the files himself."

"It's usable?"

"Yeah, it's usable. We'll need to get it verified and get cooperation from the Hong Kong police, but it's usable." Jonas closed the file and took a seat behind the desk. Nothing else seemed of interest on the laptop, but the forensics team would look it over and see if anything was hidden.

Lian came and took a seat at the corner of the desk. "So now what?"

"Now we wait for Dex."

It only took Dex and another agent an hour to get Jonas and Lian free. Dex gave Lian a hug and turned his attention to Jonas. "So now what?"

It was the same question Lian had asked him. "We'll all go back to the safe house for tonight. Tanner, I assume, is still at the warehouse. Bo told Biao to find the weapons. Right now I think Biao is going to be our immediate problem. Tell Tanner to make sure the people are safely in custody and hold the weapons where they are. I don't want them moved right now. I think moving them poses a greater risk than leaving them where they are."

"Weapons are stashed at a safe location. The warehouse is completely secured and off the books. Unless we have a mole, they're perfectly safe for now."

"Good. Let's keep it that way."

* * *

"The bomb is a fake." Dex handed Jonas the tablet with the report.

"What in the world?" Jonas took the tablet and read the report for himself.

"Smoke and mirrors. Looks like the real deal, but if it had been detonated, you would have gotten a flash and some smoke, but no boom."

Lian glanced over Jonas's shoulder. "I don't get it. What game is Bo playing?"

Jonas set the tablet down, his frustration plain for anyone to see. "A common one. He's the bad guy who turns evidence over to the good guys, so the good guys can then arrest his competition. He's not the first criminal to use the cops to his own advantage. And if the bomb is a fake, we don't have much to charge him with. He didn't say anything incriminating on the phone; he didn't say much outside his safe room. The threats he made to get us to come to him were bogus if the bomb is bogus, so nothing he said could be construed as a real threat, and he never actually pointed his gun at either of us.

He would probably claim it wasn't loaded. A good lawyer would get him off, and he can afford the best."

Dex flipped to the next report. "It gets better. Local FBI released Kang."

"What?" Lian snatched up the tablet from the table. Jonas's face was now unreadable.

Dex contained his anger. "We have his voice on a surveillance tape, and that's about it. His lawyer argued that the tape had yet to be authenticated and was not sufficient to hold his client."

"But he was arrested at a warehouse filled with guns and kidnap victims." Lian couldn't believe what she was reading.

"Someone else has claimed ownership. An anonymous source called the FBI and laughed that they had the wrong man. Kang's lawyer had a field day. We could have held him longer, but the local agents figured there wasn't much point. They'd rather let him loose and follow him than hold him."

Jonas took the tablet from Lian. "It's their call. The logic is that if someone else is claiming the crime as theirs, the hope is that Kang will lead them to the right man."

"But Biao and Bo are the right men."

Jonas understood her frustration but understood why the local FBI made the decision they did. "Bo isn't bothering to hide. And other than my word that we heard Bo threaten us and give Biao orders, Bo hasn't done anything illegal that we can unconditionally tie him to, nor can we tie him to

Kang's or Biao's activities. We can prove they know each other, but that's not a crime. Biao is hiding, and surveillance lost him as of two hours ago. Kang is still in the open, but he's not going to give his boss away. Right now, Kang will probably lay low. Waiting to see if Biao makes a move on the weapons is probably our best bet."

Dex went back to his laptop. "Unless Biao sends Kang after them. After all, Kang is the one who lost them. I doubt Biao is going to be forgiving. He may give Kang a chance to redeem himself."

Jonas knew that was also a viable option. "You could be right. This whole thing is a cluster. And I'm still concerned about Bo's ultimate goal. While he's here, he'll play the consummate businessman, enjoying his first visit to L.A. Probably hit the town, throw some cash around, and pick up a few ladies."

"Whatever way the wind blows on this one, it's late and we need to get some rest. The bad guys will still be there in the morning." Dex yawned and stretched.

Lian smiled at him. "You're probably right. Tell Mindy I said hello."

Dex stopped mid-stretch and gave Lian a dirty look. "I will. You two just need to solve this case fast so I can go home. It hasn't been so long since Mindy moved in with me; she might start changing her mind about staying after my prolonged absence."

Jonas knew how Dex felt. Lian was here with him now, but she wouldn't be for the next case or the next one.

Lian watched as Dex left the room. She glanced at Jonas. "The bed in my room is a queen."

"Yeah?" Jonas gave her a once-over.

Lian held her ground. "Yeah. Come on, we should rest too."

Everyone on his team already knew or had a pretty good idea that there was something going on between him and Lian. At this late stage, it would be silly to pretend otherwise. Jonas grabbed the bag he had left by the doorway that he always kept with him on a case. He had wanted Lian to stay here, and safely away from him, while he hunted Biao and Bo. But things changed, and he was not sure yet who he would find at the end of the trail where the guns were stashed, or what his next move was. The safe house was the best place for everyone right now. Today's bomb might have been a fake, but the next one might be real.

The pair went to Lian's bedroom together. Lian took a quick shower and dried her hair. When she got back to the bedroom, Jonas was undressed and lying in the bed. His arms were resting behind his head, and his chest was bare.

Lian left the short nightshirt on and climbed under the covers. She flipped off the bedside lamp and settled in next to Jonas. He wrapped his arm around her but made no other moves toward her.

"I don't suppose I need to ask you what you are thinking about. It must have been difficult for you today, confronting the brother you never met." Lian scooted closer, hoping he could take some comfort from her presence.

"I wasn't sure how I would feel if I came face to face with him. I supposed it was too much to hope that he didn't know who I was. What worries me is how much he knows. Where is he getting his information from? Someone has to be feeding it to him. If Naiwen really did get asylum, why haven't we heard from Griffith? It's hard to imagine he doesn't know and some triad member from Hong Kong does. And how did he know so much about you and the work you're doing? The FBI doesn't put ads out. And where did he get those papers from the Hong Kong police?"

Lian knew Jonas wasn't really asking her, so she remained quiet. His mind was working through the problems. But she wasn't worried about his job. She knew and trusted he would win in the end. But his emotions were a whole other thing. "I'll call Griffith in the morning. It's late and there's no point in calling him now. But seriously, about Bo."

Jonas's arm tightened around her. "It's hard to be detached. I know what he is. I know what he's done. But to see him face to face, to know we share blood, it is an odd feeling. There was no sense of recognition. There was no feeling like I know him. And yet it was disturbing in a way I can't explain. I can't help but think that must have been what Naiwen felt when she saw him the night she killed Howard. And I can't help but think that is how she might feel when she meets me."

Lian's voice was soft in the dark. "Did you hear what you just said? You said when she meets you, not if."

Jonas wasn't sure when it had clicked, but his curiosity about his birth mother had grown since he had learned of her existence. And unlike Bo, he would not have to arrest her. But he also didn't know how it would work. Would they be distant? Or would there be a recognition of who she was to him when he met her? "I will meet her if you make me a promise."

Lian tried to look into his eyes, but they were faint in the dark. "If it's within my ability to give it to you, then I promise."

Jonas rolled so that Lian was lying beneath him. "You be there with me."

Lian touched his cheek. "Oh, Jonas. You know I will. I keep trying to imagine what it might be like if my mother showed up, that it was all a big mistake, that she hadn't died in the accident. I think I would be both euphoric and terrified. What if she didn't recognize me? What if she didn't like the person I'd become?"

Jonas settled his hips firmly against hers. "You've really given this some thought."

Lian wriggled beneath him. "I had a lot of free time to think about stuff like that at Griffith's. I'd like to think that we would recognize each other and that she would be proud of me and the work I do."

Jonas kissed her. "I think she would be proud. Your father, too. From what I read about them, and from what you've said about them, they were caring, loving people. How else could they feel about a daughter who is trying to make the world a better place?"

Lian smiled. "Perhaps in a different way than they did, but I get your point. Naiwen is a sweet, sensitive human being, but one who has been hurt and abused. Griffith fixed some of those hurts. I think you'll help heal a few more."

Jonas imagined that a person never fully recovered from what Naiwen had endured. Jonas liked the thought that perhaps he could help her, even if in some small way. And he was also positive that his own parents would help make Naiwen comfortable and would share with her the stories of him growing up. Many of the early stories Naiwen would never know; he would never share them with her. But his parents could share the good times and share both his victories and his failures with her.

Jonas leaned over and rummaged through his bag until he found the condom he had stashed there. Lian spread her thighs further, her hands and mouth encouraging him. He slowly penetrated her body, and she wrapped her arms around him.

Their lovemaking was slow and lengthy, both of them conscious of the other people in the house. They were both breathless when it was over.

"Jonas?"

"Hmm?" Completely relaxed, he pulled her against him.

"Thinking we were going to get blown up or shot made me think that it might be past time I told you something." Lian kept her head tucked against his chest.

"It does straighten out priorities, doesn't it?"

That stopped Lian for a second. "I guess being an FBI agent, you've been in situations before that you weren't sure you were going to get out of."

"There was a memorable time. Most stuff is routine. Though a situation might be dangerous, you take it in stride. You have to, or you can't do your job. Today I was scared for you, of what Bo might do to you."

Lian knew how he felt. "And I was scared of what he might do to you."

Jonas tugged Lian across his chest. "I will do my best to make sure you are never in that kind of danger again. But what is it that you want to say to me?"

Lian scooted off his chest and sat on her knees. "Jonas, I fell in love with you. I didn't want to, but I did."

Jonas flipped on the bedside lamp so he could see her face. "Before or after you kidnapped me?"

Lian found she could laugh around the lump in her throat. "Before. You are one charming male, Special Agent Jonas Cole."

Jonas sat up to nibble her lips. "That's Supervisory Special Agent."

Lian kissed him back. "My apologies."

Jonas lay back down and pulled Lian with him. "I suppose there is no point in dancing around the subject. I love you, Lian. And I have even forgiven you for the kidnapping."

Lian giggled, then she began laughing. She pressed her face to his chest to muffle the sound. "I'd say you're definitely in love."

They were both quiet for a while, and eventually, Jonas flipped the bedside lamp back off. But Lian couldn't sleep. "So what happens next?"

Jonas yawned. "With us or the case?"

Lian supposed the case was the easy part. They caught the bad guys and threw them in jail. "Us."

"I can say with some certainty that you're not going back to China."

Lian smiled in the dark. "Don't want to give up the FBI and follow me around the world?"

Jonas heard her teasing tone, but it did worry him. "I know you said you don't date Americans. And I know you said you planned to go back to China and put down some roots. My family is here. My career is here."

"And mine is gone, and my career is wherever I choose for it to be. I am not going to lie to you; I miss home. But if home means we are not together, then I can't go back. Not so long as we are us."

"How about we honeymoon there?"

Lian stiffened beside him. "Honeymoon?"

Jonas realized what he had said. "Are you opposed

to marriage?"

Lian's breath clogged for a second. "No. Are you asking?"

Jonas realized that now, here in this place, was not the best time. "Not right now. But I will. So be sure you know the answer when this mess is over."

Lian dropped silent, and so did Jonas. Before they could talk about the future, they had criminals to catch. Her hope was that once this case was settled, they could truly get to know one another, without all the distractions. They hadn't known each other long, and they hadn't had a normal relationship. But Lian knew what she felt, and she trusted that Jonas did, too. He would not tell someone he loved them lightly, not given his history. But Lian didn't need more time to get to know him or to think about her answer. When the time came, she already knew her answer.

Chapter Seventeen

Jonas came back into the room where his team was working. He had just gotten off the phone with the section chief. He had decided it was past time, so he told his superior that morning who Bo was to him. Now that he knew for sure Bo knew, it was in his best interests to be forthcoming on the subject. Section Chief Jacquelyn Montgomery wasn't anyone to fool with or try to deceive. She was now fuming back in Virginia that he had not told her sooner. He had given her the song and dance that he had no real proof, other than Lian's statement. She had told him what she thought of that answer, but there was not a whole lot she could do about it. He had also told her that his relationship with Lian had gone beyond what it had before. She wasn't happy about that either, but again, there wasn't much she could do about it. Lian didn't work for the FBI, and technically he was not Lian's superior; she was only assigned to his case as a consultant.

"So how mad is she?" Lian set the headphones down and rubbed her earlobes. She had been listening to chatter for more than three hours.

"She's pretty ticked, but she's also happy with our progress. She has my report and the others. Gunshot residue test was positive on Kang, so she's happy we're still putting evidence together on him. She's also happy that we've moved all the victims and are finishing up processing them. Immigration has now taken over, as almost all of them were kidnapped and need help to get back home."

Lian felt so sorry for all of them. They had to be so terrified. Interpreters were called in, so her help wasn't needed to translate for those who spoke Mandarin. That left her free to listen to live feeds, which she had been doing for two days straight.

Dex perked up as he watched the multiple screens that had footage of their quarry leaving a run-down hotel about ten miles from where the FBI was set up. "Kang is on the move."

Jonas came and stood at attention behind him. "Good. I think the theory that Biao is going to use Kang to do his dirty work again is spot on. He's been circling the city, but he's headed in the general direction of where we're leading him."

Jonas had spent the last two days, along with Dex and the team, laying a subtle trail to where the guns were hidden. Already the guns had been moved and decoys were put in place. A few guards were left outside the warehouse to make it look authentic. They had orders to allow Kang to get a good look, but not to get too close. Jonas was hoping to lure both Kang and Biao out of hiding and get enough evidence to charge both of them.

Jonas was still tracking Bo. He was making no moves to hide from surveillance, nor had he done anything that would draw attention. Lian was listening to the live feeds, as Bo spoke Mandarin to everyone he came in contact with, though Bo did hardly more than order a meal. The interpreter with him was a lovely woman who looked like she was probably more than she seemed. And probably more than Bo's interpreter.

Dex hadn't been able to pick up anything on Bo either via his computer. "We're still waiting to see if Bo leaves his hotel today. Your brother has done little more than go out for a meal since his little game back at that house. His cell phone has been quiet; no one has come knocking on his door other than room service, and he has not been in contact with Biao. His so-called interpreter is staying in his suite, but our agent posing as housekeeping says she is keeping her own room, and the bed was slept in. From the way it looks, he's just another businessman on holiday, and his interpreter is nothing more than that. Nothing fishy came back on her. She's employed through a service that hires people out to travel with rich executives to help them navigate their way around whatever country they are visiting."

Jonas was not happy to hear that. He wanted to lock Bo behind bars, and the man was not cooperating. "What about Biao?"

Dex pulled up a different screen. "We did track a brief call that he made to Kang about an hour ago. Basically, he threatened Kang that if he messed up one more time, the police would find him in pieces. It sounded quite impressive in Chinese."

Lian smiled at that. "It was colorful, no doubt. I can tell you that that kind of language is not taught in school."

Dex looked up at Jonas, who was still standing behind him. "Thoughts, boss?"

"Sorry, my mind is on Bo. He's the head. He's the one we ultimately want if we are to stop this trafficking ring. And I feel him slipping through our fingers."

Lian knew how he felt and came to put an arm around him. "Hong Kong police don't believe he's crooked. Or so they tell the public. The CIA has been watching him for years. I know you want him, but you've only been tracking him a short while. He wasn't even on your radar."

Jonas kissed her temple. "The voice of reason. Alright. We need to focus on Kang. Get men on the ground. I want us where he is. I want footage of him entering the warehouse. I want footage of him opening the crates. I want footage of him loading them up. By now he'll be about twenty minutes away, and then he'll set up surveillance. Two hours after we confirm he's there, the local office will get on the radios. They will be reporting an emergency and all units are to respond. He'll be suspicious, but I have a hunch he'll eventually move."

"Will you go?" Lian's hand tightened on his arm.

"Yes. I'm lead. I'll be back later tonight. Dex, keep an eye on her and keep tracking the team. And keep tracking Bo. Let me know if he makes a move."

"Got it, Boss."

Jonas gave Lian a rough kiss, checked his weapon, and left.

Lian ignored Dex's grin at the kiss he'd witnessed and picked the headset back up.

* * *

Bo Lee watched from the top of the hill. It was dark now, so he could not be seen by the men below. There had been two FBI agents patrolling from where he now waited, and he had taken them out. The tranquilizer would last for hours. The agents would be alive in the morning but would feel like they had been hit by a bus. He had recorded their voices, and he played them back periodically with a negative when the agents were asked if there was any activity.

Bo slid a little further into the shadows as he watched. He could see Kang clearly. The man had no sense of caution anymore. Bo knew Kang was riding high from the cocaine he had purchased earlier in the day, as were the three men with him. It would also make them reckless. And knowing Kang the way he did, he knew Kang figured he'd gotten away with murdering one FBI agent; what were a few more?

Silently, Bo slid down the hill on his stomach. He could see Kang and a couple of his men entering the warehouse. Bo pulled out a pair binoculars. He left the night vision goggles in his bag. He didn't want the lights from the warehouse blurring his vision.

"Báichī." Because it made him feel better, he said it again in English. "Idiot."

Bo watched as Kang and his men slipped out of the warehouse with some crates. Even from where he hid, Bo could see the discreet security cameras, and he could see the shadow of a drone now and again as it patrolled the area.

As he came down the hill, he saw both Jonas and Biao at the same time. Cursing his luck, he pulled a black cap down over his head. He tugged his black gloves back on and wove his way down the hillside, keeping to the shadows and out of sight.

* * *

"He's gone." Dex frantically tapped a few keys.

"What?" Lian left her post to come to Dex's side. She had taken off the headphones and had been listening to the tapes from the speakers. Dex didn't mind the noise; his focus was fierce while he worked.

"Bo. He's not at the hotel."

Lian looked over at what he was doing. "I've been listening to him. And no one saw him leave the hotel."

Dex boosted the sound on his computer. "Hear that tiny noise? That is a sure bet we're listening to a recording."

Lian shook her head. "But the television is on, and what he is watching is on. I checked."

"Layers, Lian. He has the television on, and he's got some pretty sophisticated sound equipment. I've been listening to the recordings the same as you, and I just caught it. I would bet money he's not there."

"Jonas. You have to tell Jonas."

Dex nodded. He sent an encoded message out. A moment later, he got an affirmative. "Lian, you need to relax. Jonas knows what he's doing. I just wish I were with him. This guy ticks me off. I've read the CIA files, and he's responsible for the death of an agent. No one liked White, but he died in the line of duty. That won't go unpunished."

"Do you think Bo is headed to the warehouse?"

Dex shook his head. "Not if he's as smart as everyone thinks he is. He'll stay as far away from that warehouse as this goes down. Men like him pay other men to take the risks."

Lian was only slightly relieved. She wouldn't relax until Jonas was back, and Kang, Biao, and Bo were behind bars.

* * *

Jonas stood his ground, letting the rest of the recordings incriminate Kang and his men. And Jonas had caught a glimpse of Biao. Two dominoes were lined up. Jonas doubted Bo would make an appearance; he was too smart for that, but with Biao in custody, Jonas had hopes of making him talk.

Two agents were walking the perimeter on the

hillside, but they had yet to report any activity. Two more agents were on the other side hiding in the weeds that grew high around the abandoned building. They would be moving in. Jonas had two men with him, each flanking his sides. Jonas gave the order and had the two men spread out. It was time for the show.

Jonas watched as the last of the weapons were loaded. Once completed, Kang gave the order to move out. Two of his three men hopped in the truck. Jonas saw the gunshot from the field that took out the tire. Then he saw the second shot that took out the other one. There was shouting in Mandarin from the men in the truck, and Kang dove for cover. The third man began firing blindly into the fields where the shots had come from.

The two men in the truck began firing from inside, opening the doors and sliding to the ground as they fired. Kang was shouting, but it was hard to hear him over the gunfire. Kang then dropped to the ground and out of Jonas's crosshairs. Instead, Jonas took aim at the man closest to him and took him out.

Jonas circled the area. In his comm, he asked, "Anyone have eyes on Biao?"

Agent Rogan responded. "East side of the building. Moving fast. I didn't have a clear shot."

Jonas was making his way when he had to suddenly fall back as the truck exploded. Cursing under his breath, he called to his men. "Fall back. We don't know if there are any more explosives."

His two men from the fields responded, as did the two who had come in with him. His two men from the hillside didn't answer. He shouted into the comm, but nothing. Amid the smoke and the fire that was starting to spread through the abandoned building, he kept low. He didn't need to tell his men to be careful. And though Kang and Biao didn't know it, there was no ammunition in that truck.

Jonas moved as the flames started moving his way. The wind had shifted, and the fire was spreading. He quickly called for backup and the fire department. A fire like this could take root and cause havoc. It needed to be doused quickly. And Jonas needed to secure the area before they got there.

Shouting orders to his men, he saw a second of Kang's men go down. Jonas spotted Kang as he crossed to the opposite side of the building. He lifted his rifle and got him in his sights just as Kang snuck up behind one of his men. Without flinching or hesitating, Jonas went for a headshot.

Jonas was dispassionate as Kang dropped to the ground. He saw his agent turn around, shock on his face. Before Jonas could signal him, he heard a laugh behind him.

The accent was thick, and Jonas recognized Biao's voice. "You are pathetic, Agent Cole. Bo should have killed you where you stood. I have no such problem. I am not weak or afraid. You die now."

Jonas heard two shots ring out. Jonas felt the bullet meant for his heart burn across his bicep but didn't penetrate. As he hit the ground to avoid another shot, he saw Biao clutch his own arm, then saw a second bullet tear through his shoulder. Jonas grabbed his rifle with his other arm but dropped it again as a second explosion rent the night air. The pressure from the blast knocked him to the ground.

Jonas struggled to sit up, to see through the smoke. Biao was gone. He cursed but fell back.

A dark shadow came and held out a hand. "Qǐchuáng."

Jonas tried to reach for his rifle, but a man in a black mask kicked it out of his reach.

"Qǐchuáng, Jonas. Get up. The fire is spreading. One of your men is down. And Biao got away. He must have set up a second explosion. There may be more. We need to get out of here. We need to get your men out of here."

Jonas blinked the moisture out of his eyes, the smoke making his eyes water. He could see light brown/green, red-rimmed eyes through the eyeholes of the mask. He knew those eyes.

"Take my hand. You have no choice but to trust me, Brother."

Jonas took his hand.

Jonas followed Bo as they ran toward the area where Jonas could see three of his agents. They were working on the fourth that lay on the ground.

One of his agents pulled out his gun as they approached. He kept his gun trained on the man next to Jonas.

Bo pulled the cap off, wiping his burning eyes. He kept his eyes on the man on the ground, unconcerned about the man pointing a gun at him.

Jonas grabbed Bo and started patting him down for a weapon. "You come into a firefight without a firearm?"

Bo looked up the short distance into his brother's eyes. "It would be illegal for me to have a gun on U.S. soil. The gun I used to shoot Biao was not mine. I found it on the ground."

Jonas cuffed Bo's hands in front of the man but stayed by his men. He opened the comm. "Dex, get down here and bring some men. I've got Bo in custody. Kang is dead, but Biao got away. Tanner is down, and two agents are missing."

Bo held up his cuffed wrists. "They are fine. They are asleep on top of the hill. They will wake up in a couple of hours. Quicker if your medics give them something to reverse the effects."

Jonas stood there staring at Bo as he told them what he'd used to incapacitate the men. He also told them where he would find the rest of Kang's men. "Biao will be long gone before you get even a trail on him. He always has an escape plan. And his men are in Hong Kong, not here. He came alone."

"How do you know that?"

Bo dropped his hands. "I gave him orders. He may not like them, but up until our arrival here, he has taken them."

"He's your man. You know where he will go."

Jonas waited until Tanner was loaded onto a stretcher before walking Bo toward the vehicles. Techs were still looking for any other bombs, but so far none were found. The tech nodded to Jonas that his vehicle was clear, and Jonas shoved Bo into the back seat.

"I do not know where he will go. He does not have many friends here. But he does know where Kang's men are, so he will not go there because he knows you know where they are."

Jonas cursed. "I don't care where he won't go."

Bo smiled. "True. But to say where he will go, I cannot say. Like I said, he does not have friends here. He does have a wife and daughter, but he would not go to where they are either. At least not today."

"Are you going to tell me what game you think you're playing?"

Bo laid his head against the headrest. "I will wait to tell you until I have had a shower and have some clean clothes."

"Do you think you can bargain with me?" Jonas watched, but no one was following him except the backup vehicle that kept on his tail. He made a hard right, deciding to take a direct route to FBI headquarters. The sooner Bo was behind those walls, the better he would feel.

"On this? Yes. The key card to my hotel room is in my pocket, but you can ask Ms. Kingston, my interpreter, to pack me a bag if you like."

"Oh, we'll go to your hotel room. We'll search it from top to bottom. You can be sure."

Bo was not worried. "You may search it. I give you permission, but it is a waste of time."

Jonas turned into the parking lot at headquarters. Several men were waiting for them. Without issue, they got Bo inside. At that point, Bo dropped silent and refused to speak again until he got his shower and a change of clothes.

After being processed and supervised as he took a shower, Jonas finally sat across the table from his brother, now dressed in prisoner's garb. Jonas's men were at the hotel room. Ms. Kingston had been picked up and was being questioned. The only thing his men had gotten out of her was a bunch of tears and her claim that she didn't know what they were talking about.

Jonas adjusted the earbud he was wearing as he listened in on the search of Bo's hotel room. So far, they hadn't found anything incriminating.

Bo relaxed in his chair, keeping his hands on the table between him and Jonas. "Can I get something to eat? It has been a long night."

Jonas had already anticipated that question. He pulled a paper bag from under the table and tossed it to him.

Bo picked up the sandwich inside, and though he did not recognize much of what was on it, he took a bite. "Not half bad. I suppose it was too much to hope you would have brought in Chinese food."

"Do you think this is funny?" Jonas leaned back in his own chair, though he didn't feign relaxation.

Bo polished off his sandwich before he spoke again. "The combination to the safe that is hidden under the floorboards in the closet is fifteen, seven, twenty-one, and twelve. Inside you will find a black satchel. Inside that, you will find a metal case."

"And what will they find inside it?" Jonas relayed the message and told the men to proceed with caution.

"You will see."

Jonas waited. When he heard what the man said, he couldn't believe it. The man repeated it. Jonas sat in shock for a moment, his eyes on his brother. After several moments, he found his voice. "You're a cop."

Chapter Eighteen

"You won't believe what just came in." Though calm, Griffith's voice was filled with happiness.

Lian smiled into the phone at his tone and abrupt greeting. "Naiwen's asylum came through."

"How did you know? I just found out." Griffith's voice was rough on the other end.

"That's one of the things Jonas plans to find out. Bo Lee told us. We didn't want to tell you in case it was a ruse."

Griffith cursed. "Where is that bastard?"

"Right now he's in custody. Jonas called and told me a couple of hours ago. Kang is dead and Biao is missing. Jonas has a manhunt underway to find him, but it's doubtful that he'll be found, at least not tonight. Bo came in without a fight. According to the reports coming in now, Bo saved Jonas's life." Lian's voice shook as she remembered reading what had come in.

One of the agents had seen Biao take aim at Jonas and saw Bo shoot Biao twice. He had watched in the distance as the man had helped Jonas to his feet and taken him to his men as the warehouse burned around them. They had fled the burning field to go help tend to Agent Tanner, who had taken a bullet to the chest. The bullet managed to do little damage, though Lian doubted Agent Tanner would feel better for it.

Griffith's voice interrupted Lian's thoughts. "We need to make sure he doesn't get loose. He'll use this knowledge to track her down."

"He claims to have no plans to hurt her. Says he owes her for taking his father out. He claims she saved him the trouble. I don't know, Griffith. Something isn't right. Why would Bo save Jonas's life?"

Griffith wanted to reassure her, but he had seen too much in his career. "It's hard to know, Lian, until he makes his next move. I've seen men do some crazy things. Bo never struck me as crazy; he strikes me as logical and methodical."

"I'm nervous. I know Jonas knows what he is doing. The arrest was clean, as was the shooting at the warehouse. But there were two explosions, and all of Kang's men were killed. Jonas thinks Biao set the whole thing up to explode, but Bo gives the orders."

Griffith was quiet for a moment. "Until Jonas is sure he has Bo under control, you need to stay put."

"I will. Jonas left a couple of men to stand guard. His man Dex left a little while ago to help get the scene taped off and help coordinate the forensics team. He also had to coordinate a manhunt for two of Jonas's men. They were found unharmed but drugged. Open gunfire and two explosions, but only one injury. The men were lucky tonight."

"They were. Jonas did a good thing. You can be proud of him."

Lian felt a few tears gather. "I am. And when this is all over, we can reunite Jonas and Naiwen."

"It's something to look forward to. Be safe."

Lian hung up her phone and glanced around the room. She was in a room with FBI agents standing guard. She couldn't be any safer.

* * *

Bo rubbed his wrists as Jonas undid the cuffs. "Thanks. You never get used to them."

Jonas, still a little shocked, simply nodded at his brother. Jonas had left the interrogation room and had made a few discreet phone calls. Section Chief Montgomery made a few herself back in Virginia. An hour later, Jonas had confirmation from some of the highest officials in the U.S. and in Hong Kong that Bo Lee was an undercover cop and had been for years.

Jonas continued to stare at the man. His hair was tied back and now clean from his shower. He had been quite disheveled and covered in smoke when they had gotten to headquarters.   The clothes accentuated his broad shoulders and lean body. Jonas didn't think he looked a thing like his brother, but there was no doubt this man was. Jonas could admit to himself that he was relieved he wasn't a criminal. He would have had him prosecuted to the full extent of the law, but part of him did not want to take on that burden.

Before Jonas came back, he too had a shower and changed his clothes. He had stunk of smoke so badly he could barely stand smelling himself. So now he sat across from his brother, his hair damp and his clothes fresh.

"You probably have dozens of questions."

Jonas nodded. "Probably more like a hundred, but we should start with the more important ones. I spoke with your superior in Hong Kong. He said you got permission from the U.S. government to come here and try to locate Biao and Kang. He didn't say which department."

"You of all people should know I cannot tell you that. But it was sanctioned. I had been closing in on Biao in Hong Kong. I had turned over quite a bit of evidence against him. An arrest was imminent. Then I got news he was going to flee. My superiors thought Biao might lead us to Kang, and in turn, locate the people he had taken. The count this time was almost a hundred. And though the numbers have been bigger in the past, we had nothing to go on this time. It was arranged that I would go to the U.S. and follow Biao. And if he wanted to maintain his cover that he was loyal to me, he could hardly argue."

"I suppose that cover was blown tonight." Jonas tossed Bo a bottle of water.

"Perhaps in a way. But what was my motive? That will be the question he is asking himself. Perhaps I saw an opportunity to take Biao out without alerting the other triad members. Or maybe I had gone soft and would not let him shoot my brother. He will be stewing about it. But either way, the knowledge will make its way back home, though few men would dare question me. It is hard to say how this will play out once I am back in Hong Kong."

Jonas took a few notes. "It is rumored that you own and operate one of the largest export businesses in Hong Kong."

Bo's lips twisted a bit, but otherwise didn't move. "Legitimate, too, now that my father is dead. Howard had a lot of illegal dealings, and the business was a perfect cover. Problem is that there are thousands of people employed by the business. My superiors wanted me to shut it down, but I could not do that. We compromised, and it went straight. No one was the wiser."

Jonas rubbed at a sore spot on his forehead. "If the triads find out what you are, you're a dead man."

Bo casually shrugged at that. "I have been a dead man walking since the day I was born. I was groomed to take over my father's business since birth. Straight or crooked, I have a target on my back. It was either the cops, the triads, or rivals. You can take your pick. Most cops would have no knowledge of my undercover work. My superiors would have denied it had I made any mistakes. And triads, like any other business, try to take over and win territory. I had to fight them all."

"At least I know now how you got your hands on

those police records. Why the games?"

"It was safest all around. The FBI had not been read into the mission, and having you chase me made everything look more legitimate. If I had not had to take a shot at Biao, we would not be having this conversation."

Jonas digested that. "Your superiors didn't sound happy."

"I do not suppose they are. They wanted me to stay undercover, even here. They warned me not to break any laws, as they would not bail me out. They would not have been pleased to hear I blew my cover, not even to save a fellow officer."

Jonas had one more question he needed to ask, at least about the case. "Did you know about the explosives?"

Bo shook his head. "Explosives are not Biao's usual style. But he uses them from time to time. I did not think he would have had the opportunity to set something like this up. He must have had a lot of inside information to pull this off. And I am pretty sure he got it from me."

Bo looked at the camera recording their conversation. "Let's say, hypothetically, I had access to some sensitive information. Information I should not have. Say that is how I knew where you were tonight. And let's suppose Biao found his way into my files. He would know what I know."

Jonas bit off a curse. "Okay, so hypothetically you had intel on the trap we set. Biao figured he could get the weapons and get Kang out of his hair for good. We did get Kang, though I would have preferred to bring him in alive."

Bo disagreed. "It is better this way. I am sure your men have already arrested the rest of Kang's men by now who were not at the warehouse. Some will be found guilty. Some will be found not guilty and be deported. Either way, you win. With Kang dead, there is no leader here they can trust. Anyone not found and detained will not have the know-how or the contacts to start the business back up. To be sure, they will cause trouble wherever they end up, but they will not have triad backing."

Jonas made a few more notes. "We're working now to find Biao's wife and daughter. They will need to be put under surveillance. And Biao is now on the FBI's most-wanted list."

"The wife is innocent, though not without knowledge. The daughter is only five. But the wife does not have the knowledge or the skills to disappear. She will be easy to find. I have already started on my end, though you will probably have more luck."

"Innocent or not, right now she is our best bet to find Biao. When they arrived with Biao, they went straight to a hotel. They have not been seen since. I am pretty sure Biao arranged to have them go into hiding."

Bo looked skeptical but did not argue. "That should cover business. Any personal questions you would like to ask me? Off the record, of course."

Jonas looked up at the camera in the corner of the room. He motioned to the operator to cut the feed. "I don't know where to start. Until I met Lian, I didn't know I had a brother. My parents are fuzzy memories, though I think I remember brief snatches of our mother."

"Lian's friend Griffith has been working very hard to get Naiwen free. I applaud his efforts."

Jonas thought he heard something shift in Bo's tone. "You helped, didn't you?"

Bo neither admitted nor denied. "I am just happy he got her free. It was not an easy thing. His feelings for her run deep. A woman can be a great asset or a great weakness. Rumors are that Lian is yours."

"She is going to be shocked to find out you're a cop."

"I suppose it is too much to hope that you would not tell her or Naiwen."

Jonas rose from his seat. "Why would you not want them to know? Naiwen is your mother."

Bo's voice was cold. "No, she is not. Her greatest wish was that you would find a home and happiness. She will be happy to know that her dreams for you came true."

Jonas opened the door and led Bo through the building. Since he was no longer a prisoner, he was free to go. "As I imagine Howard's dreams were of you taking over one day. But not as a cop."

"My father got what he wanted, for a time,

anyway. Those are my secrets."

Jonas didn't miss the fact that when Bo referred to their father, he referred to him as his father. "Howard was both of our fathers."

Bo stopped and waited for Jonas to do the same. "Naiwen is your mother, and Howard was my father. It is best you believe that deep in your heart. Do not take on Howard's burden. He was not your father. Your parents are nice, ordinary people in Chicago. Keep that in your heart and in your mind. Naiwen does not replace; she just adds."

"That's very philosophical. And how do you know so much about me?"

Bo looked around and did not see cameras or recording equipment now that they were outside the building. "I hacked your girlfriend's records. Imagine how surprised I was when I found out my brother was alive. Shock is a mild word. Lian was trying to figure out if you knew about me, if you were straight or crooked. And she found out the truth very quickly. She was an asset to the CIA and the Chinese government at different times. This time she was a great asset to the FBI. You may want to tie her to you before someone else realizes that."

"You can count on it. Where will you go?" An SUV with a driver was waiting to take Bo wherever he wanted to go.

"Not far." Bo pulled a card out of the pocket of his jacket. An agent had brought Bo's things from the hotel. He wrote on the back of the business card.

Jonas took the card. "Untraceable number, I presume?"

Bo smiled. "Good night, Brother. Should you need anything else in the way of information about the case, you may call that number."

"And if I need anything in the way of information on more personal matters?"

Bo slid into the seat of the open car door. "You may call for that, too. I cannot promise anything beyond listening to your calls."

Jonas nodded. "Fair enough."

Jonas watched as the car pulled away. Bo would probably get dropped off somewhere and disappear. Jonas looked at the number written on the card. It was a U.S. number. When he flipped the card over, it was a card for a Chinese takeout place in Virginia. Jonas smiled and tucked it into his pocket.

* * *

Lian lay with her head on Jonas's bare chest. She was still sweating a little from their somewhat torrid lovemaking. Lian wasn't sure if "torrid" was the right word, but it was the one that came to mind. "I never would have guessed, you know."

"Mmm?" Jonas was exhausted now.

"Naiwen is going to be shocked, too."

Jonas realized Lian was talking about Bo. "I got the impression there isn't going to be a big family reunion at the end of this."

"I think I understand. He is Howard's son, not Naiwen's. As you are the opposite."

"You got that in one. I've been trying not to think about what Bo must have gone through being raised by a man like Howard. And I have a hard time believing a man raised by someone like him became a cop. But the facts are facts. After digging a little further, he is a decorated cop, though only his superiors know it. And I can't help but think that if he goes back to Hong Kong, he won't survive a week."

Lian kissed Jonas's chest. "It will depend on how much of this gets covered up, or how much of this can be pinned on Biao. It would be a befitting punishment if this could all be pinned on Biao. Bo might find life easier if it became common knowledge that Biao turned over evidence that led to Kang's death."

Jonas tugged Lian closer so he could kiss her. "I love the way your mind works. And I love you."

Lian kissed him back. "I love you."

* * *

"So that's how the story ends, huh?" Mindy curled up against Dex at Dex's apartment. Dex, Mindy, Lian, and Jonas had just finished dinner.

Lian nodded. "Official reports went out yesterday. Jonas's boss let us have the week to relax and recover before the news hit the press. The news is telling everyone that the attempted arrest of Kang was aided by one Ping Biao, a former triad member turned witness. Authorities told the public that Biao was being protected by the U.S. government for his own safety and that his whereabouts are classified."

Dex put an arm around Mindy. "And your pal Griffith made sure that the news made it to certain people in Hong Kong and to the mainland. Biao is a dead man should he go home. Bo's cover is still intact, and the Hong Kong police, in a coordinated effort with certain U.S. government officials, have arrested several members of Kang's crew in Hong Kong and several of Biao's men as well. Overall, I'd say the brass is happy. Biao might not be caught yet, but progress has been made in the fight against organized crime and human trafficking."

Lian raised her wine glass to that.

Jonas took a sip of his own wine. "Maryanne Biao, Biao's wife, is under surveillance, but he has yet to turn up. His paperwork will be rejected should he try to take any type of public or private transportation out of the U.S. Though not impossible, I'm confident Biao is still somewhere in the States, lying low until he thinks it's safe to surface. Surprisingly, Bo has not left Los Angeles. FBI is keeping an eye on him while he's here."

Mindy had heard the story. "It's still so hard to believe he's a cop. You said all the evidence was solid against him."

Lian nodded. "His cover was airtight. I worry, though, that some of this is going to come back on him, whether he thinks it will or not."

Jonas finished his wine and set the glass on the table. "Given how long he's been undercover, I think he's pretty safe. Or as safe as a man can be in his position. But I wish I knew why he is still here and not on a plane back to Hong Kong."

"Do you think he's looking for Biao?" Dex asked.

Jonas wasn't sure. "Maybe. He's not been in touch, and as far as I know, he's not working with any U.S. agencies. If he is looking for Biao, he's doing it without sanction."

Lian shuddered. "Let's just say I can sympathize. But I have no plans to get any further involved. I did what I promised to do. I'd hate to have to make Jonas arrest me."

Mindy choked on her wine but didn't say another word. Mindy and Lian had still not told Dex or Jonas that she had been involved. The two women agreed it was better not to tell.

Jonas gave her a brief kiss. "It's much appreciated."

Chapter Nineteen

Lian was finishing up cooking dinner two weeks after they had gotten back from Los Angeles when Jonas's phone buzzed. Lian had moved into Jonas's apartment but was still waiting for the rest of her things to arrive from storage. And she was already arranging to have what possessions she had left at her apartment in China packed and shipped. Jonas had told her they could pick up her stuff on their trip, but Lian didn't want to spend time on her honeymoon packing. There was so much she wanted to show him, and her small efficiency apartment was not on the agenda.

Jonas came into the kitchen, frowning while he read the message. "Dex just texted me. Bo flew into Virginia an hour ago."

Lian turned the heat down and faced Jonas. "Did Bo message you?"

"No. I've not heard anything from him since we said our goodbyes in L.A."

"You have his number." Lian pointed to the drawer where Jonas had tucked the card Bo had given him.

Jonas shook his head. "We both need to think about what we do next."

"He's your brother, Jonas. If I found out I had a

long-lost sibling, I would do what I could to build a relationship."

Jonas wasn't as sure. "We know he's a real cop. But he's done some bad things. And unless he's willing to change his name and erase his past, I'm not sure I want him around. Not around you, and not around Naiwen."

Lian supposed Jonas had a point. "So what now?"

"Dex is tracking him digitally, and we've got a few men keeping an eye on him. I ordered the men to follow him should he show up here. I just never expected he would. He's not reaching out to me, so I want to know who he is reaching out to."

Lian finished dinner, and the two of them went about their newly established routines. Later that night, with Lian sleeping quietly beside him, Jonas couldn't help but wonder why Bo was here. Jonas didn't necessarily think Bo was a danger to him or Lian, but he was a dangerous man. Jonas didn't tell Lian, but word had come down that Maryanne Biao was now in Virginia. Jonas had a feeling Bo was indeed keeping an eye out for Biao. Jonas gave strict orders to his men to contact him immediately if Biao surfaced. Bo didn't have the authority here to hunt the man down, but Jonas doubted that would stop Bo. He was a man who had been living by his own rules for a long time.

It was a little after three a.m. when Jonas's phone buzzed again. Doing his best not to disturb Lian, Jonas eased out of bed. He picked up his phone and saw the message was from Dex. Biao had surfaced.

"What is it?" Lian's voice was sleepy from where she lay.

Jonas went to the closet to grab a fresh set of clothes. "I've got to go. Intel has Biao surfacing here in the city."

Lian sat, clutching the sheet to her breasts. "Are you sure?"

Jonas nodded. "The message came from Dex. He would have verified before contacting me. I want you to stay here. Keep the doors locked and the alarm armed. I am going to send a couple of men to watch the apartment building. There's no reason to believe Biao is here for any other reason than Maryanne or Bo, but I'd rather be sure. Biao wouldn't hesitate to take out a few FBI agents or anyone else who got in his way."

Lian got out of bed and crossed to Jonas. She wrapped her arms around his neck and gave him a lingering kiss. "Be careful."

Jonas deepened the kiss, walking Lian back toward the bed. "I'll be back. Get some rest."

Lian let him go and remained in the bedroom until she heard the front door close and the alarm set. Knowing there was no way she was going back to sleep while he hunted Biao, she pulled Jonas's robe from the closet and went to the living room to wait for his return.

* * *

"I'll be glad when this is all over." Dex was awake and alert beside Jonas as they watched from a nearby building. This part of town was not exactly known for its age and charm. This was the ghetto, plain and simple.

"Agreed." Jonas kept his eyes trained on the surrounding area while Dex kept his eyes on the building.

"You'd think a man would do better for his wife and daughter than this dump."

Jonas had spotted Maryanne Biao going into the building about half an hour after his arrival. The fact that the woman had been outside in this neighborhood at five a.m. didn't bode well. The daughter had not been with her.

Jonas agreed but kept silent. Biao had gone in, but he hadn't come back out. If Bo was here, he was hiding well. But Jonas had a feeling Bo was indeed nearby. "I'm going to take a closer look. Tell the agents to stand by."

Dex nodded and primed his weapon. He opened his comm device and told the team to standby. FBI agents were waiting for the signal.

Jonas slid from the vehicle and kept to the shadows as he made his way toward the building. The street was mostly dark, as most of the streetlamps had either been smashed or had burned out long ago. He crept up to the house and moved to the rear. There was a faint light coming from the basement, and he could hear voices. He could hear the voice of a woman who was crying. He could hear a man shouting, but the words were muffled. Jonas was pretty sure that was Mandarin he was hearing. Biao was still in the building.

Jonas almost missed the faint sound due to the yelling inside, but he caught the small sound. He continued around the house and froze. Because of how dark it was, he could see a faint light. Unless he was mistaken, and Jonas was rarely wrong, a bomb had just been armed.

Jonas pulled away from the building and back against the side of the building next door. He typed a quick message, not wanting to be overheard talking. He kept the phone low to the ground so as not to attract attention from the lit screen. Jonas tucked the phone back in his pocket and was about to retreat to the waiting vehicle when he caught movement from the corner of his eye. It was barely discernible, but it was definitely a man.

Jonas kept on his knees as he followed the man. Drawing his weapon, he moved in. Then he caught a glimpse of the man's face and cursed. He moved a little faster but approached the man from behind. He kept his voice pitched low when he spoke. "I had a feeling you would show up."

Bo froze as he recognized the voice behind him. "What are you doing here?"

"Same thing you are. But I'm doing it legally."

Bo dropped back next to Jonas. "Who says I am

not legal?"

"I mean you don't have the authority to arrest Biao."

"Who says I want to arrest him?"

Jonas pretended he hadn't heard that. "Before you take another step, you should know the house is wired to blow."

Bo's eyes followed where Jonas's finger pointed.

Jonas didn't have to understand Mandarin to understand the expletive. "Maryanne is in the house. I don't know if the daughter is inside. Surveillance has not seen anyone come or go since Biao arrived, and then Maryanne."

Bo prayed the daughter was not in the house. "What is the plan? FBI storms the house? Biao will flip the switch. He would take himself out with the house and your agents rather than surrender to the FBI."

"That's what I'm afraid of. I have a team nearby, but I have asked them to stand down for now. If the house blows, I don't want my unit to go with it."

Bo pulled a mask over his face. "I will go in. I will try to get the woman out. Get her to safety."

"What kind of plan is that? Biao will kill you where you stand."

Bo shrugged. "I am ready to die if that is what it takes. I saw the way you look at Ms. Albright. I saw the protective way you stood in front of her when you thought I might kill you both. You are not ready to die."

Jonas tried to stop Bo, but the man was fast and already on the move. Jonas drew his weapon and followed. Jonas came around the back and saw Bo slip through the backdoor. Jonas peeked into the house through a window that didn't have a curtain. He couldn't see much, but he did see Biao as he continued to yell at his wife. His arms were flailing erratically, and he started throwing things.

Things happened pretty fast once Bo was inside the house. Jonas kept his weapon trained on Biao. He watched in amazement as his brother tackled Biao with a rear kick. Bo pivoted and got Biao again, this time in the middle of the back, sending the man sprawling to the floor.

Jonas met a screaming Maryanne at the back door. He grabbed her and tried to subdue her. "FBI. Just relax."

If anything, Maryanne fought him harder. She managed to get a good kick to his shin before he had her pinned. "I'm not going to hurt you. Is your daughter inside the house?"

Maryanne's voice was hoarse with tears. "No. She's not in the house. Just my husband and some strange man in a mask."

Jonas could see the two men fighting. No way was he going to let his brother die in that house. Jonas pulled out his phone. "Dex. I have Maryanne Biao safely out of the house. She says no one else is there except Biao. Bo went in and I'm going in after him. Get Maryanne to safety. I'm sending her out."

Maryanne shook in Jonas's grip, tears still streaming down her cheeks.

Jonas loosened his grip. "Across the street, there are FBI agents waiting. The house isn't safe. It's rigged to blow."

Maryanne let out a strangled breath but nodded. Jonas pushed her to get her moving. He watched as she rounded the house. Maryanne was wearing a bright white t-shirt, so his men would see her and detain her.

Jonas entered the house, his thoughts solely on Bo. He could hear the grunts and sounds of fists as they met flesh. Keeping his weapon in front of him, he entered the basement. He didn't see any more devices but knew it would only take one to topple the poorly built home.

Jonas saw as Bo landed a blow across Biao's cheekbone, the man losing his balance and dropping to his knees. Jonas saw the man as he started crawling towards a table. Then he shot to his feet and tore out of the room. Jonas knew he wouldn't be able to stop him before he set off the detonator.

"We've got to get out of here!" Jonas grabbed Bo's arm and started dragging him out of the house.

Bo realized where Biao was headed. He had forgotten about the bomb in the heat of the fight. He ran behind Jonas, the two men rushing for the exit.

When they got outside, they kept running. The blast rent the night air, and the shock wave of it sent both men flying. Jonas lay on the prickly, dry grass, stunned for a moment. Then his vision cleared, and he saw Bo struggling to get back to his feet.

"Boss. Here." Dex leaned down and helped first Jonas, then Bo to their feet.

"Where is Maryanne?"

Dex kept a hand on Jonas's arm until he was steady on his feet. "Gone. We saw her come around the corner of the house, but then she bolted through an alley and disappeared. We have men looking for her now."

Jonas watched as the house erupted in flames. "We've got to get out of here. Did anyone see Biao escape?"

"The film will show us for sure. There was a flash of light before the blast when the floodlights on the front porch lit. I'd say that Biao had this planned for a while. I would also bet that he had an escape plan."

Bo looked at the burning house, his body and fists now hurting from the fight and the subsequent blast. "One can hope he is not alive. He would not be afraid to die."

Jonas leaned against Bo as the man started to wobble on his feet, both men suffering the effects of the blast. "If he's alive, I will find him."

Bo smiled and glanced up at his brother. "Of this, I have no doubt."

* * *

Lian came tearing through the FBI offices in

search of Jonas. Dex had called and given her a brief recap of what had happened at the house. She saw him sitting at a desk in a chair next to Dex and Bo. Jonas looked like he'd been to war.

Jonas rose to greet Lian. He grunted when her fist landed in his midsection. He took a step back and put a hand to his stomach. She hadn't punched him with all her strength, but it hadn't been a love tap either.

"I swear, Jonas, if you ever run into a house that is wired to blow up again, I will never forgive you."

Jonas wrapped a trembling Lian in his arms while he shot a dirty look at Dex. Dex gave him an apologetic shrug.

Lian hugged him with all her strength. She could have lost him tonight. "Are you okay? Dex said the paramedics looked you over, and you refused to go to the hospital."

Jonas brushed Lian's pale blonde locks away from her face. "As you can see, I'm fine. Bo and I got out in time to miss the blast."

Bo lifted an eyebrow at the blatant lie but kept his own counsel. "He has just a few bumps and bruises. He will be fine after a little pampering."

Lian glanced at Bo. This was the first time she had come face to face with him since learning he was a cop. She wasn't sure what to think. This was the man she had been hunting. But looking at him now, his eyes wary as he watched her, she told herself to relax. He was not a threat to her, Jonas, or Naiwen any longer. He was just as disheveled as Jonas. His face was swelling up though. She could tell he'd been in a fight but refrained from inquiring. Bo didn't look so friendly right now. "I think you could use a little pampering yourself."

Bo got to his feet, his entire body now throbbing. "I need a hot shower and a meal. How about we meet up for breakfast at my hotel at nine?"

Jonas accepted. "I could use a shower myself. And I doubt I'll sleep anytime soon."

Lian led Jonas to her car after they saw Bo into a cab. Lian was torn between tears and wanting to strangle him. Instead, she drove sedately back to Jonas's apartment. Once inside, she helped him strip his clothes and put him in the shower.

Lian stripped her own clothes off and helped Jonas wash up. Jonas had bruises starting to form. She touched them lightly but didn't say anything. She would bet he got them from slamming into the frozen ground.

Jonas tipped her chin up as the water poured down on them. "I told you I'd be back."

"Yes, you did. But what you did was crazy. You could have been killed."

Jonas's wet hands slicked over Lian's body. "I couldn't let Bo die, not if I could help it."

Lian felt a sob well up but choked it down. Jonas was an FBI agent. He was also the type of man who would do anything for his family. And while Bo was still a stranger, he was blood. "All right. I won't talk about it anymore."

Jonas felt Lian's arms come around him, and she pressed her wet, naked body against his. He felt his body stirring against hers, his need for her now fierce. "This time we'll do this right."

Lian laughed, remembering the only other time they showered together. "I thought you did it right the last time."

Jonas smiled. "I got it half right. This time I want to be inside you while your cries echo off the shower walls."

Lian felt herself lifted, and she wrapped her legs tightly around Jonas. There were no soft words or soft touches. Her need for him was immediate, as was his for her. And this time he was buried deep inside her while both of their cries echoed off his shower walls in unison.

* * *

Bo was leaning negligently in a booth at the restaurant while he was waiting for them. He had no doubt why they were late for breakfast. Lian looked like she was glowing, and Jonas looked satisfied.

"Zǎoshang hǎo."

Lian sat down opposite Bo. "Good morning. Sorry, we're late. I fell asleep."

Bo didn't dispute her words. He had no doubt his brother had worn her out. "I had some coffee and a massage. I had a feeling you might be late."

Jonas asked for coffee, and Lian did the same when

the waitress came. Lian ordered a hearty stack of whole-grain pancakes, while Jonas ordered a loaded omelet. Bo declined a meal.

"Not hungry?" Lian took an appreciative sip of the coffee.

"My stomach is not feeling well."

Jonas grunted and downed his coffee. "Getting kicked in the stomach several times will do that. You and Biao were evenly matched."

"One day, perhaps, we will see how well you and I are matched."

Jonas heard a bit of anticipation in Bo's tone. "Does that mean you're staying here?"

Bo took a sip of his coffee and winced as his split lip protested the movement. "I told my people I had business in the U.S. that would keep me here for a while. Let me just say that with Biao gone, or at least missing, and suspected of conspiring with the FBI, things are going to get heated back home while people fight for position and power. I find that I am tired and not interested in playing the game right now. And I have some unfinished business."

"Biao?" Lian waited for Bo's answer. Jonas had told her that his body had not been recovered from the blast and subsequent fire. The FBI was operating under the assumption that Biao was very much alive.

"No. Not Biao. He is now Jonas's problem, and I am content to let him handle it. I would hate to force him to have to save me again."

Jonas acknowledged the unspoken thank you. "I

would say we are now even. You kept me from getting shot, and I kept you from getting blown up. But what business?"

Bo added a bit of cream to his coffee before he spoke. "It is a personal matter. I may call on you, depending on how it all works out."

"And Naiwen? Griffith is getting on a plane today to go get her."

Bo contemplated Jonas over the rim of his coffee cup. "I can assure you I am the last person, other than my father, who she would want to see."

Lian touched a hand to Bo's, but he pulled away. "I know Naiwen well. When she finds out you are a cop, she will be happy to see you."

"You are naïve, Lian. Cop or not, it makes no difference."

Jonas put a hand on Lian's shoulder to stop her. "I am nervous to meet her. I am also a reminder of all that she lived through."

Bo was silent for a moment, taking a minute to gather his thoughts and to decide how much to say. "Brother, I wish you much luck. Naiwen loved you, despite my father. You were her hope for a better future for her family, to restore the honor she lost when she was taken. I know you and Griffith will take care of her and see that the rest of her days are not spent in the past, but in a hopeful present and future."

Lian didn't understand why Bo did not want to embrace his mother. "Bo, you are her son, too."

"Blood, yes. Of the heart, no. If she were to look upon me, I would be a reminder to her of all that is now past. As I said, I wish you much luck. I will be flying out tomorrow. I have decided to finish up my actual business in L.A. before I get started on my personal business."

Jonas knew he wasn't going to change his brother's mind. And he felt much as Bo did. Bo was a reminder of all that was awful, all that was painful. There might be a time when Naiwen would be able to embrace her second son, but this was not the time. "I wish you luck as well. Do not leave the U.S. without saying goodbye."

Bo rose and bowed slightly. "I will not. Now that our paths have crossed, there will be no going back, only forward."

Jonas knew what his brother had left unsaid. There was no reason, as they moved forward, that those paths would cross again. They would both move forward, but not necessarily together. But Jonas had a feeling he would see his brother again. And if he did leave without a goodbye, the FBI was good at finding people.

* * *

Jonas's mother slapped his hand for the dozenth time. "Stop fidgeting with your tie. It's fine."

Lian squeezed the hand that she held, opposite the side where Jonas's mother was trying to get a hold of his other hand tugging at his tie. "You look great. But Naiwen isn't going to even notice what you are wearing."

Jonas let his mother take his hand again. He was flanked by the two women he loved most in the world. His father was behind them, his strong hand giving his shoulder a reassuring squeeze from time to time.

Jonas had imagined, when he was a little boy, what it would be like to meet his birth mother. By the time he was a young teenager, any memories he might have held onto of his mother had faded under the weight of time and anger. The woman beside him was his mom, the woman who had taken him into her home when he was not yet a man. But both women, the one who had been in his life and the one who was coming back into it, had molded him into the man he was today. And the man behind him had shown him and taught him to love and to cherish the women in his life.

"Griffith was as nervous as you are now when he left. He hadn't seen her in months." Lian straightened the tie where Jonas had skewed it.

Jonas stopped long enough to kiss Lian. He wasn't sure he could have faced Naiwen without her. She understood how he felt and encouraged him to take this next step. His parents had also demanded to come with him, to be there to support him during this turning point in his life.

Griffith was the first person he saw. The older

man waved to him and paused to bring the woman who had been hiding behind him to his side.

Jonas came face to face with his birth mother for the first time in over thirty years. She was smaller than he expected, her height barely over five feet. Her black hair was slightly streaked with silver, and her face was lined with signs of age, but in that moment her face came to him as it had been the last time he had seen her. He was barely aware of the tears that wet his cheeks but was fully aware of both his mother's and Lian's tears of happiness as they stood beside him. Naiwen cried, too, her arm wrapped around Griffith's waist, as if he were the only thing keeping her on her feet.

Suddenly, all his nerves dropped away. Jonas's arms were released, and he took a step toward the woman who was his mother.

"Huānyíng huí jiā. Welcome home."

<u>From The Author</u>

I hope you enjoyed All Of My Days! I have always found China to be a fascinating place. If you strip out the politics and strip out all the biases people have, China is a place filled with beautiful landscapes and a rich, diverse culture. I am not sure how the idea of an American character who had grown up in China evolved, but Lian was a strong presence in my mind as I wrote this book, and how hard it must be to feel like you don't belong anywhere. I think many of us can relate to that feeling to some degree. And be sure to pick up your copy of the sequel, All Of My Nights.

You can sign up for my newsletter @ elizabeth-castle.com/contact. Or follow me on Facebook @ facebook.com/elizabethcastle.romanceauthor.

Also, if you enjoyed this book, or any of my other titles, please consider leaving a rating at your favorite retailer, Goodreads and/or Bookbub. And if you have the time, a text review would be lovely. Indie authors rely on readers like you to tell others how much you enjoyed their books.

Happy reading,

Lizzy Castle

Single Titles:
    Going Home
    This Kind Of Love
    Chasing Hope
    The Babe & The Librarian (novella)
    Ghosts Of The Past

The Heart's Way Series:
    For Now and Always
    Ask Me To
    Say You Love Me
    Forever Love

Bennett Family Series:
    This Time Love
    A Bride For David (novella)

All Of Me Series:
    All Of My Days
    All Of My Nights

Cantwell Series:
    Falling Slowly
    Unraveled
    Hidden Away
    Entangled

Contemporary "Retro" Romance Series:
    Loving Jordan

Visit elizabeth-castle.com for newsletter sign up and up-to-date releases.

www.ingramcontent.com/pod-product-compliance
Lightning Source LLC
Chambersburg PA
CBHW020743310726
48969CB00002B/396